# Crozier: Four Days in September 1865
## Murder in Newberry, South Carolina

*A*
*Historical*
*Novel*

*By*
**Charles Hanson**

Illustrated by Betty Hanson and Charles Hanson

Note for Librarians: A cataloguing record for this book is available from Library and Archives Canada at www.collectionscanada.ca/amicus/index-e.html
ISBN 1-4120-5755-8

*Printed in Victoria, BC, Canada. Printed on paper with minimum 30% recycled fibre. Trafford's print shop runs on "green energy" from solar, wind and other environmentally-friendly power sources.*

# TRAFFORD
**PUBLISHING**™

*Offices in Canada, USA, Ireland and UK*
This book was published *on-demand* in cooperation with Trafford Publishing. On-demand publishing is a unique process and service of making a book available for retail sale to the public taking advantage of on-demand manufacturing and Internet marketing. On-demand publishing includes promotions, retail sales, manufacturing, order fulfilment, accounting and collecting royalties on behalf of the author.

**Book sales for North America and international:**
Trafford Publishing, 6E–2333 Government St.,
Victoria, BC V8T 4P4 CANADA
phone 250 383 6864 (toll-free 1 888 232 4444)
fax 250 383 6804; email to orders@trafford.com
**Book sales in Europe:**
Trafford Publishing (UK) Ltd., Enterprise House, Wistaston Road Business Centre,
Wistaston Road, Crewe, Cheshire CW2 7RP UNITED KINGDOM
phone 01270 251 396 (local rate 0845 230 9601)
facsimile 01270 254 983; orders.uk@trafford.com
**Order online at:**
trafford.com/05-0655

10 9 8 7 6 5 4 3 2 1

# Preface

In telling the story of the events of September 7 and 8, 1865, in Newberry, South Carolina, I have attempted to give my interpretation of history based on limited but detailed facts. The story of a fight between an ex–Confederate soldier traveling home after the war and a member of the US Colored Troops and the eventual outcome has been recorded in Newberry history since it occurred. There is a detailed description of the events of the fateful night and of the following morning that was written in the *Weekly Herald* newspaper of September 13, 1865. That documented history along with interviews with witnesses and exaggerated stories from years after the fact were documented in 1892 by Mr. John A. Chapman in his part of the *Annals of Newberry*. Some of that history is written in stone on a monument in Newberry. A story was published in the *Confederate Veteran* magazine, retelling the story of Calvin Crozier in 1901. An interview with his sister also appears in that article. Mr. Thomas H Pope, Jr. wrote his description of these events in his book, *The History of Newberry*, again taken from Mr. Chapman, the *Weekly Herald*, and the oral history of the community. Even today, long time residents of this small but historic southern town who are familiar with the story concerning Crozier will tell you their own version of the events.

I was told of this story in 1992, as a fairly new resident of the town of Newberry; due to developing circumstances, I soon found that I would need additional information on the subject. I was able to obtain more detailed facts from official military records that had not previously been researched. Some of these records will be revealed in the epilog to my story, so I ask your patience until you reach that point in my book.

These military records have allowed me to present an explanation of the events preceding the tragedy of that Friday in September 1865. It is also through these documents that I can present what I consider an accurate understanding of some of the personalities and mental states of many of the characters involved. Other historical documents have helped in my understanding of the conditions in the South and especially in South Carolina in the fall of 1865.

I have intentionally used real names where those names are known and have relied on truly fictitious names only when I felt it necessary. The two ladies whom you meet in the first chapter are

i

known only as "two young ladies" in history; so I have created Sarah and Jenny Dekalb. You will also meet two traveling companions of Calvin, Jim and Josh. These men are known in the history of the event as "a traveling companion". The events I created in the traveling of Crozier until he reached Newberry are strictly fictitious, as no actual documents exist concerning his travel from Point Lookout, Maryland, until he reached Newberry. But this fiction is based on events that may well have happened as I created them in my interpretation of the story.

Other fictitious characters in the story are Mr. Earl Morris, Zek Summer, and Mr. Ben Shealy of Newberry and Sergeant Robert Smalls of the 33rd US Colored Troops. These characters represent people who may have been there and performed as these characters do. I have also introduced real people who in history are known to be involved in the story or else were present in or near the town of Newberry and may have been involved. My purpose in using the names of these people is to present them in the story in a positive and useful manner or at least not in a negative way.

My perception of this "living history" is based on the newspaper report of the *Weekly Herald* of September 13, 1865, and military records that I have discovered through the National Archives in Washington which are mentioned in the epilog. It is also because of the latter source that this description varies somewhat in the more locally accessible versions of the story. I consider this account to be the most historically accurate to date, with the exception of some imagined and fabricated conversations throughout the book. But I will caution the reader that you will most likely fail in trying to separate fiction from fact. My intent with the use of fiction is to fill in undocumented gaps and to provide a better understanding of what happened in Newberry during those two days in 1865.

I hope the reader in this case will find history enjoyable and entertaining, as well as informative. I purposely avoided a nonfiction document based on this hope. To the average reader in today's society, I feel that a good, fairly accurate knowledge of our American history will suffice. And if a historically based story written as I have done can inspire people to seek out other such knowledge of our history, then I have achieved one of my objectives for this book. To the historian and amateur historian, if you find facts in this book contrary to your knowledge on a particular subject, then I challenge you to do as I have done when that happens to me. Research the subject through other sources as much as you can and reach your own conclusions on the matter. Prove me wrong if you can (but then share your knowledge with me).

To those who have encouraged me on my endeavor to write this story in book form, my sincere gratitude is given. And to that special person in my life who has always sought to encourage me and has pushed to see my writings in print, I continue to give all my love as well as my gratitude. My wife has been my major critic in this endeavor as well as my number one victim. For that she is priceless.

I would also like to thank my uncle, Jack Hanson, and his beautiful wife, Aunt Betty, for their support and encouragement.

And I would like to give a special thanks to Karen Ruff for her solicited time and suggestions in the final writing of this book.

Andrew Johnson
President of the United States
Washington DC

May 20, 1866
Lewis PO, Galveston, Texas

Dear President Johnson,

I seat myself to write to you asking for your coveted help in finding my brother. His name is Calvin Crozier and he served in the cavalry in the Confederate army. He has not returned home from the late war. My Pa recently received a delayed letter from him written from Point Lookout Maryland dated June, 1865. He was still a prisoner of your army but looking forward to coming home. It has been difficult trying to find out where he might be, and my family and I need your help in finding out what your army has done with my beloved brother.

Sincerely,

Mary Crozier

# Chapter 1

A tranquil star–studded sky covered the small southern town of Salisbury. On the eastern horizon could be seen the promise that a new day would soon be dawning. The town was nestled in its nightly rest except for the noisy clamor rising from the train yard on the eastern edge of town. There, men were busy making final preparations for the Charlotte train to depart. Steam bellowed from under the sides of the engine that commanded the ten–car train heading south. Orders were shouted from a boisterous Vermont sergeant from somewhere beyond the sight of the train, as a Federal regiment prepared to march toward Greensborough to board yet another train. Footsteps on the wooden platform outside the depot echoed through the night air.

This was the early morning of September 5th, 1865. The war that had divided the people of the United States for four long years had finally ended, and the southern soldiers had returned from the bloody battlefields of Virginia and Tennessee. Only a few stragglers could be seen of the boys and men who had lately been prisoners and convalescents in northern hospitals. Federal troops were visible in nearly every southern city. The trains were busy throughout the south transporting troops, supplies, and passengers. Many of the Federal soldiers were on the move daily, seemingly in all directions, separating, then rejoining, and moving from one point of unrest and rebellion to another. The southern soldiers had laid their weapons down, taken the oath, and returned to help put back together what had been taken apart by years of war and months of occupation. But surrender at home was hard for many of the citizens to swallow. Tensions remained high and army commanders were struggling to find ways to handle the situations.

Two young men sat motionless at the far end of the platform of the Salisbury station. They seemed out of place in the near darkness, as they were the only ones not in motion. The two ex–Confederate soldiers sat back to back, leaning against a post on the edge of the walkway. Daylight slowly penetrated the cool morning air and began to reveal details of their appearance. They were dressed in a mixture of Confederate clothes -- one in butternut trousers and brown jacket --

1

the other with a faded gray Confederate cap pulled down over his eyes, wearing faded blue trousers with a gray blouse. Their clothes were weathered and worn, in contrast to the new Federal issued boots revealed below the ragged edges of their trousers. Their jackets had been stripped of the buttons, as required by Federal law. They sat dozing after a night of restless sleep.

A sudden jolt unseated Josh, nearly tumbling him from the platform.

"Watch where you're going, Reb! Think you own this walkway? You still got a lot to learn about manners." The Federal soldier looked back at the man who was picking himself up. The other two soldiers laughed jeeringly, as they continued past the two boys.

"They'll learn, sure 'nough, given 'nough time and training, that is," added the corporal to his companions. They continued down the walkway, laughing.

"Where's Crozier?" asked Josh, glaring after the three Federal soldiers. "Hope that boy ain't got into some kind of trouble. What time you reckon it is?"

"Don't rightly know, to both your questions," responded his bearded companion. "I reckon Cal will be here soon. He couldn't have gone far. There should be a privy close to the station."

"Yea, that's what's bothering me," added Josh.

Both men continued to glance up and down the platform for answers to their question.

They had been on the road now for five days, sometimes walking and sometimes traveling short distances aboard the cars, wherever they could get transportation.

Josh Todd was on the way home to Gladstone, Alabama. He hadn't seen home since March of '63. He had been captured outside of Knoxville in November of that year. He had spent most of his time in that cold, northern "training camp" called Camp Douglas, just as Jim Walker and Calvin Crozier had done. That's where they had met. Cal was already there when Josh was brought in and Jim arrived a month later. Jim was from somewhere in southern Louisiana, but he would never be specific about his home. Calvin was from Galveston, Texas, although he admitted to having been born and raised in Brandon, Mississippi; but he claimed he was a true Texan. He had joined the artillery corps in Dallas early in the war and then transferred to the cavalry. "Anything to stay out of the infantry," he had said. But it was the cavalry that got him in trouble. He was on a raid into Ohio when he was captured. He spent a few days in Camp Chase, another Federal training camp near Columbus that was used as a prison. But, as Cal had put it, Ohio had been a rest camp compared to Camp Douglas. That was a hellhole. It had been a prison since '62, after the fall of Fort Donaldson and was soon overcrowded with inadequate quarters, especially during those terrible winter months. Josh and his new friends had seen many of their comrades perish in that ice box near Chicago.

Since he had been released, Josh had heard much talk about the way the Confederates had treated the prisoners in Georgia. He had been disappointed to read of the many stories of starvation there. But Josh had heard some of the stories from the Confederate prisoners who were captured near Petersburg in early '65. He had decided that the Yanks in Georgia probably had as much to eat as those boys did while they were doing their duty in the trenches.

The food at Camp Douglas was adequate for survival, but there was an irregular issue of meat. Often, some excuse about it not being fit to eat; they heard that much of their rations were being sold on the streets in southern Chicago.

Josh had been ill with typhoid, and he was still not well. The doctors in Maryland told him that he was well and could travel, but he knew he wasn't. The typhoid was still in his body. He knew. He could feel it. But it didn't matter. He was going home. He could get well there.

Jim and Calvin had been in the same hospital in Maryland with Josh after Point Lookout was closed. They were sent to Point Lookout in March for exchange, but the doctors said they were too sick to leave. The boys guessed that was why the Federals had decided to release them -- too sick to be soldiers anymore. And it was sure pure disappointment when they got there and still couldn't leave.

"When's the train going to board?" Josh wondered.

"There's Crozier!" Jim's words interrupted Josh's thoughts. Looking down the platform, Josh saw Cal standing outside the depot door talking to three ladies.

"What's he up to now?" Jim asked.

"Looks like he's putting on that gentleman way of his -- bet he

3

didn't learn that in Texas." Josh added.

Calvin had just turned twenty–five, was clean–shaven, and was the most respectable looking of the three ex–Confederates traveling together. He was dressed in Confederate gray, except for his hat, including his jacket with the buttons removed. And, like Jim and Josh, Calvin sported new Federal issue boots. He had a smile that would warm the heart of any young girl and quickly win the confidence of any southern lady. It could get him a meal at most any place he stopped on the road home. He was five foot, nine inches tall, normally of muscular build but now still showing the effects of two years of prison and continued illness. He held himself proudly with a confidence of "defeated, but not conquered" that seemed to strengthen every southerner he met and anger every Yankee soldier who saw him. That same air of confidence had made him a good trooper in Kentucky and had enabled him to survive those deadly days at Camp Douglas. Calvin had been raised with a gentleman's manners and the army and Federal prison hadn't changed that.

The two men stared as Crozier continued to talk to the women; he was now looking in their direction and pointing.

"What's he up to?" Josh wondered out loud.

Calvin touched his slouch hat he had protected with his life while in prison, nodded to the ladies, and quickly headed down the platform toward his friends.

BH

"Cal, what you up to?" inquired Jim.

With a more than usual broad smile, Calvin proudly said, "Got a job to do, boys. Don't look like I'll be riding with you for a while -- going to have to ride in one of the front cars."

"What you talking about? You ain't got nothing but pocket change, like us," argued Jim.

"The young ladies there need an escort, and I've agreed to help them out 'til they get home," Calvin continued. "The older lady is their grandmother, and the girls are going home to Macon. No unescorted ladies can travel in these times, and I've agreed to protect them. They're paying my fare through Georgia."

"Here's a man been in captivity for two years, deprived of the fairer sex, and you're to protect them!" laughed Josh.

"Watch it, Joshua," scolded Calvin. "I take my commitment serious, and I'll not have my friends insult those ladies, either, understand?" He made eye contact with Josh and then Jim.

"Sure Cal. Josh was just kidding," Jim assured him, "but personally I hope you have to fight to protect them all the way to Georgia, sitting up there in that coach while your friends are back in the cattle cars."

"Look who's suddenly complaining about the accommodations on the cars," Calvin laughed. "Maybe if you'd clean yourself up a little, cut some of that old man's beard you're so proud of, then maybe you could be recognized as that gentleman I'm sure you used to be. At least maybe your mother would recognize you when you get home," Calvin added.

"Cal is about my beard, again, Josh. Still jealous," laughed Jim. "This here beard survived those longs days in prison, and it's going back with me to Louisiana."

"The conductor said that the train would be boarding before long," Calvin said. "I'll be down there with the ladies until then. The way the conductor talked, all of us should be able to get transportation on the cars, at least to Atlanta." Then he added, "he says some tracks in Georgia still haven't been repaired and many routes have not been reopened. He told me that the trains from here south would let us ride free in the freight cars."

Calvin walked past Josh and bent to retrieve his "luggage"-- a feed sack containing a shirt, a change of under–drawers, a pair of socks, a razor a lady in Alexandria had given him, and several hand–carved keepsakes he had managed to conceal from Camp Douglas. He reached for the other sack lying between the two men.

"I'll need some of these rations up front," commented Calvin. He removed a portion of the cornbread, a third of the bacon, and two of the apples from the sack of stores they had accumulated on the road. "The ladies have food, of course, but none extra," Calvin added, as he wrapped the food in a cloth he also removed from the sack.

The two men watched as he turned and walked down the platform toward the three ladies. Even they were envious of his confidence, his inner strength, and his determination to survive all of what may lay ahead for him. Calvin had often taken upon himself to be their crutch at Camp Douglas. He would find the right thing to say at the best time to say it. It would get their spirits back up just as the days seemed they could not get any darker. Secretly, both men knew they owed more to Calvin than they could ever repay. He had helped them both survive Camp Douglas. Even during their illness at Point Lookout, it seemed that no matter how sick Calvin was, he came to their bedside at the right time. He was a twenty–five year old with the spirit of a man much younger and the discipline of a man much older. They were proud to know Calvin Crozier and call him friend.

Calvin smiled as he approached the three ladies with his sack in tow.

"Well, I guess I'm ready," said Calvin.

"Are you sure, Mr. Crozier?" asked Mrs. Pering.

"Oh, yes ma'am," responded Calvin.

"These are my only two granddaughters and I'll hold you personally accountable to your commitment for their safety, Mr. Crozier," Mrs. Pering warned. "God only knows I wouldn't send them anywhere at times like these, least it wasn't absolutely necessary. I hope you understand that."

"Of course, Mrs. Pering," responded Calvin.

"Their mother's in Macon in God only knows what kind of needs, their poor father dead in this awful war, and now my daughter demands that I send my granddaughters back home 'now that it's safe', she says," complained Mrs. Pering. "I can't imagine any place in Georgia being safe. Yankees everywhere, no law and order, they do as they please, and we hear reports every day of violence and degradation right hear in North Carolina. What's it like in Georgia? And South Carolina -- they say there're black troops in charge there -- can you imagine, Mr. Crozier?" she asked, glancing around as if looking for some unknown disaster to strike out at any moment from the early morning shadows.

"You needn't worry, Mrs. Pering," pleaded Calvin. "Your granddaughters will be safe with me, and I'm certain that things aren't as bad in Macon as you fear. Their mother wouldn't send for them if it weren't so. Most of the boys are home now, even in Georgia, and they'll do whatever's necessary to protect their homes and families," Calvin continued. "And for the black soldiers, I understand they fought honorably against us in Virginia, and like most of the Yankees, they'll be returning home soon. Our boys will restore law and order." He paused and smiled, "You know, Mrs. Pering, all of us men still need the support you ladies gave us during the war. You need to be strong for us, now, too."

"No, Mr. Crozier," responded Mrs. Pering, "I am not strong. I've never been strong. I've cried for four years for this awful thing to end. Now I just want things back to normal." Her voice began to tremble. "I want to be surrounded by my men folks, like before. I want to be protected. I want to feel safe. I want the Yankees to go home and just leave us be! I want it to be over!"

"Oh, grandmother, it'll be all right," Sarah pleaded.

CH

The older of the two girls put her arms around her grandmother's shoulders and hugged her close. "We want to stay here, too, but we want to go home. Mother needs us, and I'm sure it's safe there now. Mr. Crozier will look after us and protect us," she added, glancing at Calvin for assurance.

Jenny hugged her grandmother, crying. "I want to stay right here. I'm scared."

Her grandmother pulled her up close in her arms.

Sarah Dekalb was a very attractive young lady of seventeen. Dark hair, brown eyes, and of fair complexion, one could not tell that she had been raised on a small but profitable farm in the middle of Georgia. Refined beyond her age, she was the reflection of both her mother and her father. Her father had been killed at Sharpsburg, defending, of all things, she had heard, some stone bridge. She knew that if her mother had sent for her and her sister, she needed them, whether it was safe at home or not. Jennifer, her sister, was small boned, slender with light hair and green eyes. She was fifteen and still showing her immaturity. Sarah often felt more of a mother to Jenny than a big sister.

Mrs. Pering again looked at Calvin. "You must protect them, Mr. Crozier," she pleaded. "You must! Our world has been turned upside down, and it seems all we've ever believed in has vanished. Our worst fears are being realized." Her eyes revealed her fear. "I don't know who these people are that are here and I'm afraid -- I'm afraid for my grandchildren. These people tell me all we wanted was to keep our slaves -- such a cursed institution that God allowed to plague our society," she said, frowning. "Now they tell me I lost my only son and my son–in–law because they were fighting to keep slaves. Oh, how little do they know and understand. What will they do with us, Mr. Crozier?" she asked, as she seemed to stare deep into Calvin's soul.

He laid his hand on hers. "Those men can't take from us what's in our hearts, Mrs. Pering," Calvin whispered. "What we believed in before the war hasn't been taken away. Our values haven't been surrendered. They're ours to protect, but never surrender. Those people may never understand that. We fought to live separate from them, and many of our boys didn't make it home fighting just for that. Your sons died for that one reason that those people can deny, but never change. We fought honorably, as we were taught. We'll

8

continue to live with those values and principles that we all believe in. They won't force us to surrender them. You, your granddaughters and all of us will be all right. You will see." Calvin smiled at the woman.

"Folks, we're ready to board," announced the conductor, as he passed them heading toward the train.

Just then a blast of steam shot across the double tracks from the engine, startling the ladies. Mrs. Pering wiped tears from her eyes, gave her granddaughters a prolonged hug, a kiss on each forehead, and wiped the tears from Jenny's eyes. "Thank you, Mr. Crozier. What you said helps. If I just knew that all the men felt as you do, I wouldn't be afraid. Please remember that these are my most precious grandbabies, and I couldn't live if…"

"Grandmother, we'll be fine," interrupted Sarah. "We'll have you in Georgia with us before long!"

"Oh, God forbid. Georgia! Me in Georgia! No, Sweet Pea. You come back to visit your grandmother in North Carolina!"

Calvin laughed, as he led the girls to where the conductor was waiting at the car entrance. Calvin assisted each in turn to maneuver the three steps into the doorway. He looked back at Mrs. Pering to give her one last smile of assurance. As he turned, Calvin looked down the platform in time to see Jim and Josh disappearing into the rear car.

Calvin followed the girls into the coach and watched as they picked their seats, side by side, with Jenny insisting on the window seat. Calvin moved into the seat behind them. Others came into the car and did likewise. Two officers in uniform walked down the aisle, both glancing down at Calvin as they passed, apparently noticing his clothes. He watched them move to the front of the car and seat themselves.

Calvin noticed for the first time the position of his knife. It was uncomfortably digging into his side; he reached beneath his jacket, pulled it from his belt, and put it in his feed sack on the seat beside him. He looked up to see Sarah staring back over the seat, eyes wide with surprise.

"For your protection, if need be," he smiled. Sarah said nothing to her sister.

He had obtained the knife before he left Maryland. It wasn't new, but it was certainly a formidable weapon. He had heard of many of the dangers the boys were experiencing traveling back to the south. The knife had cost him dearly -- he had traded his watch -- his father's watch -- to purchase it. It had been hard not to lose that watch after his capture and imprisonment. But now his decision to use it to obtain a weapon had already proved its value. Two days earlier while traveling on foot in southern Virginia, Jim and Josh had been accosted by two strangers, apparently highway robbers, at their makeshift camp. Calvin was taking a late "bath" in a nearby stream. When he returned and made his presence known, weapon in hand, the scoundrels quickly disappeared into the darkness.

Now, as he sat looking at the two young girls seated ahead of him, he felt reassured by the presence of the weapon.

Calvin's journey through Virginia had been an awakening. He hadn't imagined the destruction of the cities of Richmond and Petersburg. The prisoners who had come in from that front had told him about the fighting in Virginia. But he wasn't prepared for what he saw. He had at least imagined that much of the destruction would have been removed. The papers in Maryland sounded positive, speaking of the northern money flowing into the south. Where was it being spent? Certainly not in Richmond! The farms seemed idle in much of the area he'd seen in North Carolina. Greensborough, the site of the surrender of Johnson's army, wasn't much affected by the war, material wise, but that's where Sherman's march had ended. What of South Carolina and Georgia? Was it as bad as Richmond? Certainly those northern investments were being used to rebuild some of the destruction the papers had spoken about.

His fears of what lay ahead in South Carolina and Georgia continued to grow. There had been many more slaves in those states than in North Carolina and Virginia. The Federals should have things under control. If the number of troops occupying the south was just half as many as the papers had said, there at least had to be law and order. Some of the stories drifting up north were mere exaggerations. At least, he hoped this was the case.

His thoughts began to drift toward home and his family. Calvin came from a large family, two sisters and four brothers, all living in Galveston. He had tried to write to them in prison, but it was nearly hopeless. It had been too difficult to get writing materials. His family knew he'd been captured, but he wasn't sure after that. He'd not received any mail from home since last year. He had written at Point Lookout, but afterwards he found out that even in the hospital, outgoing mail was a factor of money -- if you didn't have any, the letters seemed to "get lost."

He looked out the window to see a group of soldiers moving at the double quick -- no more than a small company apparently hurrying to board the cars. He thought this surprising, as he believed most of the Yankees were heading home. He stared at the men as they moved past, wondering where they were from. Did they know they held the future of the south in their hands?

"Mr. Crozier, do you care that you don't even know our names?" asked Sarah.

The question brought Calvin back to the moment.

"I had thought of that, but I figured when you want me to know, you'll properly introduce yourselves," Calvin responded.

"Then, I'm Sarah Dekalb and this is my sister, Jennifer," said Sarah.

"I'm delighted to meet you. If there's any service I can be to you, please just ask," offered Calvin.

"You can shoot me a Yankee!" Jenny suddenly proclaimed.

"Jenny, behave yourself!" exclaimed Sarah.

"Well, I've never seen a dead one, and I'd like to see one dead Yankee," Jenny added.

Calvin laughed. "Now, Miss Dekalb, we can't do that, now that the war's over, or we'd surely be arrested and hung."

By this time her voice had carried to the hearing of the two officers a few seats ahead. One of the men turned and looked at the girls and grinned; he turned back to his companion and said something that was followed by a laugh.

That didn't set well with Jenny. With even a louder voice she added, "They killed my pa, and I'd like to see one of them dead!". This time the officer looked back around but without the grin. He made eye contact with Calvin before turning back to the attention of his seat.

"Miss Dekalb, that was war and the war is over. Talk like that, even from an immature young lady can get us all arrested," Calvin admonished. "Now, is there anything else that I might get for you?"

11

"Yea, I want a ..."

Sarah's hand quickly covered her sister's mouth. "Stop it, Jenny. I thought you told Grandmother you were scared." Sarah said firmly.

"I did and I am scared, and that's why I want..." Jenny murmured.

Again, Sarah's hand blocked the next words that were in her mouth. "I apologize, Mr. Crozier. Jenny has been this way for a while -- since the Yankees came into Salisbury," Sarah said.

"That's quite understandable, Miss Dekalb," Calvin lowered his voice. "Sometime I feel that way myself, and I've seen a few of 'em dead. Let's just pretend that maybe one of those that I shot was for you," Calvin added with a smile, as he looked at Jenny, struggling to get her mouth free. "How about us just keeping our thoughts about this matter to ourselves, Miss Dekalb, for me?" Calvin gave her a wink.

Jenny stared and then nodded.

"Please call us by our first names, Mr. Crozier," invited Sarah.

"Thank you for your friendliness, but I prefer to keep it the way it already is," responded Calvin, politely declining the offer.

"But you can't call us both 'Miss Dekalb'. We won't know who you're talking to," injected Jenny.

"Well, then, if I see a need to distinguish which of you I'm talking to, I'll certainly call you by your first names, all right, Miss Jennie?"

This was agreeable to both.

The shrill noise of the whistle broke the silence of the sunrays as the train slowly began to move, wheels squeaking, and couplings clanking. It appeared that this was what the morning commotion had been all about.

Calvin looked out of the window at the slowly disappearing sights of Salisbury. His thoughts shifted to his two friends. Josh wasn't well, and he was concerned about him. That last long walk had taken so much out of him that Calvin feared they might have to wait for him to regain his strength. But after sleeping, curled in the pile of tobacco leaves, on that farmer's wagon the last five miles to Salisbury, Josh had regained his energy. And, now, they were back aboard the cars and heading for Charlotte. And hope was renewed by the conductor's comments about the rails being in use all the way through South Carolina.

Calvin watched as Sarah reached out and took her sister's hand. He knew that they were both nervous about what lay ahead, but Sarah was being the big sister. Calvin smiled, as he thought briefly of his sisters. He closed his eyes and let his thoughts focus on going home. It had been hard for him to do this for what seemed like eternity. He feared he would be giving himself false hopes. He had seen too many of the men not make it at Camp Douglas and then, later, at Point Lookout. There, it seemed to be even harder. They all seemed so close to starting the trip home and to see the end come there was disheartening. But now, he just drifted into those memories that seemed so long ago....

*Wednesday, August 12, 1861*

*Dear Brother Calvin,*

*It seems such a long time since I saw you last and yet it has been beet a few weeks. Neither Brother John nor Brother Wily have written and Ma is fittin to whip them both when she sees them next, according to her. Pa has been working the fields every day and misses you and the boys terrible.*

*I have been sewing a lot since you left and Ma says that we will soon have enough cotton ginned and wool sheared to make socks for the entire Confederate army.....*

*......Jimmy is home for a brief visit - his regiment is moving to Mississippi and Sis is glad and sad at the same time. She says she's afraid she won't every see him again. You and Wily and John best come home like you said you would. You promised. Remember, you said you would bring back the purse I gave you. Ma says to take care of her bible. Pa is going*

*to the PO to mail his letter to you, and he's waiting on mine to put with it. I got to close.*

*Love and kisses*
   *Your sis, Mary*

"Mr. Crozier, is this the way you look after your charge?" questioned Sarah. "You've been back there asleep for two hours, and we're just about to Concord; do you realize what might have happened to us during that time you've been neglecting your duty? Bet they didn't let you sleep like that when you were on watch in the army," questioned Sarah with a smile.

"No, ma'am, they didn't," Calvin said quickly, coming out of his snooze. "Didn't stay still long enough to get much chance to sleep like that." Another flash of home went through his mind. "I did sleep a lot in the saddle, though, Miss Dekalb."

"You were in the cavalry? I thought certain you were in the infantry, like my pa," injected Jenny. "You don't look strong enough for the cavalry."

"I haven't been in the cavalry for sometime. Seems that I got captured up in Ohio by the Yanks and spent a time as a prisoner," said Calvin with a forced smile.

Jenny looked at Calvin with renewed interest. She had heard so many things about those prisons -- terrible things.

"Did you eat rats?" she asked with a frown.

"Jenny! Of course he didn't eat rats!" interrupted Sarah. She stared right along with Jenny for what Calvin thought was a most uncomfortable moment.

Calvin answered with a smile, "No ladies, I didn't eat rats." He paused. "Well, I don't think that meat they gave us as rations was rat."

Both girls swallowed hard. Without another word, they turned back toward the front of the train in silence.

Calvin smiled at their innocence. The whistle again sounded, and a few houses came into view through the window.

*March 4, 1862*

*Dear Diary*

*It has been a dreary rainy day and I have been inside all day. There were no letters from any of the boys today and I was much disappointed by that. Mr. Dickerson and Mr. Daniel came by yesterday to see Ma and Pa and it scared us all. We were afraid they were bringing bad news. It seems that we are all getting more anxious day by day about this war and the many tragedies we have already seen.. Brother Jim writes more than Calvin, Wily, or John, and I guess I know why. Sister Betsy would come after him if she didn't get letters. I just wish I would hear from the boys more, especially Brother Calvin. He has always been my favorite and I guess it is because he has always been here. All girls need a big brother I guess, and with Calvin it has always been special. He has always taken me places and he's such fun to be with. He will always be special.*

*Mary*

"A fifteen minutes stop folks. This is Concord. Got to take on water. Fifteen minutes, that's all." said the conductor, as he passed toward the rear.

As the train came to a stop, Sarah and Jenny rose to exit the car. "Coming, Mr. Crozier, or do we trust those folks out there. There can't be more than a few dozen Yankees," commented Sarah, bending as she looked out the window toward the depot.

"Right with you, ladies," responded Calvin. He rose as the girls passed, reached back to his "luggage" and removed the knife. He quickly inserted it into his belt, concealing it with his worn gray jacket. He looked up to see one of the Federal officers looking. He ignored his stares and continued his movements, following Sarah and

15

Jenny.

When he reached the platform, Jim and Josh were standing there, waiting, both looking awkward, but with smiles, hoping Calvin would introduce them.

"These fine looking men are my friends," Calvin said, as he gestured toward them. "This is Josh Todd and the one hiding behind such a glorious beard is Jim Walker from Louisiana. We've been together since '63, in sort of…. confined company."

Jim quickly removed his hat and both men dipped their heads with a smile.

"Did y'all eat rats in prison?" blurted Jenny.

A laugh from Calvin and a startled gasp from Sarah were all that was heard, as the girl waited, expecting an answer.

"To the depot, ladies," said Calvin, nudging them forward past his two friends, who were too dumbfounded to speak.

Josh quickly caught up to Calvin and whispered, "what was that about?"

"Nothing, Josh, just a small joke," answered Calvin. "Please try to ignore young Miss Dekalb, as her manners aren't quite refined as yet."

Once in the depot, Calvin walked to a small table on the right side of the room. He scooped up a dipper of water, and, as he swallowed its contents, he watched Sarah and Jenny exit a rear door and move down a short wooden walkway to a small outbuilding.

"Care for a biscuit, mister?" inquired a voice from behind the counter, "just three cents, jam included."

They looked inviting, but Calvin gestured "no".

"I believe I will," said Jim, moving toward the plate with his hand reaching in his pocket. He removed a three–cent piece and handed it to the clerk. He spooned a large helping of homemade pear preserves onto the biscuit, and carried it out through the front door. Calvin watched through the window as Jim broke a large piece from the biscuit and handed it to Josh. Calvin smiled, thinking that kind of honest generosity probably would be the only thing he would miss about the past two years.

Jim had just turned twenty, having joined the army late in '62 at the age of 17. Josh was the same age as Calvin; he was the only married man of the three. He had talked much about his wife during those long nights at Camp Douglas and about his daughter whom he hadn't seen. She was born in the winter of '63–64, and Josh was worried when he got news that his Betsy had given birth at that time of year. Even in Alabama, the winters could be deadly. But just a few months ago, he had heard they were doing fine, his little girl walking and talking and taking the "world by the ears", according to Josh.

Calvin turned to see Sarah and Jenny come back into the station.

"Be with you in a minute, ladies," Calvin said, as he moved past them through the rear door.

Calvin had to wait his turn, but he was back in the station just in time to see the girls climbing back aboard the cars. He moved onto the platform outside and looked toward what appeared to be the center of town; it wasn't much of a town, according to Texas standards, but it did appear to be quite busy. He looked down the tracks a short distance and watched as men unloaded cotton bales from a wagon onto a freight car on a side track. It gave him a sense of relief to see cotton being marketed. He knew cotton in Texas wasn't being baled yet.

"All aboard!" shouted the conductor. "All aboard!"

Calvin entered the front car and took his seat again behind the girls. When he had sat down, Jenny turned, holding out her hand to Calvin. She handed him a piece of biscuit, covered in pear preserves.

*BH*

July 28, 1863

Dear Brother Calvin,

It's been too long since the family has received news from you. Brother Jim is home wounded and his injury is healing just fine. Sis is over him day and night tending him. He says he may stay right at home in that feather bed from now on with a wife to look after him like Sister Betsy is doing. We heard of the great battle in Pennsylvania with General Lee's army and the lists have been coming in of the Texas boys killed there. I'm glad you're not with General Lee. It seems that is where most of the fighting is. Jim says the cavalry under Morgan is now in Ohio and he thinks you may be there making raids on Yankee farms. I kind of hope so, but I can't help but worry about you and the boys. Ma had a crying spell two nights ago over you all, and Pa made her stop and all of us read the bible and pray. I trust God that it will help protect you. Little brothers Jimmy and Zek say they miss you, too.....

Your sister,
Mary

# Chapter 2

It was a relief when the train slowed to a stop at the Charlotte station. The ride during the afternoon had been hot; not much fresh air to be had, unless you wanted to breathe the smoke from the engine, even in the front car. The leather bench seats were better than a horse's saddle but that was about all. Calvin's whole body seemed to still be in motion, even after the train had stopped.

Calvin, Sarah, and Jenny entered the station house, closely followed by Josh and Jim. Charlotte was much bigger than Calvin expected. It certainly didn't look like the war ever reached here from what he had already seen.

He walked to the counter and inquired about transportation south. He showed the station clerk their tickets, who then looked at a chart behind the counter.

"You'll be taking the train to Winnsboro, South Carolina, in the morning," said the clerk. "You'll have to change trains again there and again in Anderson. Gauge differences, you know. Georgia is still uncertain, once you get to Atlanta. There're a couple of other trains due in tonight, so you might want to go ahead and make yourself comfortable."

As Calvin turned to walk away, the clerk added, "Don't mean to be nosey, but you're still in uniform. You know it's been months and the Yanks around here don't look friendly toward you fellows still in gray clothes," the clerk cautioned.

"Just been recuperating from Federal hospitality in Maryland, and I'll be home in Texas soon. These clothes will probably make a nice warm fire when I get there," smiled Calvin. He walked back to Sarah and Jenny.

"We'll be here tonight, ladies. Train doesn't leave 'til after daylight tomorrow," said Calvin. "I suggest that you take possession of one of those benches over there 'cause I suspect there won't be much sitting room in here before long. Two more trains arriving tonight. I'll be just outside for awhile, and Jim and Josh should be close, too. I'll grab a chair later or sleep on the platform in hearing range," he added.

"Mr. Crozier, if you're to be our escort, we demand that we know where you are at all times," said Sarah. "You promised Grandmother and you just can't leave us alone."

"Of course not, Miss Dekalb, I won't do that," Calvin consoled the ladies. "I'll be right outside and I'll be able to see you through the windows. Josh and Jim will be there, too. I'll sleep inside the station tonight where you'll be able to see me, if that's what you want, even if I have to sleep on the floor." The latter didn't seem such a pleasant alternative to him, but he didn't want the girls to be afraid.

Calvin watched as Sarah moved toward one of the benches at the back wall, where she could have a clear view of the platform and tracks. Jenny followed close behind, once glancing back in Calvin's direction. He smiled.

Calvin turned to walk outside. He saw the station clerk looking at him. His look made him uncomfortable about his clothes. This surprised him. He had expected to feel less conspicuous about his uniform the farther south he traveled. The clerk's comments also concerned him. He began to wonder just how the Federals were treating the southern people.

He went through the door and saw Jim and Josh sitting on two barrel heads at the end of the upper platform. Their attention was on a small group of soldiers outside a tent on the other side of the train yard.

"How was the ride?" asked Calvin. Both heads turned in his direction.

"Probably not as nice as yours, Cal." responded Jim, "but tolerable.

You see that fellow yonder?" he asked, as he gestured toward two men talking at the bottom of the steps at the end of the platform. "He's from Augusta, Georgia. Said he's been home since March. Said he'd been wounded at Richmond and sent home to repair himself; but he never returned to Virginia. He said the Federals in Augusta were taxing the people to pay for their upkeep." exclaimed Jim. "It don't make sense."

Josh added, "He said there had been trouble in Augusta since the end came -- lots of idle blacks there and getting into mischief regular. Even some robberies were being done by Federal troops, mostly after dark, against the blacks, who ain't got much anyhow."

All three were now watching the soldiers in the distance.

Josh continued. "He said there was a regiment of black soldiers who were there 'til early August. He said nobody liked them. Some of the boys in one of the Federal cavalry units rode through their camp one night, shooting. Actually shot a cook woman in the arm. They never did catch the culprits."

"Something tells me things ain't quite like the papers in Maryland said they were, boys," Calvin sighed. "I have a feeling our people have already had a rough time because of these visitors. I'll live through this thing, with the help of God, and I won't be outdone by those people," he said, as he gestured toward the Federals' camp.

Calvin had determined many months ago that if he survived the ordeal of prison life, he could live through defeat in the war and whatever it offered afterwards. He didn't consider himself any different than the other men who had returned from the war, but he did know he was a survivor. What he'd said to Mrs. Pering was how he felt. They could do as they pleased with him, as he guessed they had won that right, but he'd surrender nothing. He knew the generals had surrendered their armies to save their soldiers lives, but nobody ever considered that their honor or their beliefs were surrendered. Some of the men had refused to take the oath. Others rearranged the words slightly when they said it, but that didn't matter to Calvin now. He knew the only way for his people to pull through this was to work through it together. They would do whatever it took to survive, and he would do his part. He was ready to get started. He was ready to be home.

"What you thinking so hard about, Cal?' asked Jim.

"Oh, nothing; just tired," answered Calvin. He dropped to the edge of the platform and sat quietly.

Sarah and Jenny had placed their luggage under the bench and had removed the portion of their food their grandmother had so tenderly packed for them for their supper.

"Now, girls, I'm packing your meals for you," their grandmother had said. "Just unpack what's on top, first, and that's your next meal. There's food enough, if you eat like ladies. And remember, there will be people around looking, so eat like ladies."

Sarah smiled to herself. She wondered what it was going to be like at home. Her mother had sent them to their grandmother's in June of last year, and it seemed so long since she had seen her. She missed her mother. She had begged her not to make them go. But with rumors of

Sherman's army coming, her mother would consider nothing else. Their cousin had ridden with them to Salisbury. He was on the way back to eastern Virginia, some place called the Blackwater, south of Norfolk. That seemed so long ago, and so much had changed. Tears began to well up in her eyes.

It was a relief that morning had finally come. Sarah and Jenny gathered up their baggage and went out on the platform to join Calvin and his two friends. True to his word, Calvin had slept in a chair beside the girls, but they all had a restless sleep. People were moving in and out and talking through the night. It was nearly ten o'clock when the last train arrived from Shelby and much later before things got quiet enough to sleep. Then, the Winnsboro train had arrived just at daybreak, seemingly just as Sarah's eyes had finally closed.

"What train was that which woke us up?" asked Sarah, as she and Jenny approached Calvin who was sitting with Jim and Josh on a bench. All three men were eating apples.

"That was our train, coming in from Winnsboro," Calvin answered.

"Why isn't it here?" asked Jenny.

"It's gone to the terminal to turn around, probably will pick up a few freight cars before it gets back to the depot," responded Jim. "It's going to be at least another two hours before it's time to leave."

"Why so long?" asked Jenny.

"They have to service the engine, take on water and wood, and it's just going to take a little while," answered Jim. "You ladies want to sit down?"

"No, thank you," answered Sarah. "Mr. Crozier, would you be so kind as to escort us up the street? The clerk said there was a restaurant just a block or so from here, and we would like to go there."

"Yes, ma'am," responded Calvin, as he rose. "If you would like to leave your baggage here with Jim and Josh, I'm certain it'll be safe."

"We'll be right here," said Josh.

The girls arranged their baggage at the end of the bench and walked ahead of Calvin down the platform toward the steps. Three soldiers were just starting up when they saw the girls at the top of the stairs. They moved back in unison and waited for the girls to pass. Calvin watched the men with interest as they in turn watched the ladies. Nothing was said until Calvin passed.

"What's a Reb in uniform doing with such fine looking ladies?" one asked almost rudely.

Calvin looked back, smiled and simply responded, "Family."

The soldiers watched as the three moved up the street.

"Hey, look here, two more in uniform! What's this? You boys regrouping for another fight?" the tall lanky one joked.

"Not hardly, yank. Just trying to get home," Josh responded.

"And where's home?" asked another.

"Alabama. It's been a while," he answered. He looked into the face of the soldier and could see no malice.

"Where you been for so long, Johnny?" the soldier asked.

"I was captured at Knoxville and spent some time as a prisoner. Been getting well since the war ended," added Josh.

"I was at Knoxville in Fort Sanders in '63," the soldier volunteered.

"Well, yank, we may have seen each other there, 'cause that's where I was caught," Josh said.

"Hell of a fight you boys put up. I know I wouldn't have wanted to climb that hill with what we had waiting," he said.

"We got up the hill, okay. It was those high walls ya'll had, covered with ice, even. Nobody could stay there long." Josh smiled back. "What unit were you with?"

"20th Michigan," he responded. And you?"

"I was attached with the 16th Georgia. A couple of our companies were sent in with them for the attack," Josh informed him. "I wasn't supposed to even be there. Got trapped in that gully ya'll called a ditch and it was sure death if we tried to leave. Spent a long night in that cold ditch,"

"Come on, Will," demanded one of the other soldiers. "We ain't got time for no reunions."

The soldier from Fort Sanders smiled at Josh. "You boys be careful. I hear things ain't too safe farther south. Maybe we'll see each other some other time, Johnny," he added, as they walked away.

November 5, 1863

Dear Brother,

I have been heart broken since we found out you are now a prisoner of the Yankees. Pa has been trying to find out where they have taken you and I am writing in hopes that we will know where to mail this letter soon. The thought of those people having you in their prison frightens me beyond words. I just want this thing to be over and have you at home once again. Ma has been talking about you and Brother Wiley and Brother John every day, until we found out you were captured and now it's if she is scared to say your name. We all hope we will get a letter from you saying you are safe. Pa has us pray together every night now for you and the boys. Pa has to lead all the prayers, as Ma gets too upset if she tries. I love you dearly.

Your sister,

Mary

"And what gives you the right to make us family, Mr. Crozier?" asked Sarah.

"Just trying to avoid a fight," answered Calvin, as he followed the ladies up the street. "I hope you weren't offended."

Calvin watched as two men across the street loaded what appeared to be sacks of grain into a wagon. A third man, wearing an apron, stood by the door of the building, also watching. A little distance farther, a young black man was sweeping the walk in front of a hardware store. On the street ahead of Sarah and Jenny, a man was helping a woman into a carriage. A dog barked as it followed a rider at the far end of the street. Calvin thought that it was good to see life somewhat normal again.

"This looks like it," said Sarah, as she tried to peer into a window, mostly blocked by a pair of pink curtains. The door opened beside them, and two men came out. They were dressed in suits, minus the coats -- one heavy set, wearing a vest a size too small. The other one was a black man, also in shirt, vest and tie. He looked at Calvin, his eyes traveling down his clothes to his shoes. He paused. He then looked back up with a broad grin. "Welcome home, Reb. Welcome to the new south." Both men laughed, as they looked at each other and walked on past. Calvin stared.

"Coming, Mr. Crozier?" asked Sarah.

"Oh, no ma'am; I'll just wait out here," he said, still looking toward the two men as they crossed the street.

"We insist that you let us buy you breakfast, Mr. Crozier. You were kind enough to stay close last night," Sarah insisted.

"I can't do that, Miss Dekalb. I'll be fine out here," Calvin moved to the edge of the walk to seat himself.

"But we may not be safe in there. You just saw what came out. Lot of those men around here now. Please?" she pleaded.

Calvin glanced once more in the direction of the two men as they moved along the walk in front of the hardware store. The black man bumped the man sweeping, knocking him aside. He said something to him, frowned, and they continued down the street.

"Well, since you put it that way, I'll at least sit with you," Calvin surrendered.

He followed the two girls into the restaurant, removing his hat as he went in. The smell was of bacon, ham, and fresh baked apples. Several people he recognized from the train depot were there; all but one table was occupied. A black man was setting plates of fried eggs, ham, hominy grits, and biscuits in front of a white haired man and what appeared to be his wife.

"Good morning, folks. There's a table there," a waitress greeted them, gesturing toward the empty table. "I'll be right with you."

Calvin followed Sarah and Jenny to the table, assisted Jenny with her chair, and waited until they were both seated before he took his seat. He laid his hat on the floor beside his chair.

"You should be hungry by now, Mr. Crozier. That apple I saw you eating for breakfast couldn't have been very satisfying," Sarah smiled.

"It was sufficient," he responded.

"You sure don't seem too friendly, this morning, Mr. Crozier," suggested Jenny.

"Jenny!" Sarah looked at her sister with a scolding glance. "I doubt that Mr. Crozier rested too well last night in that chair."

"You're right, Miss Jenny. My thoughts have been distracted. I didn't mean to be rude," Calvin said, apologetically.

Jenny smiled, glad that Calvin had finally called her by her first name.

"I rested just fine in that chair last night," Calvin said, now looking at Sarah. "Maybe I'll have a glass of buttermilk, if I might. I haven't had that in some time," he added.

"Ahh," frowned Jenny. "I can't stand that taste."

Sarah again smiled. "I'm glad you finally agreed to join us, Mr. Crozier. Some eggs and biscuits would go good with that, don't you think?" she asked.

He declined with a nod of his head.

"Tell us about being a prisoner, Mr. Crozier. Was that prison really bad?" Jenny asked.

"Miss Dekalb, let's not talk about that. I'd much rather talk about Georgia. I've never been there. Tell me about your home," Calvin suggested.

"Nothing much to talk about. How did you get captured?" Jenny asked quickly, switching the attention back to him.

He looked at Sarah and grinned.

"Yes, Mr. Crozier, tell us about your war. We haven't talked to anyone who was captured," Sarah said, agreeing with Jenny.

"What can I get for you?" The lady who had greeted them was at the table. "You folks are traveling, I guess."

Sarah ordered for both her and Jenny and then said, "Buttermilk and some biscuits for Mr. Crozier."

"No, ma'am; just a glass of milk," Calvin corrected.

"Buttermilk?" she asked.

"Yes, ma'am," he answered with his usual smile.

"How did it happen? How did you get caught by the Yankees?" Jenny asked again, unwilling to let Calvin off the hook.

"Not much to tell. Just got careless, and they caught me."

"Mr. Crozier, from what I've already seen about you, careless is not a satisfactory answer," injected Sarah.

"I was a member of the 3rd Kentucky Cavalry, riding in General Morgan's command. General Morgan had been ordered into Kentucky to..."

"General John Morgan? I've heard of him. He's kind of famous or something. You rode with him?" interrupted Jenny.

"Yes, General Morgan's quite well known, but I was just under his command. We were ordered..."

"Did you know the general? Did you see and talk to him?" she interrupted again.

"No, I didn't know the general. I was just a private in his cavalry corps, but I did see General Morgan often. He was a brave man," answered Calvin. "We were ordered to attack the Federals who were threatening General Bragg in Tennessee. We were supposed to distract the Yankees so that General Bragg could retreat to Chattanooga."

"I bet General Morgan never retreated," Jenny said, smiling.

"Yea, General Morgan probably never retreated, but maybe this time, it might have been better," Calvin said. "He was determined to go into Ohio, even against General Bragg's orders, and that's what we did. It seemed that there were Yankees everywhere we turned, but the general was determined to go north. We eluded infantry and cavalry at the Ohio River and crossed into Ohio."

"How many men were with you?" asked Sarah.

"About 2500," answered Calvin.

"Bet that took a lot of boats to cross the river," Jenny added.

"We crossed on a bridge that some of the boys had captured, Miss Dekalb. We couldn't have made it on boats with all our horses," Calvin corrected. "By then, they knew we were coming, I guess. It seems that we had cavalry chasing us the rest of the time we were in Ohio."

"We just had a jolly good time, staying ahead of the Federals for a couple of weeks, generally heading east toward western Virginia," Calvin said. "I think about all of us got new horses."

"You mean you stole them?" asked Sarah, surprised.

"Well, no. We traded them most of the time," answered Calvin.

"You stole them!" injected Jenny.

"Well, we were in Ohio and that's in Yankee land, I think. By this time, the Yankees had taken most of the horses in Tennessee, so maybe we were still just trading," suggested Calvin, using some of his Texas wit. He winked at Jenny.

"Things didn't go too good after that," Calvin continued. "General Morgan had us pretty well split up, going in different directions to confuse the enemy, but he had us rejoin near Cincinnati. We passed right through that city at night heading east."

Both girls were now listening intensely.

"Again, we scattered in different directions with orders to regroup near the Ohio River, east of Cincinnati," Calvin went on. "It was there that we got surrounded. We were told we were on our own and to scatter, and some of the boys got out, including General Morgan, but..."

"Of, course, I knew he would!" Jenny added, excitingly.

Calvin glanced at her, but without his smile.

"Many of our men were killed in that fight. Our squad was still pretty much together, as we crashed through some underbrush, only to suddenly come into a clearing right in the middle of what looked like an entire regiment. I got hit from behind, and the game was pretty well up. I was gathered up with the rest of my squad that hadn't been shot, and we were soon on the way back to Cincinnati. They say we were captured near Syracuse, but it was a place called Buffington Bar, on the Ohio."

"How did General Morgan escape?" asked Sarah.

"I was later told that some of the men drowned in the river, but that General Morgan made it across with about a hundred men," Calvin answered. "But he regrouped and crossed back into Ohio, attacked the Federals and helped nearly three hundred more escape. He took those troopers and turned northeast toward Pennsylvania, but they were forced to surrender before they crossed out of Ohio."

The girls stared, looking somewhat disappointed that General Morgan had surrendered.

"But the General wasn't to be outdone," Calvin said, smiling. "They brought him and his troopers back to Cincinnati, where we had just left. We were sure disappointed when we heard that they had brought him and the rest of our unit in. We had gotten transferred to Camp Chase, near Columbus, but they kept General Morgan and the rest of our officers in Cincinnati. Soon after that we were transferred to Camp Douglas near Chicago, and it wasn't long before we heard that General Morgan had escaped and made it back to the South.

"Yea! for General Morgan!" exclaimed Jenny.

The waitress returned with the black waiter, carrying their breakfast. Calvin stared with anticipation at the cold glass of buttermilk that was set in front of him. The woman set a large plate of biscuits in the center of the table and, smiling at Calvin, said "I hope you enjoy those biscuits. Eat up."

He looked up in surprise and then smiled his appreciation. He glanced at Sarah, to see her looking at him, also smiling.

**W**hen they had finished eating, Sarah, followed by Jenny, went to the table where the waitress was sitting. She was told there would be no charge for the biscuits. She counted out the coins from her purse and handed them to the woman. Sarah looked back and saw Calvin remove two more biscuits and slip them into his jacket pocket. She smiled. Calvin caught up in time to open the door for them and followed the girls back into the street.

As they walked toward the depot, Jenny inquired, "What about that prison in Chicago, Mr. Crozier?"

"Not much to tell. It was unpleasant, and a lot of our men died there. Deathly cold in winter," Calvin responded. "Josh was brought in not too long after I arrived, and then Jim. It was good having them as friends." He paused. "And we didn't have to eat rats," he added, laughing.

Josh and Jim were still sitting on the bench where they had left them. Sarah saw Calvin reach into his pocket and remove the two biscuits, handing one to Jim and one to Josh.

*September 3, 1864*

*Dear Brother Calvin,*

*Still no word from you but we all are hopeful that our letters are getting through to you somehow. Pa and me made a trip to Dallas to try to find out news about you. When I* found out Pa was going to the war offices there, I would not take no for an answer until he agreed to take me with him. I had my first ride on the cars as that is how we traveled. The ride was exciting but frightening at first because of how fast the train was moving. I had thoughts of how much fun it could have been to have you and the boys and Sis and Brother Jim and Ma and the little ones with us, too. Oh, such a sad time. It was all sad and frustrating for Pa and me in Dallas. We went to three different offices and everyone was caring but not much help. We were finally told to write to the Yankee war office in Washington and maybe to send our letters to you there and they could get them to you. Surely, they must know where you are if you are their prisoner! We were told of the great explosion in Petersburg by the Yankees there and how they were all shot when they were trapped in that big hole. Pa said he also heard that the Yankees are now using black soldiers against us. Such a terrible people the Yankees are. I don't understand much about this war but I pray that we will win and not have to be subjected by those people anymore. Pa and I went to see a preacher in Dallas about you. He just returned home from Richmond. He told Pa that the soldiers had thought the Yankees would at least fight an honorable war against us, but they have no morals. He said the people now are losing all respect for the Yankees....

Your loving sister,

Mary

# Chapter 3

"Lieutenant! Get the men loaded and ready to travel. Now! They're moving too slowly." shouted Colonel Trowbridge. "We should have been moving an hour ago."

He watched from a distance as 2nd Lieutenant Hyde looked back in his direction, acknowledging that he had heard his command.

"You heard the colonel, boys; step to it!" he in turn shouted. He watched the progress as the several sergeants pressed their men to hurry with the boarding.

Lieutenant Colonel Charles Trowbridge stood observing the slow process of getting his regiment aboard the train. He was anxious to leave. It had been an unpleasant stop in this foothills town of Walhalla, or "Wall Hollow" as his boys called it, mocking the speech of the local people. It had been nearly a week now since Jerome Furman had been gunned down in the middle of the morning on Main Street. And nobody saw anything more "than a couple of riders that they didn't know." He was still troubled by the whole affair, and he knew they had spent too much time unsuccessfully trying to find the culprits who had done the murder. Now, he just wished that his men were aboard the train and moving.

Trouble seemed to have followed them since they left Savannah. At Augusta he lost over half his regiment to detached duty. Most of his companies had been sent to towns like Walhalla to "assist" other regiments stationed there maintain order. Almost all of his officers were detached, and it wasn't much of a military command left. He had privately questioned the motives of the department when the first of these orders reached the 33rd US Colored Troops. He had complained to General Molineux in Augusta, who in turn forwarded his "concerns" to Charleston, but to no avail. Drunken soldiers riding through their camp in the middle of the night had even attacked his men. He had strong words with Colonel Barton of the 4th Iowa Cavalry over that, but Barton still wouldn't produce those whom were guilty. General Molineux had him move his regiment across the river to Hamburg in South Carolina "to prevent further trouble", as he described it.

He had felt relieved when he had finally received orders in early August to gather up his men and return to Charleston. He procured a train for that sole purpose. But now this affair with Lieutenant Furman getting killed in this forsaken town and the continuing restlessness of his troops were making him nervous. His men had liked the lieutenant, and maybe he should have let them burn this place as they were still threatening to do. But he knew he'd be held responsible. When Lieutenant Hyde came in with that local citizen representing a group of Masons offering to conduct a funeral for Lieutenant Furman, he had felt some relief. As it turned out none of the black soldiers had ever seen Masonic Rites before, and they thought it some special way that the white people of the town were apologizing. And they seemed to have been temporarily appeased. But now their excitement had returned. He was anxious to see all the men aboard and the train moving. They had stayed there too long.

"William, let's board," the colonel said, as he stepped from the depot toward the only passenger car. The rest were modified freight cars to accommodate the soldiers.

William Crandall was the surgeon of the 33rd. He followed the colonel into the car and assisted him in storing his personal bags under the seat. He had been with the colonel almost from the beginning at Hilton Head Island.

Charles Trowbridge was twenty nine years old, five foot, nine inches in height, light complexion, brown hair and brown eyes. He sported a mustache and goatee style beard. He was born in New England and had enlisted in the army in New York in December of '61.

He enlisted as a private but was soon promoted to sergeant. He was given special detached duty handling the contraband slaves whom had been left on Hilton Head Island when they reached South Carolina. He had played a key role in turning these men into a "military" unit. Sergeant Trowbridge had worked hard to teach these men to take orders, to drill, and even march. They had been designated as the 1st South Carolina US Volunteers. He had been with them when they were carried on their first raid under an armed escort. They had been transported south and raided the small Georgia town of Darren. They had performed well and procured a good stock of supplies, which they were allowed to keep for their own use. The men were soon issued uniforms of mostly red shirts and trousers. As the men later said, "it made them easy targets for the Rebs".

"Doc, I don't know what to think of the boys right now," Colonel Trowbridge said to his surgeon as he was taking his seat. "They're good men, but lately they act like they don't want this thing to come to an end. With the way the last two months have gone, I would've thought otherwise."

"A little too much freedom, Colonel," William responded. "With so many of our officers absent, it's been rough on us all."

"Lieutenant Wood! Are they aboard yet?" shouted Colonel Trowbridge through the open window.

"Almost, sir. The last of the boys are going into the last car right now," responded Lieutenant Henry Wood, as he pointed toward the rear of the train. He and Sergeant Rivers moved on in that direction past the colonel's window and out of sight.

"Well, I think it's more than that," Colonel Trowbridge returned to their conversation. "None of the regulars have ever lost any love on the colored troops and now that the fighting is over, the boys' patience is running out."

"What the boys need is one good skirmish with the rebels, colonel," laughed the surgeon. "Too bad for them, that won't happen. It's making 'em nervous with this ambushing still going on and nothing for them to shoot at," added William. "I had hoped we could have enjoyed a few days of rest here, near the mountains, colonel. Most of the men haven't even seen mountains before. And it is a good change from the coast. The air up here seems healthier, but these past several days have us all on edge and worn out."

"I didn't think I'd be so glad to be going back to the coast, myself," injected the colonel with his thoughts still on what might lie ahead. "It'll be good when we're all back together."

It was just another matter of minutes before the train's whistle broke the cool morning air. Two more long blasts and the train jerked forward with an imitation of a rapid retreat, only to be followed by that ever so slow rolling movement of the wheels.

Colonel Trowbridge glanced out the window, looking down a dusty dirt road leading south. A man in a ragged faded shirt sat with a young girl in a wagon waiting for the train to pass. Their mule lazily swished its tail, seemingly ignorant of the train's existence. He thought briefly of New York then raised the window and turned his attention back inside the train.

33

**S**ergeant Robert Smalls pulled his cap down over his eyes as he lazily positioned himself for the train ride to Anderson. A reduced company of the 33rd was waiting there to be reunited with the regiment. That left only the three companies that were being assembled in the town of Newberry, and then they were headed back to Charleston.

This thought brought him mixed feelings. He was glad to be going back to the coast, as all the men were. It had been a tense three weeks traveling through this upper part of the state with reduced numbers. Two men had been wounded near the town of Abbeville and random shooting had occurred most every day. All the men's emotions had reached a fever pitch with the murder of Lieutenant Furman. Now they were itching for a fight, maybe even more than wanting to get back to the coast.

Jerome Furman had been with them from the first, and all the boys liked him. He had been kind to the black race, and the men felt his feelings were sincere. He and Colonel Higginson had been instrumental in getting the boys full pay since they had become an official regiment. It had taken almost a year before the army finally listened to their grievances. They had gotten back pay all the way back to March of last year when they were designated as the 33rd. Colonel Higginson was retired out of the regiment and now the lieutenant was dead, the latest victim of these renegades.

The sergeant was jerked from his thoughts as pieces of wood shattered just above his head. A bullet had torn though the edge of a side board of the car. The men scrambled to peer out through the cracks.

"Open da door!" shouted the sergeant, as he quickly raised his rifle.

"Better be careful, boss," cautioned an excited voice.

Two of the men slid the door partially open. Sergeant Small quickly surveyed the countryside for any signs of movement. Looking back, he saw the flash and smoke from another shot, but this time no other visual evidence -- just a faint report of the weapon in the distance. The train continued to rumble along, leaving the spot of the attack behind.

"Close it shut," commanded the sergeant, after peering into the now silent landscape for another minute. "Wish we could just gets at

34

'em fo' a few minutes; dat all it'd take! Look's like da colonel could get us some cavalry to assist, wid dis thing 'coming a reg'lar nuisance," he added.

"Ain't go'in do dat, sarg," came another voice from somewhere behind him. "We go'in have do it our self. If'n da cunnel would make da train stop when dey start shoot'n, I knows we could catch 'em. We owes 'em, and da cunnel know it."

"Da colonel ain't go'in stop da train, boys," the sergeant responded. "He trying to get us back together and safe in Charleston. I think da fight 'bout gone out'a him."

The men had been talking of "raids" on some of the towns they had been passing through, even before this thing in Walhalla, and Sergeant Small had felt that he'd been instrumental in keeping the lid on the boys for the past two weeks. Yet, he'd joined in with the reaction to punish the whole town of Walhalla when Furman was killed. And he thought it was going to happen, 'til the local white folks did what they did. The only officers present now were Colonel Trowbridge, Lieutenant Hyde, Lieutenant Wood, Lieutenant Child and Doc Crandall, and none of them realized that it wasn't them that were keeping the men in line. He, Ed and Prince were the real bosses. They were the ones who knew how touchy the boys were, and the boys were still listening to their sergeants. What the colonel didn't realize was how close he was to losing even their support.

Trowbridge hadn't made many friends during that first year as a sergeant. There had been a few things happen that didn't set well with the men. But, after the Emancipation, the colonel had worked hard to make them into a fighting force, and he had tried to make them realize what being free was about. He had done well to win their confidence and respect, but it was after he was promoted to lieutenant colonel that he had changed. All he seemed concerned with was the other officers. And now that the war was over, he was losing control. He'd let the army split up their regiment, and the boys blamed him for it. They'd been mistreated by the white soldiers in Augusta. Manny Brook had lost her arm after being shot by those drunken troopers and nobody was punished for the crime. They again blamed Colonel Trowbridge.

Smalls conceded that Sergeant Prince Rivers was the one who was doing the most to maintain some kind of military discipline with the

35

men. Even he was scared of Prince when he was riled.

Tall and muscular, Rivers had joined the regiment as a free man in '63. He'd lived in Charleston as a free black with his mother and his two sisters before the war. All of them had been bought by Ned Rivers, another free black living in Charleston in '48. He'd made arrangements with Prince's mother for them to work for their freedom after that, and in '55 his family was given their papers. His mother had given them his last name, as she said, "to show her thanks fo' a 'good man in what he done fo' dem." Prince had made 1st Sergeant quickly.

Robert again took his seat among the men on the bench and leaned back against the side of the car, trying to make himself comfortable. The train soon lulled him into the sleep he had missed the night before. A tiresome night it had been with the guard not only protecting the camp but making sure the men didn't wander off.

Colonel Trowbridge was jolted into consciousness by the sudden braking of the cars, as the train slowed coming into Pendleton. He hadn't slept much the night before; the uncertainty of the situation with his men deeply concerned him. He couldn't remember falling asleep.

"What's going on, Will?" he asked.

"Water stop, colonel," responded the doctor. "The conductor said we'd be here about fifteen minutes. Town's name is Pendleton."

"Lieutenant Hyde, see to the men while we're stopped," the colonel directed, looking toward the back of the car. "Only those with a necessity can get off. Make it brief and make sure the sergeants keep track of them,"

"Yes, sir," responded the lieutenant.

"I think we all need some rest," suggested Crandall. "The regiment has had pretty tough duty the last week, colonel"

"I suppose so, Will," responded Trowbridge. "We stayed too long in that mountain town."

"Maybe we could stay the night in Anderson and catch up on some sleep. I've been told that there are two regiments of regulars there," the doctor suggested.

"No. We'll have time to rest when we get to Charleston, doc," answered the colonel. "You say there're two regiments in Anderson?"

"That's what I was told in Walhalla," William responded. "The 7th New Hampshire was sent over from Greenville a few weeks ago to join the 7th Connecticut. There's been some strong organized resistance going on there. I understand they know the leader -- a rebel named Mance Jolly, but they haven't been able to catch him yet. I was even told that most likely it was some of his men that gunned down Furman."

"Looks like you've struck quite a find for information, William. Your informant a rebel or someone I might know?" the colonel inquired with a smile.

"Just heard about it this morning before we left. It was from the surgeon of the 47th New York, and you know those surgeons; they can be very reliable, colonel," he answered, coyly.

Rain had begun to fall on this cool September morning. The train slowly came to a stop with the engine in position by the water tower. Two men busily began to unfasten ropes and swing the nozzle into position. Several men were standing under the shelter of an outbuilding, curiously watching to see what this special train was about.

The men watched as two officers stepped from the rear door of the passenger car and moved toward the station, seemingly ignoring the steady rain. A third Federal officer emerged, turned and walked toward the next car in line. Black soldiers became visible as the sliding doors of the remaining cars began to open. As the officer paused at the first car, a soldier jumped to the ground and began shouting orders. This was repeated at each car. Several more uniformed men had now begun to climb from the cars. The officer soon disappeared into the station, only to quickly return and begin giving additional instructions to the men, gesturing toward another outbuilding. Several of the men who were now out of the cars were armed with rifles. These were the first black soldiers the men had seen. They stared in silence as they observed their every move.

Colonel Trowbridge moved to the table by the clerk's desk, picked up a three–day–old paper, and asked an attendant about the facilities.

On the other side of the room the doctor returned the dipper to the water bucket and reached down to remove several crackers from a barrel. He walked toward a man wearing a leather apron and peering out a window.

"Are you the clerk?" asked the surgeon.

The man nodded without moving his attention from the window. "How much further to Anderson," he asked, holding out a penny for the crackers.

Just then, the telegraph key began to chatter.

"Be with you in a minute," responded the clerk, as he quickly moved to his desk. He picked up a pencil and began to write.

The doctor watched as the balding man adjusted his glasses with one hand and continued to write with the other, the key of the telegraph continuing to click out its message. When it had finally stopped, the clerk moved into his seat and began transcribing the message onto an official looking form.

"You Colonel Trowbridge?" he asked, as he continued to write.

"No. That's the colonel there," he answered, pointing toward Colonel Trowbridge coming in the rear door.

"I have a telegram for you if you're Colonel Trowbridge," stated the man. He removed the paper from the pad and turned to hand it to the colonel.

Colonel Trowbridge read the message with interest, frowned, and folded it into his coat pocket.

"Come on, Will." he said, as he turned back to the front entrance.

The doctor followed him out the door.

"Bad news, colonel?" inquired the surgeon.

"Not good. Washington of Company G was found shot Monday past near Ninety-Six Station. Just keep this quiet right now, Will."

"Board up, men!" the Colonel ordered, raising his voice that he could be heard. He moved rapidly through the rain back to the car, closely followed by Surgeon Crandall. As the colonel moved to his seat, he observed that Lieutenant Wood was still fast asleep.

The onlookers continued to watch from under the shelter of the out building. The officer ensured that all the men were aboard and then entered the passenger car. The noise of the whistle echoed off the raindrops that were still steadily falling. The men watched as the train slowly began to roll eastward toward Anderson. They stared at the black soldiers, visible through the sideboards of the cars as they moved past, silently glad they were leaving.

"Any other details in the telegram?" inquired the doctor.

"Just that he'd been missing for three days, and that this news was forwarded to us from the 47th New York in Walhalla," responded the colonel.

"I wonder how Captain Metcalf has held up with his detachment," the doctor thought aloud.

"Lewis did look distressed when they departed for Edgefield," softly laughed Colonel Trowbridge. "Sort of looked like he was being sent to charge the entire Reb army by himself. I hated to see him leave, and I'll certainly be glad to have Captain Metcalf back, as well as the other officers. They should be waiting in Newberry -- should have arrived there yesterday."

"Well, Colonel, maybe you'll have your command back together by morning."

Sergeant Edward King was now situated comfortably, lying on his back on top of the regiment's baggage. His eyes were closed, but he wasn't asleep. His thoughts were of Charleston and his wife waiting on him there. He had married Susie in 1863 on St. Simon's Island. She had crossed into the Federal lines in '62 and had been assigned to assist the regiment with laundry and cooking. Susie, like himself, could read and write, and she spent much of her free time teaching the boys to read. Ed had done the same, but he felt his efforts were futile compared to what she was doing. All the boys were taken with her.

When orders arrived in Augusta that some of the companies were to be detached, they were told it was too dangerous for any of the women to travel with them. And when the rest of the regiment was ordered into the upstate of South Carolina, all the women were sent to Charleston to await their return. To Ed this seemed unnecessary, since they had traveled with them during the war -- they had even traveled with them to Jacksonville. Sometimes he didn't understand the officers in charge.

Ed King was the 1st Sergeant of Company E and was proud of his position. He had taken the welfare of the men in his company as his personal responsibility, and he felt that the boys had always responded to him because of that. Of course he was aware that his wife's taking time to teach them to read had some part in the matter.

"Sergeant, dig us some rations out of that sack there, 'fore you fall asleep," ordered Lieutenant Asa Child. The lieutenant was sitting on a wood crate beside Sam Stuart.

Ed rose and reached for the sack. He handed it to the lieutenant and retook his seat.

"Is the sergeant usually this quiet?" inquired Sam.

"Had guard last night," responded the lieutenant.

"I don't think nobody slept," said the sergeant. "I know da colonel was up and about half da night -- kept Lieutenant Wood on his toes."

"Is the old man always this nervous about things?" asked Sam. "And Dr. Crandall don't seem much better. Been holding onto the colonel's coat tail since I've been here."

"I ain't seen the colonel quite like he's been the last few weeks, Sam." He's always been excitable, but now it's been different," responded Asa. "And the Doc's always been where you see him," he chuckled, removing a large red apple from the sack. "This thing will be over soon and we'll be out of each other's hair."

"How come you ain't up front with the other officers, enjoying a nice comfortable seat," asked Sam.

"The colonel don't trust you two alone with the baggage, that's why," answered the lieutenant. "Besides, I'd much rather have your company than some other's just now." He finished polishing the apple, and took a large bite.

He had helped pick those apples from some of the trees near Walhalla. He and Lieutenant Furman had borrowed a wagon, had taken some of the boys and ridden a little ways to a small community they called Long Cane and gathered quite a few apples to add to their supplies. That was the day before Jerome had been gunned down. Since then, the colonel had restricted most of the men to camp, except for the special details that went out looking for Rebel snipers. The way the colonel had the details march in the middle of the roads was almost as if he was trying to draw fire with the hopes they might catch one or two of them, even if it cost them another soldier's life. The boys seemed aware of what the colonel was doing, and they didn't care much for it.

"If I might'n be so bold to ask, Doc, how abouts sharing some of dat special medicine I know you carry in dat bag of yourn," suggested the sergeant. "It ain't but da three of us back here."

"Sergeant, you know they don't allow assistant surgeons the same trust as they do the commissioned surgeons," interrupted Lieutenant Child. "I'm fairly sure Mr. Stuart ain't got any of what you're referring to in his bag. Besides, if he did, you couldn't have any 'cause you're on duty, guarding the baggage."

"And you's guarding me, I suppose," added Ed.

"That's right," answered the lieutenant. "So if Sam was allowed to have some of that special medicine you referred to, and if he was so inclined, he could only administer it to himself. But then I'd have to report him to Dr. Crandall, wouldn't I, sergeant?"

"I guess so, boss," grumbled Ed, as he pulled his cap down over his face.

The train rumbled on toward the town of Anderson.

Sunday December 19, 1864
Dear Diary

We all went to Sunday School this morning and listened to the Reverend Mr. Huggins preach a most timely sermon. Afterward, we all went home with Aunt Susanna and Uncle Robert for dinner. A terrible storm came up in the late afternoon and it caused us to be well after dark getting home. The clouds are now gone as I sit here in the window looking at a beautiful moon. It makes me feel closer to my brothers who are camped on some field or traveling on some road tonight under its bright beams of light. I would like to believe that they are also thinking of home and of me and Ma and Pa and Sis. How I miss my brothers, especially dear Brother Calvin...

Mary

# Chapter 4

Solomon Kinard had an unusually busy morning. Customers had been coming in at a steady pace since he opened. Many were just looking, but he had sold more today than the entire previous week. Business had been slow since the 56th New York Regiment had arrived in town three weeks ago.

The wounding of a soldier of the 56th and the resulting house burning had driven tensions to a fever pitch. Arrests had been made, seemingly unfounded, and the shooting was still taking place. Idleness among the blacks had now grown into a problem of much concern. Accusations of "interference with the legal authority" and threats of additional arrests were adding to the uncertainty of what the next moment might bring.

And now the black soldiers had arrived in town.

Word had spread rapidly when the first of them arrived yesterday during the early afternoon. Then news of additional soldiers arriving before dark had produced fear, anger, and hopeless anxiety among the inhabitants of Newberry.

This morning Solomon was seeing activity that was uncommon even in these times, and he related it to everyone's nervousness.

"I hear they're camped about a half mile toward Frog Level," remarked Jake Bowers. "From what I've heard three separate groups arrived yesterday, some coming from Ninety Six and some from below Dutch Fork.

Solomon removed the box of glass jars from the bottom shelf behind the counter.

"Here are the jars you ordered for Sarah," Solomon said, interrupting Jake's chain of thought. "That large order for the station also came in on last night's train, everything except one drum of oil. Appreciate the business, Jake, especially now," he added.

"It's the federals, Solomon. Their movement has had all of us busy at the station," responded Jake. "If it's not supplies from the coast going to the Yankees in the upstate, it's troops being hauled somewhere else."

Jake Bowers had been one of the more fortunate soldiers returning from the war. He had a job waiting when he got home. Mr. Chapman had seen to that. He had arranged for him to take over the foreman's job at the railroad. And it had been a Godsend.

Jake had been a farmer before the war, and he still had his farm. But with his workers gone and a house full of girls, Jake knew he wouldn't be able to make his farm profitable. It was this steady work that was allowing him to hold onto his farm and support his family. Mr. Lewis Chapman was his wife's uncle and had been helping to look after Sarah and the rest of Jake's family while he was gone. Sarah's brother, Sam, was back at the farm helping out as he had done before the war.

The cars had been running continuously until the end came, stopping briefly for a few weeks when Sherman's army passed through. Rail damage had even been minor compared to many of the other communities toward Columbia, and north. Kilpatrick's cavalry had passed east of Newberry, coming within just a few miles of the town. The trains had been sent to Laurens and then Greenville during that time. But they were soon back in service. There were even stories that the Federal army themselves had assisted in some areas getting the trains back in service, undoing what Sherman had done.

The demand on the railroads was now at a peak, and Jake was glad to share some of the Federal money with his neighbors. As foreman at the station, his greatest problem was keeping enough help. Most of the boys returning home were needed with their family farms and only a few had come in looking for work. And when they did, they didn't last long. Even the black workers weren't sure they were supposed to be working for the white men. Jake had tried to make them understand, but it looked like any Yankee soldier who came along and said otherwise could undo in five minutes what it had taken him a week to do.

And now the "new soldiers" were coming through with pockets full of Yankee dollars, looking for "financial opportunity." Lord, Jake knew they all needed the money, but these people seemed to be filled with nothing but greed -- the sinful type, he had thought. He feared what was going to happen to some of his neighbors who had already made "financial arrangements" with some of these strangers.

"Solomon, look yonder!" Jake suddenly said, pointing across the street. "Looks like some more of those welfare people."

Solomon moved from behind the counter toward the window facing Drayton Street. "Yea, looks like those three that came in last

43

night aboard the cars," Solomon answered. "I heard one of them asking one of the Yankee officers at the station about the Wilson's that came in last week. He gave them directions toward the college."

"Going over to see the new swimming hole, huh?" interrupted Earl, with a sarcastic chuckle, as he walked over to join Solomon and Jake in their observations.

"I doubt that, Earl," responded Solomon. "They seemed all business."

"I heard they brought barrels of fresh water from the creek this morning and were hoisting it to the roof of the college building," added Earl. "A regular swimming hole they built up there on top of that building and somebody's using it regularly to keep it serviced like they're doing."

The three men continued to watch as the two women, escorted by a white headed man apparently of means and obviously from some place up north, moved up the wooden walk toward Boundary Street.

"Damn those people," whispered Earl under his breath as he turned away from the window.

"**S**ergeant!" called the colonel.

"Yes, sir?" responded a youth of twenty three years, stepping into the room with sergeant stripes on his arm that appeared half as big as himself.

"Step down the hall and have Captain Loomus come into my office," directed Colonel Tyler.

"Yes, sir," snapped the sergeant, as he turned and left the room. His footsteps on the wooden floor echoed down the empty hall.

Lieutenant Colonel Rockwell Tyler stood beside his desk with his attention directed toward the morning reports that he had just now gotten around to reading. Six feet tall, with graying hair, a distinguished looking man of forty–eight years, the colonel had been quite handsome in his time. But now with four years of field service in the Army of the Potomac and a few unnecessary wrinkles from over indulgence, he looked much older than his age -- too old for his rank. But he wore the uniform well. He was a volunteer.

He had joined in Syracuse in 1861, when President Lincoln had first called for volunteers. Now, by all assumptions, it looked as if he would end his military service in this small South Carolina town no one at home had ever heard of. "Newberry?" he thought, "Is that one word or two?" He could almost hear his neighbor's words.

"Yes, Colonel Tyler?" The words said the arrival of Captain Henry Loomus, adjutant of the 56th New York Volunteers.

"Captain, I see in Captain Watkins' report that the black solders that arrived yesterday are part of the 33rd Colored Troops," the colonel said with apprehension in his voice. "His report doesn't give me any information as to why they are here nor for how long. Did he give any insight to you this morning when he submitted his report?"

"No, sir, Colonel Tyler, Captain Watkins sent his report over by messenger this morning, early, but no other information was presented," responded the adjutant.

"I need to know this information, Captain," added the colonel. "Send Lieutenant Thomas to their camp and present my greeting and tell him to instruct the officer in charge to report to me as soon as practicable. Also, tell him to restrict his men to their camp until after he has reported to me."

"Right away, Colonel Tyler," responded the adjutant as he turned to exit the room.

The colonel was somewhat worried and justifiably so. He had worked hard these past weeks to improve the situation in Newberry. But now the visit this morning by Mr. Johnstone and the other town leaders had him concerned. They had inquired about the black soldiers. Their tone had irritated him, as it could have been interpreted as threatening. But he believed their concerns were for the town and not personal.

They made it plain they didn't like his answers. But the colonel hadn't given them any. He didn't know the answers. It angered him that he didn't know.

"Morning, Solomon," greeted the recognizable voice of Ben Shealy.

"Well, good morning to you, Ben," responded Mr. Kinard, without turning around to formally greet him. "What brings you my way this morning? Business, this time, I hope. You know I got a shipment of good tools in the other day that are reasonably priced."

"Some more of those excess army tools, uh, Solomon?" Ben asked. "Shovels and such from the Confederate army that we helped provide

45

in the first place, and now we're buying them back. Don't it beat all!" added Ben.

"You here to buy something or just to waste my time as usual?" asked Solomon with a kidding grin.

"You know I don't come in here to waste your time. I come by to visit and all I get are insults," responded Ben.

"Better buy something this time, Ben," injected Earl, sitting in a chair by the back window.

"Didn't notice you back there, Earl," said Mr. Shealy. "And I guess you been putting money in Solomon's pocket this morning, too."

"What you come by here to tell us, Ben? 'Know you aching to tell us something," asked Earl.

"Well, yea, but maybe I come by to talk to Solomon and not you," Ben responded sarcastically.

"You tell anybody that'll listen, anything, Ben Shealy." Earl snapped back.

"All right, fellows, act your age," interrupted Solomon. "What news you got, Ben? Something interesting, this time, I hope."

"I just come from the college," began Ben. "I went up there with Young Pope and his daddy, the major, and two other councilmen. We went up there about those black soldiers camped down the road."

Earl sat his chair level on the floor and listened with attention. Solomon laid down his dust rag and moved to the counter.

"Who'd you see?" asked Solomon.

"Colonel Tyler, of course. You know Mr. Pope. He wouldn't waste his time with anyone less than the man in charge," answered Ben, pausing as if waiting for another question.

"Don't play your game, Ben. Tell us what you found out," Earl said, demandingly.

"We didn't find much out at all," continued Ben. "The colonel talked like they might be here awhile. Said that they were here to do their duty, whatever that meant."

"Is this what you're to tell us, that you don't know nothing?" asked Earl impatiently.

"I'm here to tell you I don't think that colonel knows much," said Ben. "'Fore we got to Platt Street one of his officers come galloping by, heading toward Frog Level. I think the colonel don't know much either."

"Well, he must of told you more," insisted Solomon.

"He just said something about obeying the soldiers and not getting in their way," answered Ben. "Boy, did Zek Summer get mad about that. Said something to the colonel about real trouble if he expected the citizens to take orders from the black soldiers."

Solomon and Earl looked at each other with the same expression, knowing Zek Summer didn't make idle threats.

"The colonel then said that the black soldiers were under the command of white officers and the men wouldn't be giving orders to anyone," added Ben. "He told Zek and us just to stay out of their way and there wouldn't be any trouble. But he added that if there was trouble, it wouldn't be good for the town, whatever that meant."

"Morning, Colonel!" greeted Earl. "What brings you into town today?"

"Same as everybody else, Earl. Just to get a look at the 'curiosity' that came to town yesterday," responded Will Lester. "What are you fellows having such a serious discussion about?"

"Same thing, Will," answered Ben. "Seems that no one knows why they're here or what this means."

"Probably just passing through, and I doubt there's much to be concerned about," added the colonel.

William Lester had been the colonel of the 13th Regiment of SC Infantry, and everyone was still calling him by his rank. A tall man with a demanding personality, he appeared to be a natural leader. At the age of thirty–three and soon home from the war, he was now finding that many of the older men in town looked to him for leadership.

So many of the young men that Newberry was basing its future on were now dead from the war. Men like young John Kinard, Dray Rutherford, James Nance, Jim and Bob Maffett, and Will Cromer could never be replaced. He had heard Rev. Martin say last week that it looked like more than 400 of the boys from the district hadn't come home. The town had its mourning, but now people were busy out of shear necessity -- life was staring them hard in the face.

"Solomon, I need a replacement strap for this broken one here," William said, changing the subject back to more important things. "I also need a ten–foot piece of that No. 40 chain."

"I guess you seen plenty of those black soldiers, uh, colonel?" asked Earl.

"I guess I have seen enough, Earl, but they were somewhat different than these men," answered William. "I understand these men are from the coast, local soldiers, most of them, been in uniform for a long time, but made into fighting men only late in the war. The ones in Tennessee were more or less fighting men and used for little else," he continued. "I'm sure you read about these men's actions on the coast and what they were being used for."

"But you think they'll be moving on, colonel?" asked Ben with apprehension.

"Think so, Benjamin," answered William. "I wouldn't worry about them so much."

"It ain't the soldiers so much, colonel," injected Solomon. "Maybe I'm just nervous as how they will fare while here. Some of the boys ain't been very friendly toward none of the Yankee troops that are already here."

"And from what Ben said that Colonel Tyler of the 56th is promising trouble for the whole town if trouble starts with them black soldiers," interrupted Earl.

"Well, word's being passed right now to stay clear of those boys, and if they behave themselves, there won't be no trouble," responded the colonel.

"Maybe you had better be sure to talk to Zek Summer, colonel," added Ben. "Sounds like he and some of the other men may go looking for trouble."

William looked at Ben with an understanding look.

"Things will be okay, boys," William said with assurance. "That colonel at the college knows the situation, and he don't want anymore trouble than us. He'll keep those boys in hand."

"Colonel, a Captain Metcalf to see you, sir," said the sergeant, standing at the door.

"Send him in, Sergeant Graves," ordered the colonel.

"Captain Lewis Metcalf, reporting as ordered, sir," said a voice with a distinct New England accent.

The colonel looked up from his desk and quickly appraised the rather heavyset officer standing in front of him. He was a man of light complexion, about thirty–three with dark bushy hair and a thick mustache to match.

"Come in, captain," responded the Colonel, rising from his desk, returning the salute. "I understand you're with the 33rd?"

"Yes, colonel, I'm commanding Company G of the 33rd US Colored Troops," responded the captain in a tone that could be interpreted as correcting the colonel for his seemingly unwelcome familiarity with his regiment.

"You're the senior officer present, is that correct?" asked the colonel in a slightly colder voice.

"Yes, sir."

"How many soldiers in your command, captain?"

"We mustered 178 men and six officers this morning, colonel -- three companies."

"What are your orders, captain?"

"We were ordered to report to a place near Newberry on the Greenville and Columbia railroad on or about September 5th to await the remainder of our regiment. They're with our colonel."

"And who's your colonel?"

"Lieutenant Colonel Charles Trowbridge."

"Do you know where he is now or when they might arrive?"

"Not sure, colonel. The last we heard was that he was in the upstate near the town of Walhalla. I understand he is to be in Newberry no later than the 9th."

The captain watched as Colonel Tyler turned and walked to the window. He stood there waiting as the colonel continued to stare out the window.

"Colonel Tyler, if I might ask …"

"Captain Metcalf, you understand that you're not under my command while you're here but that Newberry is my responsibility? I ordered you to restrict your men to their camp until we talked for a specific reason. The citizens here haven't seen Negro soldiers, and to be honest, your presence is unnerving to them. I've had enough trouble of my own during the three weeks we've been here, one soldier shot, and others being shot at almost daily. I've already heard reason enough just this morning to tell you that it won't be safe for any of your men here in Newberry."

"Colonel Tyler, if I might say a word, sir?"

"Speak your mind, captain."

"I understand the problems. We've been living them daily since we left Augusta two months ago. We lost a courier last week near Ninety Six, and had two killed in Aiken. We've had another four wounded, and we have yet to catch the first bushwhacker. The men have stood steady through this thing, and they will not be causing any trouble in this town. I'll keep the boys in camp, colonel, as you ask."

"Very well, captain," added the colonel, smiling for the first time since the captain entered the room. "Is there anything you need?"

"Yes, Colonel Tyler. I was ordered to make arrangements for replenishment of supplies the regiment will need when they arrive. Our detachment is also in need of supplies, colonel."

"When you leave, tell Sergeant Graves to direct you to the quartermaster's office. Someone can take you to Captain Fulton. Make what arrangement you can with him from what supplies he can spare and have him send the order to me and I'll sign it," directed the colonel. "I'll have some of my teamsters deliver the supplies to your camp. What transportation has your colonel arranged for your regiment?"

"I understand that he is traveling by special train that will transport us back to Charleston."

"Very well, Captain Metcalf, you're dismissed," concluded the colonel.

Colonel Tyler acknowledged the salute and watched the captain as he exited the room. He went to his desk and jotted down some notes. He again picked up the daily reports and finished his examination of them, feeling somewhat better about the developing situation in Newberry.

"Colonel Tyler?" inquired a mild voice at the door.

The colonel looked up from his papers to see a man in a black suit and hat standing in the door.

"Ah, Mr. Wilson. I wasn't expecting to see you again so soon," responded the colonel, laying the papers on his desk. He moved to greet the middle age man from Boston.

"May we come in, colonel?" asked John.

"Certainly. And whom else do I have the pleasure to meet?" inquired the colonel.

"Sir, this is Miss Susanna Shaw and Miss Margaret Benslow, both of Concord." responded Mr. Wilson. "Ladies this is Colonel Rockwell Tyler, commander of Newberry."

"No, Mr. Wilson, not the commander of Newberry," he laughed. "Just my regiment of boys from New York. Ladies, I am delighted to welcome you to Newberry." he added, taking each hand that was offered to him in turn.

"And, sir, I am Ezekiel Johnson of the Freedman's Bureau," added a white haired older gentleman, stepping from behind the ladies to offer his handshake. "We arrived last night from the coast."

"I trust you had a pleasant trip. What brings you into such hostile territory, ladies?" asked Colonel Tyler.

"School, Mr. Tyler," responded Miss Benslow. "We're here to start a school for the Negroes in Newberry. And we would like your assistance," she added in a demanding tone.

"Right now, ladies, I'm afraid the army may not be in much of a position to help start a school, but I will help in any other way that I possibly can," the colonel said.

"Mr. Wilson has already obtained a building for lease just on the edge of the village, and he has acquired some furnishing that we'll need to have transported," Miss Benslow began. "It seems that the army has taken use of most of the wagons in town, so I'm certain that you have some that can be used to move the furniture, and, of course, drivers to assist. Also, there are books and other supplies at the train station we'll need you to transport. And it's important that these items be at our school by early tomorrow morning, colonel. Can you assure us that these things can be done?"

"Oh, of course, madam!" responded the colonel, taken back by the aggressive nature of this woman from Concord. "My men will assist you, as you desire. Mr. Wilson and Mr. Johnson can escort you to my quartermaster's office, and I'm confident that Captain Fulton will fulfill your needs just as you have described."

"You mentioned 'hostile territory', Colonel Tyler?" inquired Miss Shaw in a somewhat nervous voice.

"The army is maintaining law and order, Miss Shaw, but there is still a strong rebel sentiment throughout South Carolina, just yet, and we have had some trouble," answered the colonel. "It's advisable that you ladies not travel outside without an escort, as I feel certain Mr.

Wilson has already warned you. There's an element even around Newberry that continues to interfere with the army's job and even do harm to our soldiers if the opportunity arises."

"That's your concern, colonel," injected Miss Benslow. "Our interest is to look after the Negroes' education. And that we will do. We expect the army to do their part and to provide us with what we need. I understand you have a directive from the Bureau through General Devens' headquarters in Charleston."

"Yes, Miss Benslow, and I would like to assure you and Mr. Johnson that the army will cooperate with the Bureau." answered the colonel. "We will assist you any way we can." Now, is there any other assistance I can provide?"

"Just direct us to your quartermaster's office, colonel," responded Mr. Wilson, "and we will bid you a good day, sir."

Colonel Tyler walked the group outside his door, relieved to find the sergeant back at his post.

"Sergeant Graves, would you escort these people to Captain Fulton," instructed the colonel, "and have my horse brought around with my escort."

Yes, sir," snapped the sergeant.

Rain had begun to fall as Colonel Tyler slipped his boot into the stirrup and lifted himself onto the roan mare. He felt secure sitting in the saddle of his horse. He always had. His men had rebuked him more than once for remaining in the saddle when they felt it far too dangerous, but that is where he had felt most comfortable. And today was no exception. He had taken his inspection of Newberry aboard Lilly each day since the 56th had arrived in town.

He pulled the reins to turn the horse and gently nudged her side with the heel of his boot. The mare began to slowly move toward the edge of the wooded yard to where the many rows of white tents of the men of the 56th decorated the field north of the college. The large oaks did little to help conceal the disrepair of the school building. With its facilities vacant of faculty and students, there was little to suggest to these men passing in time that there was to be bright and long future for this small southern college. The colonel and his escorts moved through the steady drizzle that seemed to be settling in for the remainder of the day. A sergeant moved up on the colonel's left to assume his usual position while escorting his commanding officer.

To the colonel it didn't matter if it was the eve of battle or a brief stop on the march or another day of routine camp life; he'd always made it a habit to informally inspect his soldiers. And no matter how routine it was, the men always seemed to appreciate his presence.

However, his visits during the days here in Newberry were somewhat different than in times past. He was using his visits to the camp to precede his rounds of the town. He had to be careful that he rode with an enlisted escort with no other officers present. There were snipers about, and he knew that a group of officers was always a temptation. Although he was careful to vary the route and time of his ride, he felt that his visible presence was necessary to the townspeople. They were aware just as he was of the danger he presented to himself with his daily ride. And now he felt it was starting to have an effect. He knew he was slowly gaining their respect.

"Colonel, you should use your oilcloth, sir," suggested the sergeant as they moved into the open field. "The air's turning cool with this rain,"

The colonel ignored the sergeant's comments, wrapped in his own thoughts, as he moved down the line of tents. Few men were now present in the camp, as the officers had most of them busy with their details and duties of the day. Two wagons were seen moving from the north end of the camp and heading south on Adams toward the railroad station. The group moved through the camp, turned west past the guard post and crossed the Greenville and Columbia tracks.

Colonel Tyler quickened the pace as he turned back south onto Drayton Street, leading into the residential areas of Newberry. His escort hurried to keep up. The rain began to come down somewhat heavier. The large trees that lined the street provided some shelter, as the men and horses moved in unison.

Colonel Tyler looked at the many notable houses that lined this portion of Drayton. From the outside it was as if the war had never been, but unbeknown to him, almost all the families who lived along this street had been touched by the death or maiming of a family member during the tragic years of the war. As the group neared Boundary Street, the colonel slowed to a walk as a carriage approached on the street.

"Good day, Dr. Mayer," greeted the colonel, tightening the reins to bring Lilly to a stop.

"What brings you out on such a rainy day, Colonel Tyler?" responded Dr. O. B. Mayer from his buggy, as his driver brought it to a halt.

"Just sight seeing, doctor," answered the colonel.

Colonel Tyler had made a point to visit with Dr. Mayer the day he had arrived in Newberry. He had read many of his articles, mainly of religious nature, in periodicals for several years. When he first found out he was being sent to Newberry, he was determined to meet the doctor. Even in New York, Dr. Mayer was known as one of the more eminent doctors in the south, not only for his profession but also recently for his writings.

"Well, colonel, as a physician, I would advise you to remove yourself from the weather," scolded the doctor.

"But, sir, do I not see you also out in this weather?" smiled Colonel Tyler.

"That you do, sir, but as you can also see, I'm under cover of my buggy. And I'm out on important business," answered Dr. Mayer. "A new birth will occur shortly, I understand, and I assure you it will occur with or without me, so I must be off."

"Certainly, Dr. Mayer, a pleasure to see you again, sir," responded the colonel, touching his hat as the buggy moved past.

Colonel Tyler again nudged his horse into a slow trot as they crossed Boundary continuing toward the south end of town. He glanced toward his left as he approached the Feed and Hardware Store. Three men watched from the window of the building as his group passed. Behind the building he noticed several Negroes standing under the shelter of a storage shed. Beyond that were the tracks of the railroad and mostly a large field. He reined Lilly toward the east and continued across the tracks to Caldwell Street. As he turned back toward the center of the small town, he noticed the large building in the center of a grove of oaks. This had been Newberry Academy and was now vacated. Halcyon Grove, as it was called, had been the site of the annual Newberry agricultural fair for many years preceding the war. On the opposite side of the street in the distance was the Village Cemetery.

As the colonel continued toward Platt Street and the Courthouse, he was unaware of what events were soon to happen in this now vacant part of this small southern town. He was beginning to feel the chill from the rain. "Maybe Dr. Mayer was right," he thought. "Maybe I need to get out of this weather. A strong drink would do much to remove this September chill."

A man stood silently watching, rifle in hand, from the rear corner of Hurd's Hall on Platt Street. He watched the four uniformed housemen gallop up Platt Street, turn and disappear down Adams toward the college.

*December 24, 1864*

*Dear Brother Calvin,*

*It is Christmas and this war will not end. Oh so many Christmases have passed with my brothers still off at war. Ma has been trying to make Christmas as special as it always was in the past when we were all one family here at home. It seems that every day we hear of another loss to someone we know. So many of the young men have been hurt or killed and I don't know why God allows this thing to continue. How many tears and troubled hearts have been almost broken since this cruel war commenced? I fear for you and I pray for you and the boys every night.*

*Ma cooked all day today getting things ready for tomorrow. Uncle Robert and Aunt Susanna are visiting on Christmas day and Preacher Williams has been invited to* dinner.

I cannot help but think of you at this time of the year. We have always had Christmas together until this terrible thing started. Your smile always makes the day special for me when I open your present and when you see what I have made for you. Oh, how I miss my big brother!

Your loving Sister,
    Mary C.

CH

# Chapter 5

The train had been hours late leaving Charlotte, and the wait had exhausted Sarah. Now, she was uncommonly nervous.

"Are you all right, Miss Dekalb?" Calvin asked, leaning forward in his seat to gently touch her shoulder.

"Yes, Mr. Crozier, just fine," she said. "I don't understand why it took so long to get the train ready. I thought trains were supposed to be punctual."

Calvin laughed, settling back in his seat.

Sarah continued her unnecessary shifting, occasionally glancing at the Federal officer seated two seats forward. There were two other soldiers seated in the rear of the car, enlisted men she had thought, but with some kind of special insignia on their uniforms. There had been more soldiers at the depot in Charlotte than she had seen in all of Salisbury. And the way they had looked at Calvin and his friends had made her uneasy. She had supposed it was because of their clothes. But the looks they had given Calvin upset her. She didn't know why, almost as if something about him irritated them.

She had become curious about the man that had agreed to escort her and Jenny home to Georgia. For a man to have been through what he must have during the past four years, she thought, it didn't seem natural for a person to be at ease with himself as he did. He had seemed so gentle when talking with her grandmother. But, now she sensed a deep inner strength in him that made her feel safe. She had seen the special bond between him and his two friends, and she had thought it was because of the situation they had been in. But she was realizing that there was something about Calvin Crozier that right now other people needed, except those Yankees. Calvin had seemed to go out of his way to avoid eye contact with them. Didn't he humble himself in Charlotte to those three soldiers who had looked at them so rudely, she thought, just to avoid trouble? His smile would make you want to smile back, so what was the matter? Maybe she just wasn't mature enough to understand. But it was unsettling.

"Sarah, what's it going to be like at home?" whispered Jenny, staring out the window at the passing countryside. "Will there be soldiers there, too?"

"Ma will be there, and Uncle Ham and Jed and Marcus," she

answered. "And you know Ma said that Mammy and Big Jim were still there."

"I don't see why Mammy and Big Jim are still there -- they don't have to be," Jenny said, dryly, turning toward her sister. "I bet they'll be gone before we get home. And how come you think Uncle Ham and Cousin Jed and Cousin Marcus will stay there long? They're probably gone back to Milledgeville already. What'll we do?"

"Jenny, please stop worrying. Ma wouldn't have sent for us if things weren't okay," again Sarah tried to reassure her sister. "Sherman's army burned out Uncle Ham and his boys. You read what Ma said. They ain't got any place to go."

"I heard Grandma tell Reverend Winslow last week that Ma said hogs and chickens had disappeared and that Uncle Ham was gone three days getting the mule back," Jenny said. "I heard her say that the soldiers were turning the other way when stealing was going on."

"You're making it up, Jenny," Sarah scolded.

"I ain't. They didn't know I was standing close enough to hear, but that's what she said was going on," she added with tears beginning to show.

"I weren't ease–dropping, ladies; you were talking loud enough for me to hear," butted in Calvin from behind. "You're getting yourselves worked up for no cause, I'm sure. If your mother sent for you, then it's safe. She wouldn't have done otherwise, and I suspect you both know it deep down. I got sisters at home and I know my Ma wouldn't put them in danger."

The car suddenly jerked and then smoothed as the train began to slow. The conductor entered the car from the front and was quickly stopped by the officer in blue.

Calvin couldn't hear what the officer was asking, just the answers from the conductor.

"This is Yorkville," answered the conductor.

"South Carolina," he again answered.

"No, just a water stop." he continued.

"Twenty minutes, at the most," again he answered, now as if irritated. "Fifteen–minute stop, folks. Water and facilities available. Back aboard in fifteen minutes." The conductor moved away from the seated officer toward the rear of the car.

Some of the passengers were already leaving their seats, even though the train had not come to a stop. Calvin waited with Sarah and Jenny until the train had stopped and then followed them from the car.

"I'll be here, ladies, until you return," Calvin said, spotting the covered wooden bucket near the depot window. It was dripping water off the sides, indicating it was freshly drawn water. He turned to the bucket as the ladies went inside. He raised the hinged cover and removed the dipper of water. As he drank, he noticed Josh near the end of the walk. He returned the dipper and walked to where Josh stood by himself.

"Where's Jim?" Calvin asked.

"Out foraging for food. He thought he saw a pear tree back a little ways as the train was slowing, and he said he was going to gather us some rations." Josh looked back down the track the way Jim had gone. "I think it were green apples,"

"He knows this is a fifteen–minute stop, don't he?"

"Ha, you're worried about him missing the train, and I'm thinking he'll probably get himself shot."

"Jim can talk himself out of any predicament. It's just that he gets lost to time when he's eating."

"You might want to wait here with me if you want your share of whatever rations he gets."

"The ladies will be back out in a couple of minutes. He better hurry," responded Calvin, anxiously.

Sarah and Jenny stepped out of the building only to find Calvin not where they had left him.

"Where'd he go?" asked Jenny.

"There he is with his friend. What they looking at down the track?" wondered Sarah out loud.

"Let's go find out, Sarah."

"No, we'll wait here."

They stood watching as both men continued to look toward the rear of the train. Calvin looked their way, then quickly back down the track.

The train whistle suddenly blew, startling the girls.

"All aboard!" shouted the conductor, standing by the door of the second car.

"Calvin better hurry," Jenny said, now looking back in his

direction.

"You better go on, Cal. The ladies look worried," suggested Josh.

"I think more like irritated at me, Josh. I'd better get. If Jim makes it back tell him to not eat my part of whatever he gets," Calvin shouted back at Josh, as he hurried to join the ladies.

"Time to board, ladies," said the conductor. "Your friend's coming."

Calvin smiled as he reached the girls, "We'd better board now ladies. I think the train is fixing to leave."

Sarah frowned at Calvin. "What were you doing back there? Something must have been very interesting down the tracks."

"Nothing much, just Jim," Calvin answered, again looking back at Josh, motioning toward Jim, who was now running to catch the train. He watched for a moment as the girls disappeared into the car. He laughed as he saw Josh trying to help Jim with the sack he was carrying and the arm full of green apples that he was now spilling on the ground.

The conductor frowned as he waited, watching the comical sight as the two young men scrambled through the open door of the freight car, tossing in apples as they went. Just as he was signaling to the engineer, an apple rolled from the open door onto the ground, quickly followed by a bearded young man in Confederate gray. Jim scooped up the apple and tumbled back into the car as the train slowly moved away from the station.

"Kindly tell us what that commotion was about, Mr. Crozier," insisted Sarah.

Calvin took his seat behind the girls and removed his knife to his sack. He looked at Sarah and smiled. "What commotion?"

"You know what commotion!" whispered Sarah. "Is this the way you value our companionship? Embarrassing us in public?"

"What public?" inquired Calvin. "There was no one on the platform 'cept the conductor and us."

"What were they up to, Calvin?" asked Jenny. "I think they were stealing! Is that it? Your friends are thieves?"

"No, they weren't stealing. Jim was just gathering rations for supper," Calvin responded. "You see, we don't have any money and the only way we've been able to travel is to ask for handouts," he continued, now somewhat embarrassed himself from the way Jenny was looking at him.

"I'm sorry, Mr. Crozier. We didn't mean to pry," Sarah quickly remarked. "Your friends were just acting like boys instead of men, that's all."

"I'm just glad to see Josh and Jim having some fun. They were pretty sick in Maryland, and Josh is still not well," Calvin said with a serious tone. "There was no intent on their part or mine to embarrass you."

"And what about, you, Mr. Crozier? Are you also having fun?" teased Jenny.

"Of course," he answered. "This is much better here with you than back in the freight car with those two." He smiled.

"But are you having fun?" again Jenny asked, smiling.

"I'm enjoying your company, Miss Dekalb, both of you. You've been a pleasure to travel with. Please understand that this is still somewhat difficult for me. I've been under someone else's control for a long time. The world I left two years ago ain't the same," Calvin continued. "And I don't quite know what to expect when I get home. Deep down, I know everything will be all right after I get there, but I fear the change that faces me, just as you do about going home to Georgia."

"I just haven't imagined you being afraid of anything, Mr. Crozier," said Sarah. "You've made us comfortable being with you."

"It's been so long since I've been home that I look forward to it maybe too much," confessed Calvin, speaking more freely than he had intended to.

Jenny interrupted "I ain't seen Ma in just over a year and it seems like half my lifetime; I can't imagine four years! I'd be an old woman by then."

Calvin smiled at the expression on her face.

"Try to have fun, Mr. Crozier," suggested Sarah. "It doesn't seem right seeing your friends having more fun than you, especially with you being younger than them."

"Younger?" Calvin smiled. "What makes you think that?"

"Well, look at them," laughed Jenny. "I saw wrinkles on Josh's face and look at that beard on your other friend!"

"That 'other friend' is Jim and he ain't much older that you. Just a kid of twenty, I think," responded Calvin. "Josh may be a year older, but he's got a wife and two children in Alabama. It's been a hard two years on us."

Surprised, both girls turned back toward the front of the car, not knowing quite what to say. The train was now moving at full steam at about seven miles per hour. To both Sarah and Jenny, this seemed fast, as the train rumbled roughly along the tracks.

"How long before the train reaches Winnsboro," Jenny asked the conductor as he was again moving to the front of the car.

"Reckon it'll be a little while yet, young lady," was his reply. "We've got to stop for water and a little wood in Chester, and I suppose it'll be past midnight 'fore we get to Winnsboro."

People stopped from their busy activities to stare at the train as it slowly passed through the outer edges of the South Carolina town of Anderson. Several of the car doors were already opening and members of the 33rd US Colored Troops were visible, crowding around the openings. Sergeant Prince Rivers stood patiently watching as the train continued its slow movement toward the depot. He surveyed the people as they stared at the passing sight. He saw three Negro children run through the rain toward the tracks, waving at the soldiers as they passed. He saw a man with one leg missing, sitting on a porch, getting his hair trimmed by a woman who had stopped her motions to also stare at the train loaded with Yankee soldiers. A man wearing an oilcloth struggled with a team of mules hitched to a wagon. The sergeant saw in the distance a park of wagons and carts under a grove of water oaks near the center of the town. A few people, mostly under umbrellas, were selling and buying produce fresh from the morning's harvest. He saw two men on horseback, at the edge of the train yard, standing motionless as the train came to a stop. He watched them as they reined their horses away from the depot and quickly trotted down a street disappearing among the row of houses.

Captain James Fowler stood anxiously watching from the shelter of the depot shed. The rain showers had come and gone throughout the morning, and now it appeared that they were here for the rest of the day. He watched as the train finally came to a stop. Several of the soldiers were already leaping from the open doors.

`"You men stand fast there," shouted Sergeant Rivers, anxious that none of the boys should wander off. Several sergeants were on the ground beside the train.

"Glad to see a friendly face, sergeant," said a voice from the edge of the depot platform.

"Capt'n Fowler, sho good to see yu, too, sah," responded Rivers, surprised that he had not seen the captain standing near the bales of cotton. "Where yor boys at, capt'n?"

"They're still in camp. You'll see them soon enough," he answered. "Looks like we'll all be here another night."

"Is that right, capt'n? I knows the colonel anxious to get to Charleston," Prince added. "Does he knows we go'in' stay tonight?"

"Not yet, sergeant, but soon enough."

Just then, Lieutenant Hyde and Lieutenant Wood stepped from the passenger car, quickly followed by Colonel Trowbridge and Surgeon Crandall. The colonel and doctor headed toward the shelter of the depot as the other two officers moved in the direction of the other cars, looking toward the men. Captain Fowler moved to report to the colonel.

"Ah, Captain Fowler, good to see you again, sir," greeted the colonel. "Hope you have your men ready to leave," He returned the offered salute.

"And glad to see you, colonel," smiled the captain, smartly returning his right hand to his side. "There's been a problem of sorts, Colonel Trowbridge, that will delay our departure, sir," he said, as he followed the two officers into the depot.

The colonel stopped and confronted the soldier. "I certainly hope this problem has nothing to do with your men, captain," he snapped.

"No, sir. There's a problem on the tracks, farther east. I was told there are other trains on the tracks and they are holding our train here 'til morning," answered Captain Fowler.

"What do you mean, 'holding us here until morning'?" responded the colonel, angrily. "They do have sidetracks between here and Columbia, don't they, captain? And these people do know how to use them, don't they?"

"Yes, I'm certain they do, colonel, but..." he attempted to explain.

"Then I suggest you inform them that we urgently need to get on to Charleston and that maybe they should reconsider their position on this matter," he ordered.

"There's the stationmaster, colonel," he responded. "I'll speak to him again, sir."

Colonel Trowbridge turned toward the basket of apples sitting on the end of the long counter. He selected one and quickly took a large bite from the apple.

"Better try one, Will. These are quite good," he mumbled with a mouth full of fruit.

"You in charge of this train?" inquired a heavyset man of about sixty years of age.

"I'm Colonel Trowbridge, and this is my special transportation," he answered gruffly. "You the station clerk that's holding my train up?"

"I'm not holding your train up. There's trouble on the tracks ahead, and you're going to have to wait here, colonel," came the reply.

"What kind of trouble, sir, that's holding my train here?" continued Trowbridge.

"There're two trains on the tracks heading west between here and Newberry, and there're no sidings available to use right now," the clerk began to explain. "One siding is damaged near Laurens and the other two are occupied -- damaged cars on one and freight waiting to move east on the other. One train will be moving off toward Greenville at Iva Station, and your train will be safe to leave after the Columbia train arrives here, which should be sometime after daybreak."

"Damn it all!" the colonel responded in disgust.

"Colonel, there's room in the camp for the regiment for the night, and preparations are already being made to feed them," said Captain Fowler. "May I suggest that the Anderson Hotel is just a few blocks from here where you and the rest of the officers can stay tonight? Our camp is near the 7th New Hampshire, and Lieutenant White and I can stay with the men."

Colonel Trowbridge looked back at the station clerk. It was obvious that he was not going to get anywhere with this man.

"Captain, can you arrange transportation to the hotel?" asked the colonel, continuing to stare at the defiant station manager. "I don't fancy the idea of walking in this rain."

"There's an ambulance wagon waiting on the street behind the station, Colonel Trowbridge, for your disposal," he quickly responded.

"Very well, Captain Fowler. I need you to instruct Lieutenant Hyde that we will remain in Anderson for the night," ordered the colonel. "You're to accompany the regiment to your camp with all the officers present, making certain that there're no stragglers. Post a marching guard for the movement. Send a driver and guard for my transportation."

"Sir, I have a driver and guard waiting with the ambulance," interrupted the captain.

"Once in camp, any of the officers who wish to have quarters in the hotel may do so, but they must come as a unit with a guard," instructed the colonel. "Have a guard posted at the hotel for the night. You'll find Lieutenant Hyde outside with the men.

"Doctor Crandall, if you would be so kind as to look after our baggage," he continued. "I'll be waiting outside with the wagon."

"Yes, sir," responded the doctor, turning toward the platform door with Captain Fowler.

The colonel turned toward the opposite side of the room to be fronted again by the station clerk. He stood waiting for the man to clear himself from his path. The man stepped to the side, still making eye contact with the soldier.

"That will be three cents, colonel," the clerk declared, as the colonel pushed past him.

Colonel Trowbridge stopped and again faced the man.

"For the apple, colonel, the price is three cents," the clerk stated, waiting with anticipation.

The colonel stared at the man briefly, then turned and walked through the open door to the street.

The ride to the Anderson Hotel was made in silence, the colonel wrapped in his own thoughts and the doctor respecting his silence. William Crandall glanced through the opening in the rear of the ambulance, observing the muddy street behind them. He saw several soldiers of the 7th New Hampshire talking to two men near the entrance to a theater. He briefly observed two riders move from a side street, stop on the edge of the thoroughfare, and watch their vehicle as it continued toward the hotel. It made the doctor feel uneasy, but he continued to keep his thoughts to himself.

The ambulance came to a stop in front of a two story brick building with an elevated porch on the front with two large oaks located at the front corners. It had been at one time the center of Anderson social life. The building next door, though a wooden structure, was nearly as large as the hotel and was the town meeting hall, occasionally serving as a ballroom. A sign on the corner of the hotel building advertised "The Two Oaks Restaurant".

The two men climbed from the rear of the wagon. The driver was there waiting to assist with the baggage. The guard stood on the sidewalk and waited as the colonel and the doctor climbed the several steps leading onto the porch. The guard followed the men, stopping at the top of the steps as the two officers disappeared into the main entrance. The guard was armed with an Enfield equipped with a bayonet.

A large chandelier of gaslights hanging from the center of a high ceiling dominated the lobby of the hotel. To the right side of the room were several chairs, a settee, and a fireplace. A likeness of Robert E Lee stood on the mantle. The entrance to the restaurant was on the right rear of the room. A thin man wearing brass rimmed spectacles was busy behind an elaborate walnut desk, beside which was a staircase leading to the upper rooms. Another entrance on the left led into a narrow hall leading to the first floor rooms.

"Gentlemen, may I help you?" inquired the clerk, looking up from his work.

"We'll need accommodations for the night," responded the colonel, as both men walked to the desk.

"Of course, sir. Do you need separate rooms?" asked the man, looking over the top of his glasses.

"One room with separate beds," came the reply, "on the lower floor. There will be several of my officers joining us later. Do you have additional rooms available?"

"Yes, sir, the entire upper floor is currently empty," the clerk responded.

"Colonel Trowbridge?" came a voice from behind.

The two men turned to be greeted by two officers just coming through the front entrance.

"I'm Colonel Jacob Abbott of the 7th New Hampshire and this is Lieutenant Colonel Bob Skinner of the 7th Connecticut," continued the officer. "We met in Jacksonville, and I have hopes that you might remember us."

"Ah, yes, now I do. We dined together with Colonel Higginson at General Gilmore's headquarters," responded Colonel Trowbridge, moving to shake their hands. "This is my surgeon, Will Crandall, of the 33rd."

"Gentleman, it's a pleasure," the surgeon said, offering his hand. "If you will excuse me, I'll finish with the arrangements, colonel." He turned back to the clerk.

"I'm not sure we've met, colonel," inquired Colonel Skinner. "Colonel Hawley of the 7th Connecticut was acting brigade commander then, and I was senior captain in charge of the regiment at Olustee."

"And, you, colonel, were still major at the time, and I see that Colonel Higginson's prediction was correct about your promotion," added Colonel Abbott. "We were told that you would be arriving soon in Anderson, and I'm pleased that you arrived safely. How long will you be with us, colonel?"

"Longer than I had liked, gentleman, but no reflection on your company, of course," answered the colonel. "It's been a trying journey since we left Hamburg, and to be honest, I desire to be back in Charleston as soon as possible. There's some kind of trouble on the tracks and they've delayed our departure 'til morning."

"Well, at least you'll have time to dine with us tonight," said Colonel Abbott. "I've been directed on behalf of the Honorable James Orr to invite you to join us as his guest here at the hotel for dinner. It seems that he has heard nothing but favorable reports of your men here in the upstate during the past two months, and he desires to meet you."

"And who, might I ask, is this Mr. Orr?" asked Colonel Trowbridge.

"Mr. Orr lives here in Anderson and is an influential man, colonel. Rumor has it that he may very well be the new governor of South Carolina," was the reply.

"If I had it my way, it would be a long time before this state would ever have a government again," injected Colonel Trowbridge. "You referred to him as 'the honorable' James Orr. May I inquire more about him?"

"Well, he was a judge and served in the United States Congress. And I think that's where he may have derived his title," added Colonel Skinner. "You'll have to ask him more about his politics, colonel, as that's all I know."

"I see that Crandall has completed the arrangements, and I'd like to get some rest, if I may ask your leave, Colonel Abbott?" said Colonel Trowbridge.

"Certainly, colonel. We can visit more over dinner, I presume? Seven o'clock?"

"Yes, 'til then, gentleman," responded Colonel Trowbridge, with a salute.

Both men answered the salute and watched as the newly arrived visitors moved into the hallway, baggage in tow.

CH

# Chapter 6

Calvin was sitting with Jim in the doorway of the freight car, eating green apples. This was Chester, and the stop had lasted longer than they expected. There appeared to be no sign that the train was getting ready to leave anytime soon.

"I know walking weren't no way for us to get home, but sometimes I think it was better than just sitting around waiting to go somewhere," commented Jim, tossing the apple core onto the ground.

"Maybe you got a point, Jim, but I think I'd prefer to be sitting here than walking right now," Calvin responded, watching the steady rain continue to fall.

"I thought Josh would be back by now," Jim added with slight worry in his voice.

"Well, maybe he better hurry 'cause there comes the conductor out of the depot," commented Calvin also in a concerned tone.

They watched as the conductor moved to the edge of the platform and looked in their direction. He paused, then quickly started toward them.

"It's your friend, boys! He's out behind the station with some Federal soldiers," shouted the conductor in a worried tone.

Jim quickly slipped from his perch in the doorway to the ground and hurried to catch Calvin as he moved toward the corner of the building.

"Boys, be careful!" the conductor's words of warning followed them around the corner of the building.

Calvin stopped and turned to Jim, "You'd better go back to the train for the girl's sake," Calvin said with authority.

"They're your responsibility, Cal. Maybe you better go back!" Jim responded.

"Don't argue. We don't want your temper flying off and getting us all in trouble," warned Calvin. "Whatever the situation, it might be better for Josh and me to handle it. Now, go back to the train, Jim. If one of us ain't there shortly, explain to the girls and you take over for me. Even if we miss the train we'll catch up down the track somewhere."

Calvin turned and walked toward the rear of the station. He looked back and added, "Wait for us in Atlanta a day or two. We'll be there."

Jim stood frozen, unsure of what to do. He couldn't let Calvin walk right into trouble like this, but he had to do what he said. Sarah and Jenny were waiting aboard the cars.

"Damn!" he whispered, as he turned back toward the tracks. "This ain't right."

Calvin moved cautiously toward the rear corner of the building, listening for signs of danger. There were none. He turned the corner and spotted the group of soldiers about fifty yards down the street. It appeared they had Josh centered in their midst. Calvin began to slowly walk toward them, listening as he went, trying to determine what they were up to. As he got closer, Calvin could see the concern on Josh's face.

"Come on, Reb, you 'bout to get yourself shot, if you don't fess up!" came a voice from somewhere in the group.

"I told you boys; this is just food the lady across the street was kind enough to share with me. I'm traveling on the train and this is my supper," Josh tried to convince them, obviously in vain.

"You already said that, boy, and we ain't having none of it!" a private said, angrily, making a move toward the ex–Confederate, as if to strike him.

"Is the war still on, fellows, or are you just some of Sherman's boys left behind when he went home?" Calvin words drew their attention quickly.

"Another damn rebel!" cussed another of the soldiers. "Maybe this ain't no concern of yourn!"

"This here is my friend, Josh, and we're both just trying to get back home," Calvin said with defiance in his voice. "And if I ain't mistaken, that's our supper Josh has got in that bundle in his arms."

Calvin moved in such a manner as to partially uncover the knife in the waist of his trousers.

"You must be mistaken in what you're doing," Calvin continued, watching each one in turn, "'cause it should be obvious he ain't got any money. And I ate some of that army chow of yours for a long time, and even it ain't bad enough for you fellows to get in trouble trying to steal food from a poor rebel on his way home."

"He's the thief, and maybe you in cahoots with him!" was the reply from another of the men.

"Well, if you really thought that, you'd be 'cross the street right now asking that generous lady standing there on her porch, watching," Calvin said, gesturing in her direction with his head. "Maybe she might've even figured what you boys are up to by now."

"You're a mighty smart–ass for such a little fellow," came the reply. The soldier turned and took a step toward Calvin. He stopped as he saw Calvin's hand move to the handle of the knife.

Josh saw the hand of the soldier directly in front of him move toward his revolver. He tensed in preparation for his next move.

"There're two officers in the depot just now," Calvin said, staring into the eyes of the man making the threatening gesture in his direction. "They probably belong to you fellows, and I just bet they would be interested in what you fellows are about out here."

Another of the soldiers looked past Calvin to see the conductor standing at the rear entrance to the station, watching the events as they were transpiring. He again looked across the street to see the woman still staring in their direction.

"It's getting crowded out here all of a sudden," said the observant soldier. "Maybe we'd better be getting out of this rain." He pulled at the arm of the private that had his hand resting on the handle of his revolver and turned back toward Josh, frowning. "Hope that grub's worth the trouble you was 'bout to make for yourself, Reb."

Josh stared back at the soldier, as he began to move away.

"Better come on, Josh, and let these fellows be," Calvin said. "The train will be leaving soon."

Josh moved past the last of the soldiers, who bumped him as he passed. Josh returned the gesture with only a smile. He walked on toward Calvin, still cradling the bundle in his arms. Calvin continued to stand his ground until the last of the soldiers began to walk away.

"You done it, again, Cal," said Josh, remembering that night in Virginia, as they both walked through the rain back to the depot.

As Josh approached the conductor, he smiled and said, "Sure glad you were there just now, mister. Saved a whooper of a fight."

Calvin just smiled at his friend's comments, as they continued down the boardwalk past the man who was standing in the doorway.

The conductor stared at the men as they walked past him toward the opposite end of the building, wondering at the spirit of these men whose lives had been in such danger just moments before. He continued to watch until both men had disappeared around the corner of the building.

"What you got in there that you so proud of, Josh?" Calvin asked. "Those boys were about to hurt you over it."

"I got us a fresh made apple pie, Calvin Crozier, and I was sure afraid them boys were going to smell it," Josh smiled, as he raised the cover from the bundle of food in his arms. The smell of the warm pie reminded them both of home.

"**M**r. Crozier, are you all right?" Sarah asked with concern, as Calvin took his seat behind the girls.

"Quite so, should I not be?" he asked in turn.

"Well, we didn't know. You were gone for some time, and we saw Jim on the platform," answered the young lady. "And don't you tell us he wasn't worried about something. He was pacing like a mother hen with new chicks."

"What were you up to this time?" added Jenny.

Calvin looked at the two girls, paused and then smiled. "Just having fun," he said.

"**C**olonel Trowbridge, I'm curious as to why you elected to do duty with the army in a colored regiment?" asked James Orr in a rather loud voice.

"I volunteered for the duty, Mr. Orr," responded the colonel. "These men desired to be free and they were willing to work and to fight for it. I saw what they were capable of during the months they were on St. Simons Island, and I knew they'd make good fighting men."

"It's been rather difficult, hasn't it?" asked the heavyset man. "I understand that the black troops were dealt with harshly whenever the Southern soldiers could get at them and even your white compatriots in arms haven't been very supportive."

"Prejudice against the black man has been the curse of this country, sir," responded the soldier, "and now that this thing has been done only free men exist in all corners of this country. Those prejudices will soon be wiped from this land, Mr. Orr; I can promise you that," he added emphatically. "Difficult? Yes, it's been difficult at times, but, sir, I feel it has been well worth the effort."

"Well said, Colonel Trowbridge," lauded the statesman. "I've heard good things of your men while they have been in the upstate of South Carolina. I haven't heard one account of trouble from your men anywhere they've been."

"I wish I could return the complement, Mr. Orr," replied the colonel, "but it seems everywhere we've been in South Carolina we've experienced nothing but trouble from your citizens."

"Yes, you're probably correct, sir," answered Mr. Orr. "The people of this state will never get used to seeing the black soldiers in uniform, under arms, that were just yesterday slaves in the very state that they now are being paraded about in. There's a strong element of fear there, sir, and I think you should be able to understand that."

"Oh, I do, Mr. Orr. But, what I don't understand," Colonel Trowbridge asked, "is how cowardly your citizens can be to bushwhack and murder in the dead of night the men who are simply here to do their duty and help those same people regain law and order in their own communities."

"As you can see, Mr. Orr, the commanders of the black troops believe in their men quite heartily," injected Colonel Abbott, offering a smile to Colonel Trowbridge.

Mr. James L. Orr was seated with his four invited guests in the luxurious confines of the Two Oaks Restaurant in the Anderson Hotel. His guests were Mr. Talbert Clinkscale, Sheriff of Anderson District, Colonel Jacob Abbott, commander of the 7th New Hampshire, Lieutenant Colonel Robert Skinner of the 7th Connecticut Regiment and Lieutenant Colonel Charles Trowbridge of the 33rd US Colored Troops.

"You said there were difficulties, colonel?" Mr. Orr asked. "Were you saying more difficulties than training the white soldier?"

"No, Mr. Orr, there were no more difficulties than dealing with any volunteer soldier," answered the colonel. "These men took to working and fighting as a unit much better than the white soldiers did. That part seemed natural to them. It was the discipline of the men that was the most difficult, I suppose."

"I can certainly agree with that," butted in the sheriff. "Being the law here I guess I see the worst of it now. There was a time when about all they knew for discipline was the lash."

"And we had to deal with the way you people down here taught them about the lash, sheriff," responded Colonel Trowbridge with anger in his voice.

"And I suppose, colonel, the army never used the lash on these men?" he questioned.

"Only early in the war, when they were still classified as contraband by the army, and then, only on the rarest of occasions," answered the colonel, "and after the Emancipation, I don't recall any incident that wasn't in line with army regulation for the discipline of any soldier."

"And I suppose now, discipline with your troops is no longer a problem?" Sheriff Clinkscale continued to front the colonel with his comments.

"Obviously not, Sheriff Clinkscale, from the positive reports I've heard," interrupted Mr. Orr.

"I understand that you've an illustrious background in politics, Mr. Orr," interrupted Colonel Abbott, trying to change the subject. "You served in the US Congress, I understand, as well as the Confederate Senate?"

"Ah, yes, Colonel Abbott," he answered, smiling, "and proudly have I served the people of South Carolina now for twenty years. In the South Carolina Legislature, I fought against nullification and in the US Congress I argued against the cause of the south and secession," he continued. "And when the people of my state elected to go a separate way, my duty was here with them, right or wrong, and I served them as well as I could, sir."

"Did you serve in the war, Mr. Orr?" inquired Colonel Trowbridge.

"Oh, yes, for a time," he responded. "I equipped a regiment that took on my name early in the war and served briefly with them until I was called by the people to serve in the Confederate Congress."

"Orr's Rifles? Is that the name, sir?" inquired Colonel Skinner. "It seems that they were on the field opposite us at Gettysburg."

"Yes, Colonel Skinner. They earned quite a reputation during the war, even without me," he answered, with a laugh.

"You speak freely about your involvement with the Confederacy, sir," commented Colonel Abbott. "Aren't you at least concerned for yourself that there may be repercussions from the US Government for your actions?"

"Oh, but no, Colonel Abbott. I have nothing to be ashamed of or fear at present," he responded with confidence. "I served the people as they called me to serve and during the last two years I worked tirelessly, though regretfully unsuccessfully, in the Confederate Congress to obtain a peaceful settlement with the government in Washington. And now with the guidance that we're hearing from President Johnson's administration, I feel certain things will progress successfully for South Carolina. As you know, a Constitutional Convention is being held next week in Columbia."

"But, Mr. Orr, there's strong words coming from some Congressional leaders that President Johnson's policies may be overridden," suggested Colonel Skinner.

"No, sir, I disagree!" he answered. "I think the Congress will move quickly to establish citizenship for the Negro and I think the people of the South will grant them the vote, as President Johnson is encouraging. I think this action, combined with the president's leadership, will assure a quick recovery for the Southern states."

"And what do you see for your future, sir," inquired Colonel Trowbridge.

"I am again offering my services to the people of the state of South Carolina, colonel. I'm offering myself to serve in the capacity of governor, if the people will have me, sir," said the politician.

"I think maybe you people of the south may be building too much hope, sir," argued Colonel Skinner. "I know that the people of Connecticut and Massachusetts aren't ready to allow the Southern states full representation in the US Congress, yet."

Just then, Sheriff Clinkscale spied one of his assistants standing at the door of the restaurant, discretely motioning toward him.

"Excuse me, gentlemen, for a moment, if I may," asked the sheriff, as he rose from the table.

The men at the table continued their conversation as the deputy began to speak to the sheriff in whispered tones. A folded paper was passed to Sheriff Clinkscale, who quickly read it and returned it to his assistant. Additional words were exchanged before the man turned to leave the room, apparently receiving final instructions from the sheriff.

"Hope that wasn't urgent business, Sheriff Clinkscale," Mr. Orr commended, as the sheriff returned to the table.

"I'm afraid this business should not wait, sir," responded the sheriff, still standing. "I need to speak to Colonel Trowbridge in private."

Certainly," responded the colonel. "Please excuse me, gentlemen," he added in a concerned voice, pushing his chair from the table.

The sheriff followed the colonel into the lobby of the hotel. Lieutenant Wood and Lieutenant Hyde were enjoying the comfort of the room as well as the cool breeze gently blowing in the window next to the fireplace. Lieutenant Hyde was quietly enjoying a fresh charge of his pipe. The men watched the colonel and his companion exit through the front entrance of the hotel.

Both guards snapped to attention when the colonel came onto the porch. Colonel Trowbridge turned and walked along the porch far enough to be out of hearing of the two soldiers.

"Is there a problem with my men, sheriff?" he asked.

"Oh, no, colonel. As far as I know your men are in camp and everything is quiet," he responded. "There has been a developing situation that involves you and your officers, I'm afraid. There was some idle talk heard around town earlier today concerning your regiment, but nothing to be taken seriously," he added. "But now a written threat has been received stating that none of the officers of the 33rd will reach Charleston alive."

The night seemed suddenly still as the colonel listened to the information that was being given him. The rain had stopped an hour earlier and just a slight breeze filled with the sounds of tree frogs and a distant whippoorwill crossed the end of the porch. Nothing more seemed to be stirring in the night shadows.

"You apparently consider this threat of much concern, Sheriff Clinkscale," commented the colonel.

"That, I do, colonel," he responded. "Things have been unsettled since the first soldiers were brought into this area, and I consider this serious. I understand you had an officer murdered in Walhalla, Colonel Trowbridge," he continued.

"Yes, and it is suspected that the work was done by someone from Anderson. Do you know who these people are, sheriff?" he asked with an accusing tone.

"I have my suspicions, colonel, but most of the suspects can't be located at present. The 7th New Hampshire was brought in because of the unrest, but they haven't been successful in locating any of the suspects, either," he answered.

"Well, sheriff, if you consider this threat serious, then I must also," said the colonel. "If you'll excuse me, sir, I must say good night to our host. I have business to take care of."

The colonel quickly turned back to the entrance of the hotel, and moved rapidly past the guards, ignoring their salutes. He stopped in the lobby and called his two officers to his side at the clerk's desk.

"Gentlemen, new orders are being issued for the remainder of our time in Anderson," the colonel stated, as he began to write on a piece of paper he removed from a stack there on the desk. "I'm sending written orders to Captain Fowler concerning the men and officers in camp. I'm also restricting all the officers in the hotel to remain in the building tonight. We'll be moving back to the train just before daybreak, but no officer is to leave here until a guard arrives from the regiment to escort us back to the station. Lieutenant Hyde, I'm ordering you to insure each officer in the hotel receives these instructions," he concluded, as he looked up from his writing to receive acknowledgement of his order.

"There has been threats of assassination against all the officers of the 33rd," he added, "but I'm determined that I'll not lose another man to these culprits."

He finished the written orders and handed the paper to Lieutenant Wood.

"Give this to one of the guards outside and have him deliver it to Captain Fowler, personally," instructed the colonel. "Warn the guard to move quickly, as I consider no place safe here in this town. He'll be returning with two additional guards."

Colonel Trowbridge dismissed both men and returned to the restaurant to say good night to his host.

The night seemed exceptionally dark to Private Rhodes, as he stood near the entrance to the hotel. Clouds still covered the September sky, and there was no source of light from that direction to offer him comfort. He was anxious for the sergeant to return with the additional guard. The lieutenant had seemed nervous when he sent the sergeant back to the camp with orders.

The hotel was now quiet, as the restaurant was closed. The

gaslights still burned brightly in the center of the lobby, sending two blocks of light across the porch to disappear into the street from the high windows on the front of the building.

A sudden snap of wood brought the private's attention toward the darkness past the tree on the right of the building. He moved toward the edge of the top step, trying to see into the blackness.

The sound of the revolver hammer clicking to the cocked position over his left shoulder caused him to tense, and then rapidly turn in the direction of the distinct noise.

"Stand your ground real still, boy, and real quiet," said the voice in the darkness behind the pistol pointed directly at him. Two horsemen had moved from the shadows of the street and the private could only see the front of the animals with the outstretched hands above each, holding Navy revolvers.

"Is this where the damn Yankee officers are staying?" inquired the threatening voice.

The soldier stood motionless.

"Better speak up, boy, if you value your life," came another warning.

"Ye... Yes'ah," came the broken response. "Dey officers is here."

Private Rhodes dove behind the column of the porch as the two riders began to fire their pistols.

Bang!... bang!... bang! bang!, followed by the dull thud of bullets striking against the brick walls and then the shatter of glass of an upper window. The echo of the gun shots rang loudly across the tops of the darkened buildings and through the tree tops above the quiet town of Anderson as the night of September 6th, 1865, came to an end.

It was nearly 1:00 AM as the train from Charlotte rolled to a stop in front of the train depot in Winnsboro. There was but little activity to be seen around the station. A single lamp burned beside the door leading into the wooden building. Another lamp could be seen through the window, sitting on the station attendant's desk. Across the tracks two armed soldiers stood sleepily watching, as steam rose from beneath the train's engine. A lone middle aged black man stood on the platform ready to assist with baggage.

A young man by the name of Calvin Crozier sat looking into the night through the window of the passenger car. His thoughts were of his mother and father. He wondered how many more nights should pass before he reached Galveston. In the seat in front of him two young ladies under his protection were still fast asleep. The stopping of the train had failed to wake either, as it had been hard for both of them to sleep during the last two days.

In a box car near the rear of the train slept two other young men, both ex–Confederates on the way home, as was their friend Calvin Crozier, who had not seen home in over two years. Their day had caught up with them not long after dark had fallen, and the steady rumbling of the cars had produced a sleep that long nights in Federal prison could not provide.

Back in the passenger car, the train's conductor stood quietly by the door holding a lantern as passengers began to exit the train. In a few minutes all was quiet inside the car. Only the sound of escaping steam from the train's engine could be heard above muffled voices of the people outside.

The conductor's voice broke the silence and Calvin's thoughts as he quietly spoke, "The train will remain where it is for tonight and there's no need to wake the ladies. This is likely the most comfortable place you'll find to sleep the rest of the night, young man. There's only one hotel, and it's closed for he night". He quietly moved on.

Calvin turned back to the darkness outside the window. He stared into the dark shadows of the night, his mind observing nothing but his continued thoughts of his family. He wondered about his brothers, as they had answered the call of their state and had left for war with their father's blessings, just as he had done. It was difficult knowing the tragedy of war and how blind its injustice was toward human life when he thought of them. He hoped he would find them safe, as with all his family. Calvin regretted what he knew his mother had to endure with his absence and the uncertainty of his fate. She loved all her sons and she had made that apparent everyday growing up in her house in Texas. How he missed his dear mother. A beautiful woman in her youth, but now covered with the marks of time, the white haired lady with the most pleasant smile and loving voice had kissed her son on his lips and made him promise he would protect himself. She had told him the morning that he left that she was putting him in the care of God's hands, and she trusted that He would also protect him and use him for His good. She had said, "I love you so dearly, my precious boy, Calvin." Her words had comforted him on many frigid nights in that cold, lonely place called Camp Douglas.

May 3, 1865

Dear Brother Calvin,

Such a sad day for us to hear that the Confederate army has surrendered and that the war has been lost, but it is pure joy to know now that you should soon be coming home. We are all told that the prisoners will be released and should be coming home by next month. I know my prayers will be answered and that you are safe and you will be home just as you promised. Oh, such a joyful day when we all see you come walking back up to the porch. I am still frightened because we have not heard anything from you but my trust remains in God.

Pa has been sick, but Ma has been humming her songs that I don't think I have heard since you and the boys left for the war. She misses you all so much. When we last heard from Wily and John they were still in Georgia, but now we look for them any day. I do not know that any of the boys have returned back to Galveston yet, but the boys that were home getting well are here to stay. We know nothing of the Confederate government, but hear the president got off safe. We hope so. We all fear what the Yankees might do to him....

Your loving sister,

Mary

# Chapter 7

Sunrise was still an hour away, as the men of the 33rd US Colored Troops began to arrive at the depot in Anderson. A regimental guard had arrived sometime earlier and was now posted around the train yard. The special train that had brought these men from Walhalla the previous day sat on a side track, its boiler fired, in preparation for its departure. A crew had added extra cars during the night to accommodate the extra baggage and men that were now rejoining the regiment. Two wagons driven by teamsters of the 7th Connecticut were moving toward the rear cars to be unloaded.

Captain James Fowler and Lieutenant Nathaniel White were the only officers now present with the regiment. They had entered the depot, following the instructions of Colonel Trowbridge to not expose themselves more than necessary. The men gathering outside the depot and around the train were under the directions of their many sergeants.

Tension among the men was growing, as they waited to leave. Most of the men had been deprived of sleep during the night. New orders had been received in camp late about an early departure, gunshots had been fired during the night, and the regimental guard around the camp had been doubled. A squad had been sent to the Anderson Hotel as additional guards. The men had not been told of the added danger that surrounded the regiment there in Anderson, but their excitement told the officers that they knew something was up.

Three sergeants stood together outside the depot watching across the tracks, as their men gathered in groups, talking, and waiting to board. They watched, as occasionally a group would look in their direction and then go back to talking among themselves.

"Prince, dey don't like dis none," Sergeant Robert Smalls voiced his concerns, as he watched the men. "Dey gittin pretty upset now, and da officers don't seem none to care. Dey ought'a be here with 'em."

"They'll be along shortly, Bobby," answered Sergeant Rivers. "I don't know what's up either, but if da colonel saw fit fo' us to know, he'd a told us."

"Well, he best tell us sump'om soon, 'cause dem boys am anxious to shoot sump'om," added the sergeant.

"And I think you, too," said sergeant Ed King, looking at Bobby.

"Yu' right 'bout dat," responded the sergeant. "Just line dem Rebs up and I shoots 'em all!"

"Bobby, I don't need no talk like dat right now," scolded Sergeant Rivers. "Them boys are excited 'nough without dat talk from yu'. Yu' best remember yo' position and do yo' job, 'cause none of da officers going to put up with dey sergeants talking like dat."

"If'n dey ain't here to hear it, dey can't do noth'in about it," he quickly responded.

"No, but I is!" Prince quickly countered, "and I'll skin yu if yu let dis thing gets out of control!"

The anger in his voice told Bob Small it was time to be quiet.

Two men now approached the three sergeants -- one a 2nd sergeant and the other a 3rd corporal, both from company E.

"When we leaving, boss," the 2nd sergeant asked, looking at Sergeant Rivers for answers.

"Soon 'nough," answered Sergeant King.

"Ain't right, boss, dem getting us out early, and dem not yet here," added the corporal. "Ain't right 't'all."

"You boys just see to yo' men and make sure none wander off, less dey wants to get killed," ordered Sergeant Rivers.

"Hey, boss! Where da cunnel at?" shouted Private Mills, in a boisterous voice from across the tracks.

"Sergeant Smalls! See to dat man and keeps 'em quiet," demanded Sergeant Rivers. "You all get back to yo' men!"

Sergeant Smalls and Sergeant King walked across the tracks together.

"Yu' heared what Rhodes say when he got back to camp 'bout dat shoot'n last night, Ed," commented Bobby, still upset over Prince's words. "Dey probably go'in' have us wear the officers clothes next and da cunnel have stripes on his arm."

Sergeant Ed King smiled at Bobby's comments, as they rejoined their men.

The colonel only dozed through the night. Every noise seemed to echo through the high ceilings and papered walls of the Anderson Hotel. He had been up for nearly an hour and it was through a struggle of exhausted patience that he allowed his officers to get the final hour's sleep.

Doctor William Crandall had been up and about for almost as long, as the colonel's early rising had wakened him. The surgeon of the 33rd had been busy getting the hotel staff to prepare a breakfast for the colonel. He entered the lobby carrying a hot cup of coffee.

"Colonel, there're eggs and some fresh biscuits in the kitchen, and the cook is slicing ham that smells mighty good," he smiled, handing the coffee to Colonel Trowbridge.

"Doctor, make sure all the officers are awake and have them in the lobby in fifteen minutes," he said, looking again at his watch. "They can have a few minutes to eat. The escort should be here by then."

"The colonel is going to eat something, I hope?" asked the doctor.

"I'm not hungry just now. Have some food packed, and I'll eat once we're on the train," he answered, as he sipped on the hot coffee. He drifted back into his thoughts. The room was now fairly dark, as he had the ceiling light turned off right after the attack. Only a lamp near the desk was illuminated. His thoughts were still on the attack that had occurred just hours before. The developing complexity of the game had changed. Those riders had his guard dead in their sites, and they didn't attempt to kill him but just made noise by firing a few shots into the hotel. It was as if the faceless cowards were trying to affirm the threat that had been given. He continued to sip the black coffee and stare into the empty fireplace.

"Two full regiments in this town, and we sneak out of here under guard and in the dark of night," criticized Lieutenant Asa Child, as he walked from the darkened room with Lieutenant Hyde. "Hell of a way to be victors in a war!"

"Easy, Asa," responded Ernie. "This thing will be over soon, and you'll find yourself back home like the rest of us. Things will settle in the South soon enough," he added, as he followed through the hallway.

As they came down the stairs, they saw Lieutenant Henry Wood already in the lobby, along with Dr. Crandall and Colonel Trowbridge. They were followed by the new addition to their regiment, the assistant surgeon, Sam Stuart.

There's breakfast in the kitchen, boys, but you'll have to help your own plates this morning," said the doctor. "I did good to find a cook at this time of day."

"Lieutenant Hyde, take this voucher to the clerk. It's for our stay," interrupted Colonel Trowbridge. "I've taken the liberty to sign it. Just finish filling it out. Tell him he can take it to the adjutant of the 7th Connecticut, and he'll see that the voucher is paid."

Lieutenant Hyde took the paper from the colonel and went looking for the clerk. He thought how glad he'd be when they had a new adjutant assigned. He watched the other officers as they entered the restaurant. He got a slight smell of what he was certain was ham, as the door closed behind them.

Two horse drawn ambulances, escorted by a squad of eight black soldiers, slowed to a stop in front of the Anderson Hotel. A sergeant jumped from the front seat of the lead wagon and moved up the steps to the porch. A corporal sat silently by the driver of the second wagon, as one of the horses raked his hoof through the wet dirt of the street.

The sergeant of the guard entered the hotel lobby and reported to the colonel that the transportation had arrived. He quickly returned to his post.

Colonel Trowbridge entered the restaurant where his officers were standing next to a waiter's counter, finishing their breakfast.

"It's time, gentlemen," he ordered. "The wagons are out front. Once outside, get your baggage loaded quickly and get yourselves in with the least amount of exposure. The trip to the station will be slow because of the guard, but at least it's not far. If any shots are fired, protect yourself, and use your side arms to assist the guard as you see fit."

The officers quickly swallowed as much of the coffee as they could and grabbed the last of the food. They caught up with the colonel at the front entrance. The clerk extinguished the lamp in the lobby, as he was instructed, and the men moved onto the porch. The colonel moved ahead of the men, quickly followed by Surgeon Crandall and Lieutenant Wood, and entered the front wagon. The other men boarded the second wagon, and the column moved out through the darkness toward the depot.

Three riders sat on horse back in the dark shadows of the alley opposite the hotel. They sat silently, weapons in hand, watching as the wagons and soldiers moved through the muddy street. They turned away in unison and disappeared into the darkness.

The shrill whistle broke the stillness of the breaking dawn as the Columbia train rolled into the Anderson train yard. It slowed to a stop in front of the depot.

The special train that sat beside the main tracks bellowed a greeting of steam to the arriving train, announcing that it was soon to depart. All the doors of the freight cars were closed as ordered. Inside, the men of the 33rd US Colored Troops were occupied with finding resting places, as sleep was now utmost on their minds. Inside the forward passenger car burned a single oil lamp. In the dim light Colonel Charles Trowbridge sat patiently waiting for the train to get underway, as Captain Fowler and Lieutenant White worked on their morning reports. The remaining officers of the regiment had been ordered to ride in the cars with the men. Two armed soldiers stood watch on the rear platform of the passenger car.

The train seemed to strain under its heavy load as it rolled onto the main tracks heading east. It slowly began to gain momentum and was soon moving at a steady pace heading through the outskirts of Anderson. From inside the first car, the colonel pulled back the covering of his window and was greeted with a view of a detachment of the 7th New Hampshire, scattered along the tracks, barely visible through the morning mist. "Colonel Abbott had kept his word," the colonel thought with a smile. He settled back into his seat, relieved to be underway.

It was a matter of minutes before the regimental commander had nodded into a restful sleep, only to be abruptly wakened by the sound of a window being shattered and glass being blown across the seat in front of him. A bullet lodged in the wall padding across the aisle.

Two cars back, William Crandall was startled awake by wood splintering from the board just inches from his side. A piece of the wood penetrated the trousers of a soldier lying prone on the floor, drawing blood from the calf of his leg. Three other bullets passed harmlessly through the cars or lodged in the wooden walls as the train continued on its journey.

In the cab of the engine sat a sleepy engineer. He reached and pulled twice on the cord of the train's whistle, signaling the crossing that lay just ahead. He lazily watched through the side of the cab as a farmer surveyed his field of corn just across a nearby creek. His attention was drawn back to the sunrise breaking through the shallow line of trees in his front. He stared into the bright morning light and the flickering shadows and thought of what lay ahead, oblivious to the world that was behind him.

The morning sunshine felt warm on Sarah's cheeks, as she and her sister exited the car that had provided needed rest after the long and dreary day before. Calvin followed the ladies out onto the platform and then into the station. Jim and Josh were already out in the bright morning sunshine, sitting shoeless on the end of the platform, talking with an elderly man.

Inside the station, Calvin was told it would be mid–afternoon before the train would be leaving for Newberry. He had hoped it might be earlier, as his last thoughts of the night had been of home; he felt anxious to be moving again. He walked back outside to wait for Sarah and Jenny.

The small southern town didn't offer any relief for Calvin. It wasn't anything like Galveston. The lay of the land was hilly and the town was engulfed in trees -- a mixture of soft pines and a variety of hardwoods, oaks and hickory, with even a few walnut trees thrown in.

He watched as a wagon moved along the street leading toward the station. The two drivers were army teamsters, obviously, from their mixed dress of uniform and other attire, with a blue army cap adorning each man's head. He watched as they turned the wagon toward the building opposite the station.

Calvin looked back toward Jim and Josh. The old man was walking away, aided by his cane, toward the same building where the wagon had stopped. Calvin walked over to where the boys sat.

"You fellows rest good last night?" asked Calvin.

"Weren't bad, plenty of straw on the floor and a cool breeze blowing through 'til we got here. Then t'was just like a quiet night at home," Jim said, smiling.

"Looks like we got us another wait. Sometimes this afternoon 'fore the train leaves," said Calvin.

"Kind of wish we could just go back to sleep and wake up already at home," Josh said, with a tone of longing in his voice. "Will this thing ever end, Cal? Sometimes it don't seem it will to me. I had another of those spells last night of longing for Betsy and the kids."

"I just dreamt about home," said Jim, "and I think I slept like I was already there."

"Cal, that man we was talking with says things are dangerous abouts," commented Josh. "He said a man was murdered two days ago by what most believed were idle Negroes looking for money. He said a soldier was shot near here yesterday -- says it ain't safe for nobody."

"Seems that they all are saying that," responded Calvin. "I'm afraid things might be worse than we thought. You know what those soldiers were up to doing yesterday. Ain't no wonder people are talking the way they do."

"Better stay close to the ladies, Cal," suggested Jim. "That fellow said the Yanks are the worst he'd seed about men insulting the ladies."

"You want to join us for breakfast? We're going to eat yonder, under those trees where those boxes are," Calvin asked, pointing toward several pines near a rail fence on the other side of the depot.

"Sure the ladies won't mind our company, Cal?" asked Jim.

"Don't think they'll mind you two at all," smiled Calvin. "Better put those shoes on, though. Hope you saved me another piece of that pie."

The three men joined Sarah and Jenny and walked with them to the spot they had selected. Jim was especially helpful, cleaning and arranging the boxes for the ladies to sit on. They shared the food that they had, as they enjoyed each other's company and idled part of the morning away.

Activity in the train yard had picked up. The Charlotte train had been moved, the freight cars uncoupled, and other cars were being attached, loaded with freight heading north. The other set of rails was empty, waiting the arrival of the train from Camden, which would continue to Newberry and Anderson. Several wagons had come and gone at the warehouse, and men were busy, handling freight to and from the cars. Several soldiers lounged near the depot. There was a small group of Negroes near the warehouse, apparently looking for work.

"Maybe we had better go back to the station, ladies," suggested

Calvin. "I'd feel better with you ladies inside."

"But it's better out here," responded Jenny, "and I don't see any danger."

"We best do as Mr. Crozier said, Jenny," insisted Sarah, noticing the group of men at the warehouse looking in their direction. "No need for us to invite trouble. It does seem there are a lot of people around doing nothing, when the others seem so busy."

"The morning will pass soon enough and we'll be back on the train," encouraged Calvin, watching Jim help the girls gather up the leftovers. Josh was standing, watching three black men talking to two Federal soldiers on the side of the street.

The five young people began moving toward the depot.

Calvin and the two girls entered the depot and found comfortable seats near an open window. The morning breeze passing through the building felt cool and clean, the way the air can be only after a long, continuous rain. Jim and Josh rested on the platform.

It was late afternoon before the Camden train arrived and then departed for Newberry.


*Camp Douglas War Prison*
*Chicago, Illinois*

*July 25, 1865*
*Lewis PO, Galveston, Texas*

*Dear General,*

*I have recently found out that my brother was a prisoner in your prison at Camp Douglas. His name is Calvin Crozier. He entered your prison in 1863 and was captured in Ohio. My family and I have not heard from him since he was captured. We need to find out where he is and what has happened to him. Please help us. You should have records of his whereabouts.*

*Sincerely, Mary Crozier*

# Chapter 8

The unscheduled train rolled into the Newberry train yard late in the afternoon. Local citizens gave little notice to the whistles, as in recent weeks trains had been coming and going at all times, day and night. The train was moved onto a sidetrack of the Greenville and Columbia rail. A train from Winnsboro was expected to pass through later in the night heading back toward Anderson.

It was only after the train had been unloaded that people began to stop their activities and stare at the colored soldiers. There had been rumors that additional colored troops were heading to Newberry to join the three companies already there. And now as the people stared with apprehension they realized that these rumors were indeed true.

Mr. Jake Bowers stood on the platform outside the Greenville and Columbia railroad station, watching the sight, as many of the passing citizens were doing. Three hours earlier he had received a telegram reporting news of the special train that would be arriving in Newberry and would remain there overnight. But it was only now that he understood what it was carrying. Five companies of the 33rd US Colored troops filled the train yard between the train and the station.

Colonel Charles Trowbridge stepped from the rear of the passenger car, his eyes scanning the scene for signs of danger. His guards were already posted and the remainder of his officers was busy getting their respective companies into marching order. He hurriedly walked toward the entrance of the depot.

"Have other colored troops arrived in Newberry," he asked of Mr. Bowers.

"There're here," came the reply, dryly.

"May I ask their where abouts?" again asked the colonel.

"They're down the tracks a ways toward Frog Level," Jake answered.

The colonel walked past the man and took a drink of cool water from the water bucket. Just then, two officers appeared at the end of the platform and hurried toward the colonel.

"I'm Colonel Rockwell Tyler of the 56th New York and this is my adjutant, Captain Henry Loomus," greeted the colonel, presenting his salute to the younger man. "Welcome to Newberry, sir."

"Colonel Charles Trowbridge, of the 33rd US Colored Troops," responded the colonel, returning the salute. "I wasn't expecting any greetings on our arrival, colonel."

"I thought I would greet you personally and invite you to dine with me at my headquarters this evening, colonel," explained Colonel Tyler.

"Kind of you sir, but we've had a bad time of it. I consider it best that I remain in camp with my officers and men tonight. Have any arrangements been made for our camp?" asked the colonel.

"Captain Metcalf told us that you would be arriving," responded Captain Loomus. "There's a field just to the right of the tracks about a quarter of a mile distance, colonel, just past where the tracks turn. I have three wagons on the way to the station to assist in transporting your baggage and supplies."

"Do you know where Captain Metcalf is, captain?" asked Colonel Trowbridge.

"Not at present, sir," answered the soldier. "His camp is located east of here about three quarters a mile."

"Wish you would reconsider my invitation, Colonel Trowbridge," Colonel Tyler offered.

Colonel Trowbridge looked toward the civilian standing at the edge of the platform, turned and began walking down the platform. The two officers followed.

"Colonel Tyler, I've had several men shot and one officer killed since we left Augusta," the colonel began in a lowered voice. "There has been a threat issued against all of my officers. We ran short of supplies in Walhalla and when Lieutenant Furman was killed there, the men wanted to burn the entire town," he continued. "My men are tired of this duty and are in an agitated state. I'm afraid what might be the outcome should anything else happen before we reach the coast. It's my duty to see that all of my officers remain in camp tonight."

Colonel Tyler stopped and looked at the colonel not knowing what to make of his comments. He paused, waiting for additional information that didn't come.

"Well, Colonel Trowbridge, I will say that Captain Metcalf has done well in keeping his soldiers in line since he arrived two days ago," commented Colonel Tyler. "I'm certain you'll be able to do the same. Things in Newberry are much improved since I arrived and I need to keep it that way. If you feel the only way you can control your men is by being in camp with them, then do it, sir. This is still a dangerous town, colonel, and it might be best that you restrict all your men to camp while you're here."

"Thank you, colonel. I'm glad that you understand. Now if I might be excused, I'll return to my men," answered the colonel with a salute.

He turned away from the two officers and started back toward the train.

Colonel Tyler watched the young lieutenant colonel as he walked toward a group of his officers in the yard. He was still uncertain of what to make of the colonel's comments.

"Captain Fowler, we'll be moving the men into camp a little farther down the tracks," Colonel Trowbridge said, as he approached the captain, Lieutenant White and Lieutenant Wood. "Make sure all the officers understand that they are restricted to camp tonight. Lieutenant Wood, I want your entire company on regimental guard once we're in camp. All the men are restricted to camp tonight, gentlemen, and it's important that this be enforced."

"Colonel, may I have permission to move my detachment to Captain Metcalf's camp?" asked Captain Fowler. "I am anxious to get the entire company back together."

"Once we get to our campsite, you and Lieutenant White may move your men," answered the colonel. "But I also want it understood no one is to leave that camp."

"Speaking of the captain, he sure is a sight for sore eyes," interrupted Lieutenant Wood, gesturing in the direction of the officer leading a horse toward them.

Colonel Trowbridge turned to see Captain Metcalf heading in their direction with a smile on his face.

"Sure glad to see you again," said the officer with a smile, rendering a salute. "Maybe this means this duty is about over."

"We hope so, Lewis," responded the colonel with a dry laugh. I hope you and the men are doing well."

"As well as can be expected, colonel, with the regretful report that I have lost three men since I saw you last," answered the captain.

"When we gwi'in to camp, colonel?" came a voice from the ranks.

91

Colonel Trowbridge turned to see a sergeant quickly in the face of a private, reprimanding him.

Colonel Trowbridge stared for a moment and then turned his attention back to Captain Metcalf.

"I received word yesterday of Private Washington and I understand a man was killed in Aiken," commented the colonel.

"Also, Corporal James of my company has been missing since we were in Trenton, three weeks ago," added the captain.

"Captain Fowler wishes to return with his detachment to your camp, Captain Metcalf, which I told him he could do," said the colonel. "Have you made arrangements for additional supplies for the regiment?"

"Yes, sir. Captain Fulton of the 56th said he would have supplies brought to the station as soon as your train arrived," said Captain Metcalf.

"Very well, Lewis," responded the colonel, now feeling somewhat better than when he first arrived in Newberry.

A young man wearing an apron stained with ink came from the front entrance of the depot and walked toward Jake.

"Jake, you got any idea which of those men might be Colonel Trowbridge?" asked Benny.

"That tall fellow there with the bars on his shoulders talking to those other officers is him," responded Mr. Bowers, pointing in his direction.

The station clerk stepped from the platform and walked across the yard, limping from his leg wound that still hadn't completely healed.

"You Colonel Trowbridge?" asked the man as he approached the officers. "I got a telegram for you if you are."

The colonel took the paper from the clerk and immediately began to read. Benny turned and walked back to the station.

"Damn it, more bad news. General Molineux sends word that Captain Heasley was killed last night in Augusta," said the colonel with anger.

"Alex was just a kid, colonel," said Captain Metcalf. "Any details about what might have happened?"

The colonel handed the telegram to the captain and said no more. He walked back toward the depot leaving his officers to discuss the latest news among themselves.

Three wagons driven by black teamsters slowly moved along Platt Street, crossed the tracks, and turned into the train yard. The drivers halted them near the rear of the train. Lieutenant Ernie Hyde and Gus Chamberlain, his quartermaster, were there to greet them. Gus walked to the first two wagons, briefly examining their contents.

"Take the supplies to the second car there and leave the empty at the rear car," he instructed the drivers. "Lieutenant, if you could get me a detail, we'll have these supplies on the train in no time, and the baggage ready to move in a tick," he added, looking back at the officer.

The drivers moved the wagons as instructed, parked them, and climbed from the driver's seats. All three men moved to the other side of the tracks to meet the newly arrived soldiers.

The supplies were soon aboard the train with the exception of a barrel each of meal and flour, two bags of dried beans, and a box of salt pork. Gus had the baggage loaded onto all three wagons, covered and tied, in less than thirty minutes.

"Colonel, the wagons are loaded and ready to move," reported Lieutenant Hyde, standing at the edge of the station platform.

"Very well," he responded. "We'll be moving shortly."

"Would you like for me to arrange transportation for you, sir?" asked the acting adjutant.

"No, lieutenant, that won't be necessary. I'll be walking with the men," responded the colonel.

Lieutenant Hyde walked over to join the conversation with the other officers.

"In my opinion, this problem won't be solved until permanent commands are set up in all the towns in this state and military law is officially declared," argued Captain Metcalf. "The idea of allowing the rebels to set up new governments now is foolhardy!"

"Well, they're going to do it, right here in South Carolina next week and with the blessing of our president," added Captain Fowler.

"He's a southerner, even if he didn't secede with the rest of 'em," commented Ernie, as he joined in the group.

"Alex was killed in Augusta, yesterday. The colonel just got word," Lewis told the lieutenant.

"Alex Heasley? Not him, such a sweet and honorable kid," said Lieutenant Hyde with surprise and disappointment. "I assume another assassination by the rebels?"

"We don't know, Ernie. Nothing in the telegram about who or how -- just that he was shot," answered Henry Wood.

"All right, gentlemen, fall your men in at attention," commanded Colonel Trowbridge.

The officers quickly separated, joining their respective companies.

Officers gave commands followed by the bark of the sergeants, as soldiers slowly moved into formation. Attention was called first at the head of one company, soon followed by its echo down the line, then echoing across the yard, as movement began to decrease and chatter became quiet murmuring.

"Men, listen and understand me clearly," came the voice of Colonel Trowbridge, as he began to address the ranks. "We're moving into camp for the night and will depart in the morning for the coast. We're glad to have Captain Metcalf and his detachment of three companies rejoining us for the remainder of our trip. I've been told this is a dangerous town, just as most of the towns we've been in lately." This comment was followed by chuckles and laughter in the ranks, followed quickly by commands of the sergeants for attention. "All officers will remain in camp tonight with your men and all men are restricted to camp. Company A will have the regimental guard tonight. Officers take charge of your companies. No straggling will be allowed," concluded the colonel.

Jake Bowers continued to watch from the edge of the platform, as the officers moved their men into columns of four preparatory for the march. It was the first indication in Jake's mind that there was a military unit in front of him. He watched as the regiment marched beyond the rear of the train and formed in line behind the three supply wagons. As the wagons began to move out into Tarrant Street, the columns followed in turn until they were moving in unison. He continued to watch from his vantage point, as the procession turned onto Boundary Street, once again crossed the rails and disappeared beyond the station.

Colonel Trowbridge had taken his position beside the ranks with Sergeant Rivers walking by his side. The other officers were scattered down the column, as the colonel wanted none of the officers grouped when exposed as they were now.

"Not far to da coast, now, is it, colonel?" asked the 1st Sergeant.

"Couple of hundred miles, Sergeant," the colonel responded, as they walked beside the men.

"Dat won'ts take long, colonel, now dats all da men is back and den Capt' Heasley and Capt' Samson comp'neys be joining us from Georg'a when we gets to Charleston," continued the sergeant with a smile.

"Captain Heasley was killed in Augusta yesterday," responded the colonel, without looking at the sergeant. "Just don't say nothing about it just now. The men don't need to know."

Sergeant Rivers watched ahead as the wagons began to turn right onto another street putting the slowly descending sun over their right shoulder. He watched the ground and the many moving shadows of the men and thought how many times he had seen that in the last two years. "Soon it be over," he thought, "but how many more shadows be missing 'fore dat time?" He looked about him, seeing the many people who had come out to stare at the curiosity that was being moved through their midst. Again, he saw several black children waving, as they moved across the tracks down Caldwell Street away from the last residences. Not far on his left he saw a cemetery, already one of age, with many tombstones visible. He looked ahead to see an open field with a large grove of trees near the far end. An abandoned building stood near the trees. On his far right continued another street beyond a line of trees now blocking the sun's rays. Several outbuildings jutted into the field back near the railroad, part of a business of such, apparently.

Captain Fowler and Lieutenant White had already moved off, following the tracks with their half company, accompanied by Captain Metcalf on horseback.

Lieutenant Hyde had halted the wagons and was giving directions to the different companies, as they moved into the field. Men were stepping more rapidly now, eager to discard their large backpacks and stack their weapons. Details were already being formed to draw supplies from the wagons.

Colonel Trowbridge was standing beside Gus Chamberlain at the rear wagon when a gunshot rang out.

"Who discharged that weapon?" shouted Lieutenant Wood.

A second shot echoed across the field, this time with a bullet striking the wagon near the colonel. Shouts rang from the men, quickly followed by a small group of men heading toward the eastern edge of the field, weapons in hand.

"Lieutenant Wood, have your guard stop those men at once!" shouted the colonel. "Nobody is to leave the camp!" he said angrily.

Lieutenant Wood hurried toward his guard near the eastern edge of the field, their backs turned toward the rapidly approaching gang of soldiers. The lieutenant's shouts got the attention of the sergeant of the guard, who quickly ascertained the commotion behind him. He shouted for the approaching men to halt, and then ordered the two accompanying privates to lower their weapons at the running soldiers. The men slowed to a walk, as they continued to approach the guard.

"Bet 'er 'in step asides, Jim. Das a Reb in dem woods yonder, and we's go'in gets him," warned a large private, breathing hard with excitement.

"The lieutenant says fur yu' to halt, and I means fur yo' to halt, too, Sam," answered 2nd Sergeant Goins. "Don'ts makes us shoot yu, 'cause da cunnel sho watching, too."

Colonel Trowbridge watched at a distance, as the men seemed to be confronting each other. Lieutenant Wood was soon upon them, and the situation was now back in hand.

"Colonel, I can takes a scout out yonder and sees if we can finds da shooter," suggested Sergeant Rivers. "I'll keeps them under control and we get dat man, colonel, if'n yo' gives us permission."

"No, sergeant; it's best we stay together right here," answered the colonel, still staring at the men as they slowly moved back toward the center of camp. Other men stood ready to move, weapons still in hand, now splitting into small groups again, talking amongst themselves, occasionally looking toward any officer standing near. Colonel Trowbridge was anxious as the early evening slowly approached. He watched Lieutenant Wood as he returned, sweat running from his forehead and a look of frustration on his face, as he headed toward the duty tent.

Captain Loomus approached the table where the colonel and major were almost through with their dinner.

"Sir, there have been shots fired near the camp of the 33rd. I understand no damage was done, but I'm afraid it might be a long night, sir," said the captain.

Colonel Tyler finished chewing his last bite of beefsteak and looked at his major, with a smile.

"Captain Loomus, have Captain Walker take three squads of four men and a sergeant each," the colonel began, now looking back at the captain, "and soon after dark has set in, have him post each squad near the camp of the 33rd, under cover in case another incident happens. I won't use these newly arrived men as bait, but we might as well take advantage of their presence to try to catch some of these rebels that continue to cause us trouble."

Captain Loomus responded with a grin, "Yes, sir, colonel".

"But remind Captain Walker not to let his men get too close to their guards. I understand they are 'quite agitated' and we don't want them shooting any of our men by mistake," added the colonel, also with a grin of sarcasm. He filled the major's glass, as well as his own, with more brandy.

War Department, Office of the Adjutant General
Washington, DC
September 8, 1865


Dear Colonel Robertson,

I have been told that you were in charge of the prison records at Point Lookout Maryland in 1865. I have recently found information that showed that my brother, Calvin Crozier, was at Point Lookout Maryland in June of this year. My family and I have heard nothing further of him. I am anxious to find out what happened to him there and why he has not come home.

Sincerely
Mary Crozier

# Chapter 9

The Winnsboro train was beginning to slow as it approached the sleeping town of Newberry. Inside the passenger car, three young people were finally asleep. They had spent several of the hours since they had left Winnsboro talking, sharing childhood dreams and plans for the future. Two sisters, heading back home to a world that no longer existed, had spoken of their uncertain future. They were not prepared for the hardships of reconstruction and the cruelty of having to grow up too soon that lay just ahead for them. The other, a young ex–Confederate soldier, was trying to return home to a family that would be forever scarred by the cruelty of that war.

The shrill whistle woke Calvin into semi–consciousness. He opened his eyes to the dark interior of the coach. Sarah and Jenny were asleep in the seat ahead. The whistle screeched once again, but this time a constant whistle. Calvin was wide awake when the train suddenly jolted, followed by the crack of the train's wheels striking debris on the track. The sound and motion now had the two girls wide awake. The train continued to move erratically when suddenly Calvin was thrown forward against the back of the seat ahead, and then just as suddenly, his head struck the window as the car swerved abruptly to the right. The train continued to slow rapidly. The passengers were bounced roughly as the front wheels of the car struck the ties of the rail bed. Jenny screamed as she bounced from her seat into the aisle. Sarah was also thrown with the erratic motion of the car.

As the train came to a final stop, flickering light began to fill the car. Calvin quickly righted himself to see the shadows generated from the flames somewhere behind him. He turned to see a man already on his feet and extinguishing the fire from the broken lamp that had been tossed onto the floor. Calvin just as quickly turned back to attend to the girls. Jenny still lay prone in the aisle but was now in motion trying to get to her feet. Sarah was sitting in the seat, holding her head. She would have a nasty bruise come morning.

"Jenny, are you hurt?" Calvin asked excitedly, as he offered his hand to assist her in getting to her feet.

"I… I don't think so," she responded. She turned to look after her sister, who was still seated, holding her hand to her forehead. "Sarah, you're bleeding!" she shouted.

Sarah removed her hand to see a trickle of blood on her fingers. She gently touched the laceration and the rapidly growing bump.

"Let me see, Miss Dekalb." Calvin leaned close in the dim light. Jenny quickly produced a handkerchief and handed it to Sarah.

"A bad bruise and slight cut, Sarah. I'm certain that the hurt is worst than the damage; what do you think, Jenny?" asked Calvin, smiling at the shaken seventeen–year–old.

"Scarred for life, Mr. Crozier," responded the girl.

"Shut up, sis! What happened, Mr. Crozier?" Sarah asked.

"Well, ladies, I'd say we just survived a most disastrous train wreck, and I'd also say at least one car is off the track," Calvin answered, this time more seriously. He moved to get up and felt the pain in his knee.

"Mr. Crozier, you're hurt!" exclaimed Jenny.

"Just a bruise, I think," he said, as he fell back into his seat.

Other passengers were also looking after themselves and others whom were bruised and shaken. No one seemed to be seriously injured. The conductor soon entered the car, also to check on the passengers, lantern in hand.

"What happened?" inquired a middle age man of the conductor.

"Not certain, just yet. But we do know this car has wheels off the rail," he responded. "Are you ladies all right?" he asked, looking at Sarah and Jenny. Sarah was holding the handkerchief to her forehead.

"We're all right," responded Sarah, with a slight smile.

"We're in Newberry, and the car is but a short distance from the depot," added the conductor, looking at Calvin. "You ought to take the ladies there. Ya'll have to leave this car anyway. Ya'll find light and water in the station." He walked on through the car, stopping to check on an older couple in the front seat.

Calvin rose to assist Sarah from her seat.

"Are you up to walking?" he asked.

"I'm all right, Mr. Crozier. I was just dazed. You look to your own injury and that'll make me feel better," responded Sarah.

"Are you certain you aren't injured, Miss Jenny?" Calvin asked, looking at the younger girl.

"I think I banged my foot, maybe," she said, with a frown. "It's starting to hurt a little." She put her weight on the foot and tried to

99

take a step. "I can walk. It only hurts a bit."

"You wait here and I'll see how far it is to the station," suggested Calvin.

"No, Mr. Crozier, we're all right. Help us with the baggage and we'll go with you," answered Sarah.

Calvin reached under the seat to feel for the ladies bundles, only to find that they were now under the seat ahead. He found his own sack, removed the knife and inserted it into the waist of his trousers. The one remaining lamp in the car gave little assistance as they gingerly walked toward the rear door of the car.

Four soldiers of the 33rd Regiment of US Colored Troops watched from a distance as people began to exit the passenger car. They remained hidden in the shadows, struggling to keep their voices low. They heard footsteps in the gravel along the tracks as two men slowly became visible in the starlit night. The four men moved further back into the darkness, afraid that they may be discovered.

"It looks like cars are off the track, Josh," exclaimed Jim, as they moved rapidly up the track.

"Uh," came the trailing voice behind Josh, who came to a sudden stop.

"You okay, boy?" asked Josh, as he reached down in the darkness to help Jim back to his feet. "What'd you trip over anyhow?"

"Don't rightly know. Looks like a large piece of wood, crosstie maybe?" replied Jim. "Looks like another big piece there. Reckon that was on the tracks, Josh?"

"Come on, Jim," encouraged Josh. "Calvin may be hurt. I think that might be the passenger car up front that's out of position." Both men hurried toward the damaged cars ahead.

Three men were standing outside the passenger car examining the situation by lantern light. As foreman of the railroad, Jake Bowers was already there, as were the station clerk, Benny, and Hayne Dominick, waiting to help service the engine when the train arrived. "Well, it looks as if my work is cut out for me tonight," commented Bowers, ruefully. The three railroad men began to walk past the passengers toward the rear of the train.

Calvin stepped from the car first and assisted the two girls from the single step of the car. He looked back at the second car in line to notice that the front wheels were off the rail, along with both front and rear wheels of the passenger car.

"It's just a little walk to the station, ladies," Calvin said. "It's best that we get you there and let you check to make sure you're not hurt anywhere else."

They had moved but a few yards when Josh's voice was heard from behind.

"Ya'll okay?" he asked, breathing heavier than Calvin thought was necessary.

"Just bruised some," answered Calvin. "I'm taking the ladies to the station to make sure they're not too badly hurt. You boys didn't get hurt?"

"Kind'a scared us a little," admitted Jim. "Know what happened?"

"Cars just jumped the track, I reckon," responded Calvin.

"Might have been something else. Looked like crossties might have been put on the rails back a ways," commented Josh, still showing difficulty breathing.

"Who'd do that?" asked Jenny.

"Don't know, Miss Jenny, but it sure looks like the case," answered Jim. "Near broke my neck stumbling around in the dark. They're thrown everywhere back yonder, mostly in pieces now."

The group moved toward the station, following the older couple just ahead of them. Two black men came from around the side of the station and headed toward Jake and the other men.

The boys assisted Sarah and Jenny up the steps to the platform, and they all entered the station.

Once inside with better light, Calvin and Jenny could see the size of the bruise on Sarah's forehead. The cut was minor, but there was no doubt that the spot would be sore by morning.

Calvin looked toward Jim and Josh seated on a bench on the side of the room. Jim was talking to Josh in a low voice, looking concerned.

Calvin saw the flush of Josh's face and knew the fever had returned. He watched, as Jim removed a worn handkerchief from his pocket and walked over to the water bucket. He poured water from the dipper onto the cloth and returned to Josh.

"Do you have any injuries, Mr. Crozier," asked Sarah with concern for his slight limp.

"Just a bruise and another tear in these old trousers," responded

Calvin, looking at the new hole at the knee. "Don't guess it'll matter much, with all the patches, already."

Calvin looked around the room at the other passengers who had entered the building. The older couple sat together on the opposite end of the bench from Jim and Josh. The woman, still somewhat distressed, was favoring her arm. The man who had extinguished the fire could be seen through the front window on the platform outside. The other two male passengers stood near the water bucket, talking. Jenny discretely examined her foot and ankle.

The conductor and station clerk soon entered the depot, both seemingly in an agitated state.

"Folks, it looks as if we'll be here awhile," said the conductor. "We have two cars off the tracks that'll have to be fixed. The railroad foreman is checking the rails, but so far they look okay."

"Do you know what happened?" asked the older man, still trying to calm his wife.

"There may have been debris on the track. Who knows how it got there?" he said.

The rear door of the station opened and a man in his late fifties entered, carrying a doctor's bag, accompanied by a stout, dark headed lady.

"Dr. Gary!" greeted the clerk. "Glad to see you. Doesn't look like anyone is seriously hurt. The lady there has a nasty bruise." The clerk pointed toward Sarah.

"Are you a doctor?" asked the elderly man. "It's my wife, doctor, her arm is hurt, and she's not feeling well at all."

Dr. John Gary walked toward the two people seated on the bench. His wife moved toward Sarah and Jenny.

"Someone is checking to see if the hotel will open up for passengers desiring to stay there the rest of the night," said the conductor "All the boarding houses are closed. Anyone who wishes to remain in the station tonight is welcome to do so, but it's most likely going to be busy here all night."

"May I look at the bruise on your head?" asked Mrs. Gary, looking at Sarah.

"It's not much to bother with. I'll be fine," said Sarah, trying not to draw attention to herself.

"You just let me determine that," insisted the woman, kneeling in front of the chairs where Sarah and Jenny were seated. She removed a bandage from her apron pocket and handed it to Calvin.

"Moisten this for me, young man," she instructed. Calvin quickly stepped to the water pail and dripped water on the cloth from the dipper.

"It's a bad bruise, but only a slight cut," she assured the girl. She dabbed the wet bandage on the wound, cleaning away the blood. "Not bad at all," she said, rising to her feet to get an ointment from the doctor's bag.

"This won't look very pretty on such a pretty young lady, but it will help the healing and help keep the swelling down," said the woman.

Jenny watched the lady, as she tended to her sister and then turned to Calvin, "What are we to do tonight, Mr. Crozier?" she asked with concern. "We don't have money for any hotel."

Calvin looked toward the narrow bench where Jim and Josh were seated and the doctor was busy tending to the older couple.

"Are you ladies traveling far?" asked Mrs. Gary.

"We left our grandmother's in Salisbury Tuesday morning and we're going home to Macon," Sarah answered. "This is Mr. Crozier, and he's escorting us until we get home."

Mrs. Gary smiled at the young man in his well–worn Confederate gray. "That's kind of you, Mr. Crozier. It's certainly not safe for a lady to travel anywhere now," she added, as she applied the ointment to Sarah's cut.

"The doctor and I have an extra room for you for tonight if you like," offered Mrs. Gary. "The young man can sleep in an out shed that's fixed up with a cot."

"Oh, no ma'am," answered Sarah, quickly declining the offer. "We'll be fine here. Mr. Crozier's friends are also traveling home with him and I think we can all find a spot right here to rest 'til morning."

Mrs. Gary looked toward the two young men seated on the bench. She stared at Josh with some concern.

"Is your friend ill, Mr. Crozier?" she asked.

"I'm afraid he may be getting the fever again," Calvin answered, with concern. "All three of us were ill when we left Camp Douglas, and I'm afraid Josh may be traveling too soon. His fever came back for a day while we were still in Virginia, but he insists he'll be all right."

"Camp Douglas?" she asked, "Where's that?"

"Near Chicago. We were all ill with dysentery and camp fever, mostly" answered Calvin. "Sarah, you and Jenny should take the lady's offer; don't you think? There aren't many options around here right now," added Calvin, looking back at the girls.

"Can't ya'll find us a comfortable spot in one of those freight cars on the track?" suggested Sarah. "There's probably room in one near where Jim and Josh were riding."

"I don't know, young lady," said Mrs. Gary. "There is a large group of soldiers near here, and it may not be safe for anyone in the cars tonight."

"It'll be fun, Mr. Crozier," added Jenny. "You and Jim and Josh will be there with us."

"Yes, Mr. Crozier, that's what we'll do," decided Sarah. "It'll be quiet, and we won't have to worry about you and your friends here by yourselves."

Calvin looked at Mrs. Gary, who showed concern at the girl's suggestion.

"Maybe you and Jenny should go with the doctor and his wife," argued Calvin.

"No, we will stay here tonight," Sarah said with finality.

"Well, I do have a couple of quilts in the carriage," conceded the woman, "which you are welcome to use, if it would help. You can leave them here in the station with Benny in the morning."

"Thank you kindly, ma'am," responded Sarah, smiling.

"Mr. Crozier, would your friend mind if I look at him for a moment?" asked the nurse.

"You can try, but Josh can be stubborn about things like this," he answered.

The nurse cleaned the excess ointment from around Sarah's wound and went to the opposite end of the bench from where her husband was still attending the elderly lady.

The nurse and Josh were talking in lowered voices, and Calvin couldn't hear what was being said, but it was obvious to him that Josh was losing the argument.

Calvin watched as she opened the doctor's bag and removed a medicine and carried it back to Josh. Jim quickly went to the bucket of water and returned with a dipper full. Mrs. Gary handed two pills to Josh, which he swallowed with the help of the water from the dipper. He smiled at the lady, who patted his cheek and also smiled. She then went to the doctor's side to see if he needed assistance.

Calvin looked through the front window to see the foremen standing in the light of the lantern by the front entrance. Several black men surrounded him. It appeared that he was giving instructions, and then they separated.

It was but a short time before Jim accompanied the doctor's wife out the rear of the station and returned with two quilts in his arms. He took them to Calvin.

"You ladies sure you want to stay in a freight car tonight?" asked Calvin one last time. "I think we could make a comfortable place for you here in the station."

Just then two of the black workmen came into the room. They asked the clerk about the keys to one of the sheds and then returned outside.

Calvin rose and approached the clerk. "The ladies are determined to remain aboard the cars tonight," he told the clerk. "We need a lantern, if you have an extra."

"Certainly, mister," answered Benny. He turned and went to a closet in the corner of the room. "You'll need to fill it. There's oil just out the rear door, there in a can on the porch."

Jim and Josh went out the front of the building while Sarah and Jenny waited on Calvin to fill the lantern. Jim was carrying the ladies baggage. He watched Josh with concern, as his breathing was still somewhat labored. Calvin and the ladies emerged from the depot a few minutes later.

With the lantern casting a glow in the darkness, the five young people started back toward the rear of the train. They passed the work crew, who now seemed to be organized and were already busy at work. It was becoming clearer that it would be sometime after daylight before the task could be completed.

"Better watch your step. There's wood scattered everywhere here," cautioned Jim.

With Calvin holding the light the two ladies carefully picked their steps through the debris.

"Believe you're right, Jim. Sure looks like what the train may have hit," commented Calvin. "Wonder how that happened?"

"Here's an empty," stated Jim, peering into the partially open door of a freight car. "There seems to be plenty of room."

Calvin and the ladies stepped closer to the opening to look inside. There was some straw on the floor, and only a small part of the car taken up with freight.

Jim slid the ladies baggage inside and quickly tossed the two quilts in the door. Calvin set the lantern just inside behind the door and assisted Jim in lifting both girls in turn into the car.

"We'll be right down there, Cal," Jim said, pointing further down the tracks into the darkness toward the rear of the train.

"You going to be all right, Josh?" asked Calvin with concern.

"I'll be okay after I get settled. The lady said the medicine will help hold down the fever," answered Josh, having difficulty with his breathing.

"Jim, you look after him. If you need anything, you know where I'm at," added Calvin. "You need some light to get settled?"

"We're fine, Cal. You just look after the girls," said Josh.

Calvin watched the two figures disappear into the darkness, and then he hoisted himself through the door of the car.

Unknown to any of them a soldier watched silently from the darkness.

"This should be comfortable for the night," commented Sarah, taking the lantern to expose the interior of the car. "There's even more straw piled in that corner."

Jenny began to spread the straw evenly toward one side of the floor with her feet and then laid one of the quilts on top of the bed she had made. Sarah watched in approval.

"What will you do Mr. Crozier? There're just two quilts," asked Sarah.

"There's plenty of hay that will keep me comfortable, Miss Dekalb," Calvin answered.

"But you'll need something to lie on other than hay," she responded. "Take one of the quilts. It's really not that cool tonight."

"I did notice some burlap near the end of the platform back at the station house," Calvin commented. "Maybe I'll go fetch it, and you can keep your cover. I think that'd be better."

"You going to leave us?" asked Jenny.

"I'll be right back, no need to be worried," assured Calvin. "The men working on the cars are just back up the tracks."

Calvin was down and headed back toward the station in no time. His eyes had adjusted to the darkness now, and he had no problem maneuvering through the obstacles along the way. At the depot he gathered several pieces of the torn burlap in his arms and was soon headed back to the car.

As he approached the open door, Calvin thought he saw movement off to his left in the shadows being cast from the lantern burning in the freight car. He stopped for a moment and listened. He heard nothing but silence. He saw no movement. He hurried to the door of the car.

"Everything all right, ladies?" Calvin asked, tossing the burlap into the far corner opposite from where the girls had made their bed.

"We're fine, Mr. Crozier," answered Jenny. "Those rags what you're going to sleep on?"

"They'll do nicely," responded Calvin, still standing on the ground looking into the car. "I've got just one more errand to do. I'm worried about Josh, Miss Dekalb. If you can excuse me just for a few more minutes, I need to check on him."

"Take the lantern, Mr. Crozier," suggested Sarah. "You can't see much in the dark. We're settled and, most likely, we'll be half asleep by the time you return."

Jenny carried the lantern to the door and handed it down to Calvin.

"I won't be long," Calvin added, as he moved away from the car with the light of the lantern to lead his way.

"You boys in there?" called Calvin, as he approached the entrance to the last box car in line. He sat the lantern inside the doorway.

"Cal, that you?" responded Jim, leaning around the edge of the sliding door. "What you doing here? Where're the ladies?"

"I came back here to check on Josh," answered Calvin, lifting himself into the car.

"I'm right here, Cal, and I told you no need to worry," answered Josh, his voice sounding somewhat better.

"Got to make sure for myself. I'm in no mood to think about stopping in Alabama and trying to explain to that Betsy of yours how I let you die trying to get you home," smiled Calvin, as he slid closer to his friend.

"I swear, you treat me better'n those brothers of mine," chuckled Josh.

"The medicine helped, Cal. He's better," added Jim.

"You just stay warm tonight and rest. That fever pops up every time you get too energetic," ordered Calvin, feeling Josh's forehead with the palm of his hand. "And, Jim, you make sure he rests.

"I should get back, else the ladies will be down here in the dark looking for me," added Calvin, feeling somewhat better about Josh. He rose and headed back toward the opening.

"Thanks, Cal. You rest well, too," added Josh, as Calvin disappeared out the freight door.

"That you, Mr. Crozier? What happened to the light?" asked Sarah in a nervous voice.

"What yu gals doin' in here?" asked a gruff voice from the darkened entrance of the car.

"Get out! You got no business in here," commanded Sarah, trying to hide her fear.

"I's just looking fo' a place to sleep, and yu ladies got plenty room in here," responded the voice.

A sudden light flashed from a struck match, illuminating the face of the black soldier, now standing inside the entrance to the car. There was a sinister grin across his face that quickly terrified both Sarah and Jenny.

"I think we'uns can all be cozy in here, with all this here hay and dose dare quilts 'ready made into a bed," he suggested, as the match burnt out.

"You get out now!" Sarah's voice became louder, "or we'll scream! You're going to get into a lot of trouble!" she added with Jenny now pushed up close to her sister in the dark.

"Yu'uns jus might be worth a lit'le trouble," responded the soldier, striking another match.

Calvin heard voices from inside as he reached the end of the boxcar. A man's voice was clearly heard, followed by Jenny's short scream. Calvin threw himself inside the door, leaving the lantern on the ground. He made out the frame of a large man standing in the shadows.

"Get out!" Calvin ordered with authority. "I don't know who you are, but you've no business here; now get out!"

The soldier was startled by the sudden appearance of the man in gray clothes, now standing in the entrance.

"I's ain't doin' noth'in, but try'in to gets a place to sleep. Yu look likes one 'em Reb ghost, and mighty small a dat," answered the soldier, turning quickly toward Calvin. "Maybe yu da one ought 'a get out," he suddenly lunged at Calvin, striking him in the chest and knocking him hard against the rear of the car.

Calvin was trying to regain the breath that had been knocked from him when he felt the big hands grab at him in the semi-darkness. He was thrown hard onto the floor. He heard both girls scream as the soldier came down heavily on top of him, again striking him in the midsection. Calvin struggled with all his effort and managed to move the man just enough to slide his hand to the handle of the knife in the belt of his trousers. Another blow struck him in the face, stunning him, as the man rolled off his prone frame. A foot struck out at him from the soldier beside him on the floor. Another foot shoved him across the rough boards of the boxcar. Calvin pulled at the handle of the knife, freeing it just as the full force of the soldier's weight landed on top of him. Instinctively, Calvin struck out into the darkness across the soldier's back, the knife finding its mark on the back of the man's neck.

Calvin felt the man release his grip; a low growl from deep in the soldier's throat was quickly followed by the shout of a wounded animal. The man moved to a bending position, and then bolted upright, holding his hand to the back of his head. He lurched to his feet and jumped through the door opening. Calvin lay motionless on the floor, still trying to get his breath.

"Oh, Mr. Crozier!" shouted Sarah, clinging to Jenny in her arms. Both girls crouched near the freight at the opposite end of the car. "Are.... are you hurt?".

"Just so," came the gasping reply. "Give me a minute, ladies."

Sarah and Jenny remained motionless in the dark. The shadows on the walls of the car from the lantern outside revealed no movement. The only sounds that could now be heard were the heavy breathing of the ex–Confederate lying on the floor and the gasping of the two girls.

Calvin sat up, checking his body for damage. The knife was still in his right hand. He looked down at it in the darkness and felt relieved.

"Are you ladies hurt?" inquired Calvin with concern in his voice.

"Just scared," responded Sarah. "Are you injured, Mr. Crozier?"

"Just bruised. I'm going to get the lantern from outside," Calvin said, as he pulled himself to his feet. "Don't be scared anymore. The man's gone."

Jenny began to cry. Both girls remained where they were, staring at the entrance, waiting to see Calvin reappear. It was but moments before he set the lantern inside the car and pulled himself back in. He held the lantern up where he could see for himself that the girls were all right.

"What happened?" inquired Sarah.

"Just a man up to no good," answered Calvin. "He won't be back. I'm afraid I cut him pretty badly."

"Good for him," cried Jenny.

"But he was a soldier, wasn't he?" There was distress still in Sarah's voice. "What if he comes back with others, Mr. Crozier? What'll we do?"

After a long pause, Calvin said, "Maybe its best I take you back to the station, just in case."

"He knew we were in here, Mr. Crozier," Sarah commented, nervously. "He must have been watching all the time. His intent was evil. All the soldiers will know that!"

"I'm sorry I let this happen, ladies. I should've never left you alone," apologized Calvin.

"I'm not going outside," Jenny cried, looking at her sister.

"We best do as he says, Jenny," answered Sarah, looking at Calvin's discouraged expression. "It is too dangerous out here now. Help me gather the baggage."

Calvin assisted the girls in folding the quilts and moving the baggage to the door. He jumped to the ground and assisted Sarah from the doorway. They both helped Jenny out of the car.

"Don't you think you should let your friends know what happened, Mr. Crozier?" asked Sarah.

"No, not yet. It's best to leave them where they are for now," responded Calvin. "In case anything comes of this, it's best that they stay clear."

Calvin led the ladies back along the track to where the men were still busy with the cars. Several of the men looked at them as they passed. Calvin walked with the girls into the station. It was now empty. The only sound inside the room was the slow tick of the clock on the wall. It indicated 1:15 a.m. It was now the morning of September 8, 1865.

*Dear Miss Crozier,*

*The records from Point Lookout Maryland show that the soldier you inquired about was a prisoner there in 1865 until late June when the prison was closed. He was then transferred to Hospital #6 where the records seem to be incomplete. It is supposed that he was discharged from there and went home. Why you have not seen nor heard from him is beyond any records we have. I regret that I was unable to answer all the questions you have about your brother.*

*Regretfully*
*Colonel D.S. Robinson, Assist Adjutant*
*US Army Adjutant's Office*
*Washington, DC*

# Chapter 10

"Hep me! I's been mudered!" exclaimed Private Gloster Mills. "Hep me, lord, hep me!" he continued, his voice weakening.

"Sergeant of da guard!" cried another voice across the darkened field.

"Some Rebel dun kilts me! I's bleed'n bad, ohhhh!" the private moaned.

Two soldiers grabbed at the man as he began to stumble. They started walking him toward the duty tent.

"What going on here?" asked the sergeant, as he approached the men.

"It's Mills, sarg, he done got cut!" responded one of the guards.

"What yu get into, boy. Who done cut yu?" demanded the sergeant.

"I's jus sleeping out yonder when dis Reb jumped me and cut me. I seen him boss, he's a rebel sho 'nough," Mills panted, as he continued to walk between the two men.

"Whar yu at boy? And don't tell me out yonder!" snapped the sergeant. "You dun snuck off and got yo'sef cut!"

"I's kilt, boss, ain't sompbody go'in' get dat Reb fo' me?" moaned the private.

The men continued to carry the wounded man toward the center of the camp, supporting his weight on their shoulders.

"Can't find nobody out yonder in da dark, private!" shouted the sergeant. "Yu best tell us wheres yu at when yu gots cut." The private was now panting for breath. Blood was running down the sleeve of his blouse. The back of his shirt was wet from his wound. One of the soldiers pressed a cloth to the back of Mill's neck.

"Who done woke me up?" asked Sergeant King, as he came out of his tent. "What's going on here? Dis man's hurt; get da doc!"

"Mills dun snuck off and let some Reb cut him, Ed," barked the sergeant of the guard.

"Might knowed," responded the now awake Sergeant Ed King. "Where you been, boy? Speak up, you hear!"

"D...down by da station, boss. I's jus sleep'ng." insisted the soldier, again with a howling groan. "Dat man dun kilts me..."

Two other men who had joined the group grabbed for the private as he began to lose consciousness. They lifted him and hurried him to the duty tent.

Sergeant Robert Smalls stood by the opening of his tent as the group passed. He was one of many who were coming out of their tents to see what the commotion was about. Bob had heard the private's comments about the station as they passed. Three privates approached the sergeant.

"Yu boys get yo weapons and some mo of da men. We's go'in on a raid'in party. Go'in get us a rebel." ordered the sergeant to the other soldiers.

"Hots damn!" came a shout.

"Keeps it quiet, and make it a hurry," scolded the sergeant.

"Sergeant? Yu's 'wake?" came the almost whispering voice of a soldier as he stuck his head into Sergeant Prince Rivers' tent.

"I am now. What you waking me up fer?" answered the man.

"The mens all just 'bout up, sarg; lots talk and excitement, boss. They done brought Mills of Cump'ny 'C' in all cut up." answered the corporal. "Thought yu might better know."

Sergeant Rivers rose from his night roll and grabbed at his belt. He was quickly dressed and out of the tent. In all areas of the field where there was glimmering light from the many campfires, he could see movement; this wasn't good. The men were already stirred up enough, as it was, to have them aroused like this. He didn't like what he saw. He immediately headed for the duty tent.

"We gone go get 'em, sarg?" asked a private, as Prince passed a group of soldiers standing near one of the teamsters' wagons.

"What you men doing up? Ain't nobody sounded reveille!" the sergeant responded as he passed. He continued moving toward the large tent in the center of the camp. He could see that there was more light there than the colonel would have liked if he was there. An adjacent tent was illuminated from within, as well.

As he approached, he could see the large number of men milling around the outside of the tent. He stopped to look inside the first tent. He saw a soldier on a cot, lying on his stomach, emitting a low groan. The assistant surgeon was examining him. Blood covering the man's back.

He approached Lieutenant Wood inside the open tent.

"Sergeant Rivers, see if you can do anything about getting these men back to their tents!" ordered the lieutenant. "The other noncoms don't seem much interested in following orders right now."

"Yas, sir," responded Rivers. "Peterson! Franks! Get those men back to where they belong, now!" shouted the seasoned sergeant.

"But boss, some rebel done sneaked into camp and cut Mills. The boys wants to find him," came back a response.

"You hear me, if Mills got cut, it cause he was outside of camp," growled the sergeant. "Nobody done got pass da guard. Use 'em stripes on yo arm and gets dese boys back to bed, else I see da colonel takes 'em off dat arm. Those men have no business here; do as you told!"

Prince spotted Ed King coming out of the darkness. "Ed, help get dese boys away from here. Dey 'spose to be in their tents..."

"Private Williams report'in as ordered, sur!" shouted a private under arms, as he hurriedly entered the tent.

"What is it, guard? Who ordered you here?" asked the officer of the day.

"It was Sergeant Jones, sur. He say fo me to report that men have left camp, sur." answered the soldier.

"Who left camp, private?" asked Lieutenant Wood.

"Twas Sergeant Smalls, sah," replied the guard. "He say he was ordered to take a detail out on scout'in duty, but Sergeant Jones say he don't have no orders about no scout'in party. He told me to report it to headquarters."

"How many men did he take with him?" asked the officer.

"Dozen, at least, sah," came the answer.

"Damn!" exploded the lieutenant.

"Sah, lets me gets a detail and gets 'em back to camp?" asked Sergeant Rivers. "I can have 'em halfway back to camp by da time da colonel finds out.

"The colonel's being sent for now, Prince. Might better wait 'til he gets here," answered Wood.

"Pardon, lieutenant, I knows those boys dat gone, and dey out to hurt somebody or at least do no good. I thinks it best dat dey be brought back now," added the sergeant.

Lieutenant Wood hesitated, and then looked again at Rivers.

"All right. Take at least ten men you can handle and make sure everyone is armed," ordered Lieutenant Wood. "Mills said he was near the train station when he got attacked, so I would guess that's where Smalls has gone. You send a messenger back to me in thirty minutes to let me know what's going on," he added, emphatically. "Wait 'til I write you a pass for the guard."

Solomon was startled from his light sleep by the sound of distant voices coming from the rail tracks. He rose quickly and moved to the back window of his store. He could see nothing in the darkness. He shuffled to the rear door, unbolted and opened it, letting in the cool September night air. Now he could hear the voices more clearly but could still see no movement. They were clearly the sounds of soldiers, black soldiers, moving down the tracks. He could make out but a word or two as the men continued to pass. It was also clear that they were excited about something. He listened as the voices gradually dissipated into the darkness as they moved further away, heading in the direction of the depot. Solomon Kinard had decided to spend the night at his business, since the arrival of the new soldiers earlier in the afternoon. The edge of their camp was not far from his outbuildings behind his hardware store. He could see the distant lights of their camp in the openings between the several sheds. The sounds of the passing soldiers could no longer be heard and the only noises were barking dogs in the direction the soldiers had gone.

He closed and bolted the door, set his pistol on the table beside the rocker, and sat back down to a restless sleep. It wasn't long before he thought he heard muffled voices again in the distance. He listened, but heard no more. He drifted back into a light sleep.

The group of men led by Sergeant Smalls hurried along the tracks in the direction of the station. There was little resemblance to a military unit as they moved through the darkness. As they continued around the long curve in the tracks, the end of the Winnsboro train sitting silently on the rails was slowly revealed.

Inside the rear freight car, Jim and Josh were both wakened by the voices of the passing soldiers. They listened in silence to the excited mob moving toward the station.

"What you reckon that was about, Josh," asked Jim. "Was that just more men going to work on the cars?"

"Don't think so," he responded. "They sounded too excited just to be going to work. Sounded like they were all black, though. Jim, could you get me a drink of that water from the jar?"

"Sure," Jim said, as he found the jar of water beside their sack of food. He removed the lid and carried it to his traveling companion.

"Josh, you're hot with fever again," Jim whispered, as he touched his hand in the darkness handing him the jar. Jim waited until Josh had drunk and then poured some of the water on the cloth that lay beside him. He put the cool rag on his friend's forehead.

"I'm worried about you, boy," commented Jim.

"I'm sweating, and as long as I'm doing that, I know the fever will break as before. It'll just take a little time," he responded, lying on his back in the darkness.

Jim lay there silently worrying about Josh. All appeared quiet again except for an occasional sound of the work being done to the cars.

Jake Bowers had his back to the approaching soldiers as he directed the placing of another jack at the rear of the passenger car. He heard a shout and then angry voices. He rose and turned to see a black soldier grabbing the arm of one of his workers.

"What yo know 'bout one our soldiers getting hurt down here?" asked an angry voice.

"Get your hand off that man!" Jake shouted, before the black man could respond.

Sergeant Smalls looked at the large white man and saw the knife in the sheath strapped on his belt.

"What yo know about a soldier getting cut?" asked the sergeant, as he approached Jake.

"I don't know anything about no soldier getting hurt," he responded angrily at the threatening move by the black soldier.

"He got a knife, boss!" shouted one of the other soldiers.

"I's sees it," Smalls said, as he approached the man. Another soldier raised a musket and pointed it at Jake.

"You men have no business here," added Mr. Bowers, looking at the sergeant coming toward him.

"I think maybe yu knows something, all right, like maybe yu the one who done cut him," accused Smalls.

116

"Lets me shoots him, boss," shouted a private from the rear.

The group of soldiers began to gather closer to the foreman, as he stood defiantly facing the sergeant. The other workman began to back away in fear of what was taking place.

"He ain't cut nobody," an older black worker said, as he also backed away.

"Stay out'a this, nigger!" shouted one of the privates.

Two men suddenly lunged out at Jake from behind, grabbing both arms. He struggled to free himself.

"Get your hands off me!" shouted Mr. Bowers. Other guns were now pointed at the struggling man at close range.

"Yu better settle down, now, Reb, or else we shoot yu right now," threatened the sergeant.

Jake stood still, breathing excitedly, beginning to feel the fear that he should have already realized.

"We take him to da colonel, boys, I thinks we got our man," smiled the sergeant.

"Uh, uh," came another threatening comment from the private with a gun now to his shoulder. "Da cunnel ain't go'in do noth'in to him. I thinks I shoots him right now."

"Easy, boy," warned Smalls. "What 'bout it Reb? Yu wants us to shoot yu right here, or maybe yu's willing to confess 'fore we takes yu to da colonel?" added the soldier.

"I ain't done anything to confess to. I don't know who gave you the authority to come down here and threaten folks, but you've no business here. Either you let me go right now, or take me to your commanding officer!" shouted Jake with defiance.

"Shoots him, boss," shouted a voice.

"I's shoots him," shouted another private, cocking the hammer of his musket.

Sarah had heard the voices first, and when they looked through the side window of the station, they saw the group of soldiers standing with the railroad workers. Calvin was looking at what he had felt sure would happen. He had hoped there would be an officer with them, but all he could see were black soldiers.

"I'm scared," cried Jenny. Sarah put her arm around her sister's shoulder and looked at Calvin as he stared at the men crowded near

117

the train.

"What do they want?" Sarah asked

"Looking for the man who cut their soldier, I reckon," sighed Calvin, still observing their every movement.

"You've gotta run, Mr. Crozier," cried Jenny. "They're looking for you!"

Calvin remained motionless and silent as he stared through the glass. Jenny began to sob.

"No, Jenny. I won't run. I won't run for what I done," Calvin said. "That man had no business near you, whatever his intentions were. I regret having to hurt him, but he brought it on himself." He turned and looked at Jenny. "Whatever happens, I did what I had to do. You and Sarah didn't do anything to cause what happened. That soldier did. I did what I would do again, if need be" He glanced at Sarah. He could see the fear in her eyes.

"Look," exclaimed Jenny, pointing out the window. Calvin turned back to the window and saw the soldiers grabbing the railroad foreman. Guns were being raised and the other workers were backing away from the soldiers.

"I've got to go," exclaimed Calvin. He looked at Sarah. "You and Jenny stay right here. Whatever happens out there, you stay here! Jim and Josh will be looking for you if they arrest me, and it's important, Sarah, that they stay away from those soldiers!. You tell them that I need them to look after you. If they come near their camp, they might get shot. Do you understand?" Calvin asked.

Sarah nodded with tears beginning to run down her face.

"You can trust Jim and Josh, just as you've trusted me," he smiled. "They're fine brave men, and they won't let anything happen to you."

He smiled at Jenny as he saw the tears of fear also staining her cheeks. He gently wiped a stream of the tears from the left side of her face. "You make Jim stay with you and Sarah, young lady. Don't let them come near wherever they might take me. I don't want them hurt because of this thing. Will you promise me that?" he added.

Jenny nodded, now crying.

The girls watched in fear as Calvin turned and walked quickly through the front door. They both moved back to the window, staring as Calvin walked from the platform toward the area where the soldiers were now shouting.

The young man in Confederate gray walked toward the men from the depot.

"Who that?" came another voice in the crowd.

"It's a sure 'nough Reb soldier, still in sec'cess clothes!" shouted another.

The sergeant looked beyond the man they were holding to see the man standing about ten feet away.

"Yu da one who cut our man?" shouted the sergeant.

"I know he's not the man you're looking for," answered Calvin, calmly.

"Dens yu know who done it, I sup' pose?" added Smalls.

"Might, but you need to turn that man loose." added Calvin with authority.

"They both done it, boss! Don'ts yu lets 'em go!" shouted another soldier. Several of the soldiers were already pointing their weapons toward Calvin.

"Yu cut our man, boy?" the sergeant now asked in a more threatening tone.

"I told you, that man didn't do it and you're still holding him. Let him go!" demanded Calvin.

"Yu"s da guilty one, ain'ts yu?" Smalls now accused with a growl.

"I'm the one who fought with your soldier," Calvin finally admitted.

"Yu one dead Rebel, man!" a private shouted, now raising his musket and cocking the hammer.

"Hold on right there, soldier," ordered Sergeant Rivers, as he rapidly approached the group just ahead of him. "Yu lower dat gun, now!"

Sergeant Smalls turned quickly to see Prince and the other ten soldiers of his detail almost upon them.

"Bob, what's yu up to?" asked the 1st Sergeant.

"We's got our man, boss," stated Smalls.

"Yu don't know what yu got. Looks to me yu got two of 'em," Prince added.

"I's arresting both of them," Bob smiled.

"And yu don't look like yu arresting nobody, either," he snapped. "Looks to me yu about to shoots 'em."

"They done kilt Mills, sarg!" shouted a private, excitedly. "They needs shoot'n!"

"Shut up, boy!" snapped the sergeant. "We're going to find out who's guilty of what, but we's ain't go'in shoots nobody. Yu boys arrest dat man there, and we'll take 'em both backs to the colonel."

"That man ain't done anything," interrupted Calvin, pointing to Mr. Bowers. "He's here with the rail crew working on the train, and he ain't guilty of anything."

"What's 'bout you?" asked Prince, now moving toward Calvin aggressively. "You cut our soldier?"

"He attacked me, and we fought," confessed Calvin.

"Yu damn murdering Reb, I's shoot yu right now!" shouted a private rushing out from behind the sergeant, raising the muzzle of his gun toward Calvin.

Prince moved quickly and grabbed the barrel of the gun. The soldier jerked it hard away from the sergeant's grasp and raised it again at Calvin. This time the 1st Sergeant swung rapidly at the soldier, grabbing the gun from him, almost pulling the man to the ground. The soldier gained his balance and turned quickly toward the sergeant. Prince caught him cross the face with the back of his empty hand, drawing blood from the private's mouth.

"Arrests dat man!" shouted Sergeant Rivers, in a posture to strike again if need be. Two corporals moved quickly, seizing the private before he could respond to Prince's blow.

Satisfied that the man was restrained, Prince turned back toward Calvin.

"These boys ain't playing, Dey's ready to shoots somebody, namely yu!" exclaimed the sergeant. "Our man says he was just sleeping and yu done tried to kill him. Did yu cuts him or not?"

Calvin stared into the black man's dark eyes. "Your soldier was where he wasn't supposed to be, and he attacked me when I told him to get off the train," commented Calvin.

"He attack yu with a weapon? He says he was asleep. Is dat what yu done, found him asleep on da car and yu cuts him?" snapped the sergeant.

"He wasn't sleeping and he didn't have any weapon that I saw. I was just defending myself when I cut him," responded Calvin. "And that man there wasn't anywhere around when it happened."

"Yu best be careful 'bout what yu saying, boy. These boys looking for blood." the sergeant threatened. "Dey don't believe yu done cut Mills in no self–defense, and I don'ts either. I think yu one of them bushwhackers been after us for days, and we's go'in take yu to da colonel."

"That do no good, boss," injected Sergeant Smalls. "The cunnel ain't go'in do nothing. Still thinks we should shoot him right here."

"And yu best be quiet, man. Yu in bad 'nough trouble as is," snapped Prince, now glaring at the sergeant. "Lets that man go and yu take those boys of yos and report back to camp immediately. Lieutenant Wood wants to see yu something bad!" the 1st sergeant added with authority.

Sergeant Smalls looked at Prince with barely concealed anger. "All right, boys, yu heard da sergeant. Let's go," he said, turning away from Prince's threatening glare. The two men released the railroad foremen with a shove.

Jake looked at Calvin as he passed, trying to read his face.

"You look after the ladies in the station for me 'til my friends get there, and tell those boys to stay away," Calvin said to Mr. Bowers, as the soldiers roughly began to lead him away.

"Look here, boss!" shouted one of the men holding Calvin's arm. He reached down in front and removed the knife from Calvin's belt. "Dis boy's guilty as sin, boss. Maybe we can goes ahead and shoots him and save da cunnel da trouble!"

Mr. Bowers hastened off toward the station, looking back as the soldiers began to disappear into the darkness. He rushed into the depot.

"What are they doing with Mr. Crozier?" shouted Jenny, as Jake entered the station house. "Where're they taking him?"

"He's been arrested. They're taking him back to their camp, to their commanding officer," responded Jake, angrily. "They'll get it straight once they get him back to their officers. Do you know what happened between him and some soldier he was supposed to have cut?"

"Mr. Crozier got into a fight with him," answered Sarah, her voice quivering. "The soldier attacked him aboard the cars. Mr. Crozier had gone back to the rear of the train to check on his friend. He wasn't gone but a few minutes, and... and this black soldier came aboard the car. He was scaring us both when Mr. Crozier returned. The soldier attacked him and they were struggling on the floor when the man jumped up hollering and ran from the car. We thought Calvin... Mr. Crozier... was hurt bad, but he said he had cut the soldier pretty badly. That's when he brought us back to the station," Sarah was now crying.

"Is he a friend?" asked Jake, now with more compassion, choking back his anger.

"He's a soldier trying to get home. He told our grandmother he would escort us home," answered Sarah. "We've been traveling since Salisbury."

"What are they going to do?" cried Jenny. "It looked like they were going to shoot him!"

Jim and Josh listened intently as the men passed again, this time moving in the opposite direction. The two groups that had passed seemed to be together, now, but they couldn't see in the darkness enough to tell what they were about. They knew they were black men, and maybe even soldiers, but they couldn't tell for certain. They remained silent until they had passed.

"I think they be black soldiers, Josh!" Jim whispered excitingly. "I think I best go check on Cal," He began to get up.

"Not without me, boy! You just wait," Josh exclaimed, struggling to get up.

"You're too sick. Josh. You best wait here; I won't be long," said Jim.

"You're not listening! Help me up. I ain't that sick, Jim Walker!" insisted Josh.

Jim assisted his friend to his feet and then exited the boxcar to help him to the ground. Both men were anxious, as they headed through the darkness toward the boxcar where their three companions were. Josh was breathing heavily but kept up with Jim, as they moved rapidly toward their friend.

"Cal, it's us, Jim and Josh! Ya'll awake?" asked Jim. There was no response. They moved quickly to the door and looked into the darkness. "Cal, you in there?" repeated Jim. There was still no response.

"They must have gone back to the station, don't you guess?" asked Jim.

"Suppose so; come on!" responded Josh, more anxious than before.

They continued along the tracks heading toward the light where the men worked with the derailed cars. They could see the distant light coming through the window of the depot. It was now Jim who was struggling to keep up with Josh. As they approached the damaged cars, they saw the workers standing near the train, but they were standing idly. The foreman wasn't with them. Josh studied their faces in the dim light, trying to find a hint of what might be going on. He saw only staring faces watching the two young men in Confederate clothes pass by.

Josh hurried as fast as his weakened body would allow him. The light from the station house was getting closer, but there was no evidence that anyone was there. He hurried up the steps to the door, closely followed by Jim. He entered, quickly glancing around the room for Calvin. He stopped when he saw Sarah and Jenny sitting on the bench against the wall. The foreman was standing beside them.

He glanced once again about the room. "Where's Cal?" he shouted to the ladies.

"Easy, young man," answered Jake. "He's been arrested, but there's nothing you can do right now."

Josh stood poised in the doorway to reverse his direction. "Where's he at?"

"These two young ladies need your attention and protection. You boys best keep your heads about you and look after them first," added Jake, firmly.

Josh struggled to keep from going back out the door in the direction the soldiers had gone. Jim walked slowly toward Sarah and Jenny. Josh stared at the three people for another few moments, before he finally released the door and followed Jim.

Jenny jumped to her feet and ran to the big man, throwing her arms around him. "They're going to hurt him, Jim," she cried, "and I can't help him!"

"Don't worry, Miss Jenny. We'll take care of Cal," Jim tried to comfort her and put his arms around the young girl.

"He said you got to stay with us. He said that if anything happened, to tell you to stay away, or you might get hurt," she continued to cry, holding on to Jim tightly.

Josh was looking at Sarah. He could see the fear in her face. "What happened?" he asked, now a little calmer.

"A soldier came in the car while Calvin was with you, and Calvin had to fight him when he came back. He had to use his knife," Her eyes showed him she realized the consequences of what had happened. "The man was going to hurt us," her voice shook, as her lower lip quivered and tears slowly rolled down her cheeks. She struggled to remain still.

"Boys, I'm going to see what we can do for your friend. I need for both of you to stay here with the girls, you hear me?" Jake asked in a firm and determined voice. "That boy saved me some hurt out there, and I owe him, too. If you two show up anywhere close to those boys' camp with those clothes on, they'll shoot you, sure, no questioned asked. You understand?" added Jake, as he looked at both men.

Jake quickly headed for the front entrance of the station. Josh watched as Jake hurriedly shouted something to the men who stood idly by the train. Then he raced toward the rear of the station. All was soon quiet inside the large room except for the soft sobs of the girls and the ticking of the wall clock.

CH

# Chapter 11

Mr. Kinard was again wakened by the shouts of voices coming from the tracks. This time they were louder and the soldiers seemed more excited. Solomon rose quickly and opened the rear door, straining his eyes to see movement in the dark. Again he could see none. He listened as the movement continued into the field heading toward the soldiers' camp. The voices became distant murmurs, interrupted occasionally by another shout. Soon he could see the blinking of the campfires, as the movement of men throughout the camp momentarily blocked the light from Solomon's view.

Lieutenant Wood stood behind Surgeon Crandall who was bandaging the wound of Private Mills. The soldier continued to moan, occasionally hollering in distress. Several men continued to wander near the tents despite the repeated effort of the lieutenant to force them to return to their quarters.

"That's a nasty wound, soldier. I've bandaged it the best I can," said Surgeon Crandall. "You lay still and we'll see the outcome," He turned away from the private, moved past the lieutenant and stepped out into the open air. Wood followed him out.

"He might not make it; lost too much blood," began the doctor.

Suddenly a new clamor of activity came toward the two officers. Soldiers were again moving away from their tents toward the group of men that were now visible through the shadowy light. It looked like a growing mob as the men crowded close to the returning soldiers, shouts now ringing out above the noise.

"Sergeant, report immediately," shouted the lieutenant to Sergeant Rivers, as he approached the duty tent.

The sergeant moved away from the others and rapidly headed toward Wood and the doctor.

"Reporting as ordered, sur. Sergeant Smalls and his men are back in camp, lieutenant. I ordered da sergeant to report to yu," said Sergeant Rivers, delivering a salute. "We also brought in a prisoner, sur. Da rebel dat cut Mills."

Just then, Lieutenant Wood saw two corporals pass with one of their own soldiers in tow, moving toward the duty tent. The lieutenant looked at the sergeant. A young white man was brought

125

forward escorted by three guards. He was dressed in the remnants of a Confederate uniform, a slouch hat tight on his head and his hands bound.

"Take him to my tent," ordered the lieutenant, looking at the prisoner as they passed. "Find Sergeant Jones and have him report at once. Sergeant, you come with me. The rest of you men return to your tents. There's no more to see here. Do as you are told, or you'll be put on report."

Sergeant Rivers followed Wood back to the duty tent, behind the other men and prisoners.

"What's the private under arrest for, Prince?" asked the lieutenant.

"Disobedience, sah," answered the sergeant. "He tried his best to shoots dat man, even after I told him to lower his weapon. It might be best if da lieutenant keep him under arrest da rest of da night."

"Tell me about the other prisoner," commanded the officer.

"Whens we got to da station, Sergeant Smalls had another man under arrests, along with dat one there," answered Sergeant Rivers. "Dey's about to shoots 'em both, sah, and if I'd been much longer, I thinks dey would've, too. Dat man said da other man was innocent and knows nothing about Mills getting cut. He says he be da one dat cut Mills. Says Mills attacked him."

"Did he say why?" asked the lieutenant.

"No, sah, He just say he was defending himself," responded the sergeant.

"What do you, think, Prince?" Henry asked.

"I thinks he be one of dem mens that's been after us. I thinks he follows us to dis place and he caughts Private Mills alone and cuts him, dat what's I think. Looks here, lieutenant," the sergeant said, as he withdrew the knife from the rear of his belt. "He didn't have no gun, but he had dis here knife."

The lieutenant took the weapon from Prince. "He didn't have any other weapons on him?" Henry asked.

"No, sah," just dat there knife," he answered. "He mighty brave, tho', boss. He comes right out and say he da one dat cut our soldier and dat da other man knows noth'in' 'bouts it. I told him he best watch what he say, 'cause those boys looking for blood, but he say he not go'in let no innocent man get hurt fo what he done. Dat's why I

126

lets da other man go. I thinks he just working on da train, lieutenant."

"Lieutenant, what's going on here? I understand one of our men was hurt?" asked Colonel Trowbridge.

"Yes, sir, colonel," responded the lieutenant, turning in the direction of his commanding officer. "Private Mills was brought in about an hour ago, and this prisoner was bought in just a few minutes ago."

"Was Mills in camp?" asked the colonel.

"No, sir. It appears he may have been at the railroad station," answered Wood.

"How bad is he hurt? Is Crandall here?" again he inquired, now with anger in his tone.

"Doc Crandall has bandaged him, but he says he may have lost too much blood. He's in the tent over there, colonel," answered the officer.

Colonel Trowbridge looked toward the man now sitting on the ground, his hands bound behind him, being guarded by three soldiers. "Have you talked to him?" Trowbridge asked.

"No, sir, not yet. I've been busy trying to get the men settled, colonel. They're excited over this thing, and none of us are having much success getting the boys calmed down," the lieutenant said.

Colonel Trowbridge turned and walked over to Calvin. He stared down at him. Calvin remained still, trying not to provoke the situation.

"You a soldier?" he asked.

"I was, sir. Just trying to get home now," responded Calvin.

"And getting a few last licks in before you get there, huh?" suggested the colonel.

"No, sir. I'm not looking for trouble," responded Calvin, now looking up at the officer.

"But you already found it, boy! You injured one of my men, didn't you?"

"I weren't looking to hurt him, colonel. He attacked me, and I had to fight him,"

Colonel Trowbridge continued to stare down at Crozier. "What's your name?"

"Calvin Crozier. I'm on my way home to Texas."

"Mighty long time traveling, seems to me."

"I was a prisoner."

"And with the war over, you just had to get revenge on somebody, is that it?"

Calvin didn't answer but again looked away.

Colonel Trowbridge looked at the man sitting before him, feeling satisfied that they had finally captured one of the assassins that had been causing so must strife for his men.

He turned and walked out of the tent toward Will Crandall, who was still with Private Mills.

"Reporting as ordered, sur!" saluted Sergeant Jones.

"Sergeant, select four of your men not on perimeter guard right now and have them report to me for special guard duty," Lieutenant Wood ordered. "You make a round and make sure all your guards are at their posts, and then appoint two corporals to make the rounds the rest of the night. You remain close to the duty tent."

"Yas, sah," responded Sergeant Jones.

"The men are still excited and don't want to get back to bed. I'm concerned about guarding the prisoner," added the officer. "You be sure to choose some men you trust for guard duty here."

"Yas, sur. Is dat all, boss?" asked the sergeant.

"You're dismissed. Just don't take too long getting back here, Jones," added the lieutenant.

Wood turned and walked over to Calvin.

"You say your name is Crozier?" asked Henry.

"That's right," he answered, looking at the ground.

"You care to tell me what happened out there?"

Calvin sat still, not responding to the officer's question. He wasn't sure of the lieutenant, but he did seem to be the only calm man in the crowd.

"Your soldier came aboard the train, and I ordered him out," Calvin slowly answered.

"Why did you tell him to leave?" Lieutenant Wood asked, hoping to find out why Mills was at the station.

"He was insulting some ladies aboard the car," answered Calvin, now looking at him, trying to judge his intentions.

"And he attacked you?"

"I have already said that, but your men don't seem to want to hear it."

128

"But, it seems you were the one armed. Why'd you use the knife on him?" again asked the lieutenant.

"I couldn't fight him with my fists," Calvin responded. "I was in the hospital near Point Lookout until the army finally released me. Did I kill him?"

"No, he's still alive right now, but it doesn't look good," responded Wood.

"Sergeant Smalls!" called the lieutenant, as he saw the man entering the tent. He turned away from Crozier and met the sergeant as he entered.

"What yu go'in do wid dat killer?" asked Smalls, as he looked toward Calvin.

"Let's talk about what trouble you're in for disobeying orders and leaving camp," responded the lieutenant emphatically.

"Somebody's had to go gets him, and I's decided to helps," responded the sergeant.

"Bob, you've got a good record and I hate to see it spoiled now that the end is about here, but willfully disobeying the colonel's orders like you did may get you a courts–martial, you understand?"

Smalls stared back at the lieutenant then relaxed. "Yas, sah, I's understand, boss."

"The colonel knows you left camp and that I sent Sergeant Rivers out, too," added Wood, "but right now I'm not sure that's on his mind. This situation with that man over there is what he's concerned with. For your sake, I hope he won't say no more about your actions, and if he doesn't, then I won't either."

"Thanks yu, lieutenant," answered the sergeant.

"Sergeant Rivers may not be as patient as I am, though, He's pretty mad at you, and I can't say whether he's going to mention it to the colonel or not. Maybe you best talk to the sergeant and see if you can't settle it with him."

"What's the cunnel go'in do wid dat man, boss?" asked the sergeant.

"That's not your concern. The colonel will handle it. You best make yourself scarce for awhile. You can help by getting those men out there calmed down and away from this tent!"

"Is thats all, lieutenant?"

"For now -- remember this thing may not be settled yet."

129

Lieutenant Wood watched as the sergeant left. Several of the men were watching some ways from the tent. He saw the sergeant walk into their midst and begin talking, looking back toward the duty tent.

"Colonel, I need to transport Mills to a hospital. I understand that the 56th has a facility set up near their headquarters," stated the surgeon, as he entered Colonel Trowbridge's tent.

"I'm sending a messenger to Colonel Tyler of the 56th, Will. I want the colonel to see me on this matter. It's best to leave the wounded man here until the colonel arrives. One of the teamsters is taking a messenger now to the colonel's headquarters."

"Then, I'll need to go ahead and sew his wound," responded the doctor. "Colonel, it might be good if you order all those teamsters out of camp, sir," added Crandall. "When I walked past them just now, they were inciting the men, colonel, saying that there would be nothing done to the prisoner. They were talking about burning houses! When I arrived at the duty tent, Mills was screaming for revenge for the rebel 'that done kilt him'. Lieutenant Wood has had his hands full keeping the boys in line and away from the prisoner, already, colonel."

Colonel Trowbridge looked at Crandall, concern on his face.

"You just tend to your patient, doctor," the officer finally answered. "Colonel Tyler will be here soon."

The doctor quickly headed back to the duty tent as the colonel ordered. He saw Asa Child and Henry Hyde moving along the line of now empty tents heading toward the colonel's quarters.

The rear door of the station house opened, startling the girls who were cuddled on the bench together. Josh and Jim rose to their feet, not knowing what the disturbance was. Mrs. Gary entered the room, followed by the doctor and another man.

"Are you young ladies all right?" asked Mrs. Gary, as she approached the girls. She bent to tend to them when Sarah quickly embraced her. Sarah's maturity and motherly instincts for Jenny suddenly disappeared as she released her emotions on the older woman's shoulder. Mrs. Gary put her arms around the girl. Jenny clung to her sister.

Dr. Gary touched his wife's shoulder. "Are you ladies hurt? Did that man injure you in any way?" he asked.

"I'm Walt Houseal," the man said, as he looked at Jim and Josh. "I'm the sheriff of Newberry. You must be the friends of the boy the soldiers arrested."

· "Yes, sir," answered Josh. "We're all three trying to get home."

"Mrs. Gary is going to take the girls to her house not far from here," began the sheriff, "and I need for you to go with them. Jake told me he was concerned about what you might do on your own about your friend, but there's nothing you boys can do right now."

"You don't understand, sheriff. I owe Calvin my life, and I'll do whatever it takes..." Josh began.

"I think I do, son, but now's not the time," interrupted Walt. "Jake has gone to see his uncle, who's the county magistrate. He's going to get him to see the colonel of the colored troops or at least Colonel Tyler of the white regiment stationed here. Jake and Sam will do more than you can. There's a lot of excitement in that camp by the tracks, and all you boys can do is get yourself shot if you go near there."

Josh turned away from the man and walked to the window. He was hiding the tears that filled his eyes. Jim remained motionless, looking sadly at the two girls, as the doctor and his wife tried to comfort them.

"We've got a buggy outside." Dr. Gary said. "You can ride with us and your friends can ride with Sheriff Houseal. You boys get the ladies' baggage."

"But what if Mr. Crozier gets free and comes back here looking for us?" asked Jenny.

"Mr. Crozier will find you, I'm certain," reassured Mrs. Gary.

Josh turned back to see Jim picking up the girl's bags and the two quilts belonging to Mrs. Gary. He watched as Jim picked up Calvin's sack.

"Our stuff is still on the train," Jim said.

"It'll just have to wait 'til daylight, son," answered the sheriff. "It ain't going anywhere."

The boys reluctantly followed the others out the back of the station.

The knock on the door roused the colonel back to consciousness. He lay there in the dark room trying to clear his head.

"What is it?" asked Captain Loomus, as he sat up on his bed.

"A messenger to see Colonel Tyler," responded the corporal. "He's from the 33rd, captain."

"Just a minute, soldier," answered the colonel, also raising himself to a sitting position. Captain Loomus was up, lighting a lamp on the table. The colonel rubbed his eyes as the light began to penetrate to the back of his head.

Loomus soon had his trousers on and headed to the door. He opened it to be greeted by the guard and a black sergeant.

"Sergeant King, to see Colonel Tyler. I's got a message from Colonel Trowbridge, sah," said Ed King.

"I'll give it to him, sergeant," answered the captain, reaching for the paper.

"No, sah," responded the sergeant. "I's told to see da colonel and nobody else, sur. We's had a man muddered at da train station and da colonel wants Colonel Tyler to come to da camp."

Colonel Tyler was now on his bare feet behind Captain Loomus. He was wearing just his under drawers. "Give it to me, sergeant," he ordered.

The sergeant reluctantly handed the paper to the man standing in the dim light. He stared at the older man with the ruffled hair.

The colonel moved over to the table where he could read the message. He stood there silently while the captain and sergeant waited.

"A soldier of the 33rd has been stabbed, and they have the man who did it in their camp, captain," commented Colonel Tyler. "Colonel Trowbridge wants me to come to their camp. I don't understand what he needs me for," he added, looking at the sergeant.

"This man the colonel arrested, is he a soldier?" asked Tyler of Sergeant King.

"No, sa. He a rebel, colonel. He in Confederate clothes, sur."

"Captain, get dressed. You're going in my place. I'm running a fever and am not well enough to go riding about in the middle of the night," ordered Colonel Tyler.

The captain moved to the door and told the sergeant he would be along shortly. He also ordered the corporal to get his horse and another saddled and brought to the side entrance. The corporal was to escort the captain to the camp of the 33rd.

132

"Colonel, can we speak with you?" asked Lieutenant Child, as he entered Colonel Trowbridge's tent.

"Ah, Asa, I needed to see you. Is that Ernie with you?" asked the colonel, getting up from his campstool.

"Yes, sir, colonel. It's the men, sir..." began the lieutenant.

"Walk with me over to the duty tent," he ordered, as he walked past Child. The lieutenant hurried to catch up.

"Looks like we finally caught us a bushwhacker, gentlemen," stated the colonel.

"We know, colonel," responded Asa. "It's the boys. They're beyond following orders, Colonel Trowbridge. They're demanding that we do something to that man they brought in. It seems some of the boys heard him confess, and they want him executed, colonel," Child added.

"It's not that bad, lieutenant," answered the colonel, "The boys have always listened to our officers..."

"It is, colonel," interrupted Lieutenant Hyde. "I walked up to Sergeant Smalls talking to some of the men. He was talking about burning houses if the officers didn't punish that rebel soon. I rebuked him for his comments, but he was insubordinate, colonel. I even ordered his arrest, but the two corporals I ordered to arrest him refused to do it."

The colonel stopped and looked at both officers. "Are you men telling me you can no longer control your men?"

Child and Hyde looked at each other, but neither spoke.

"Well, gentlemen?" asked the colonel again, angrily.

"Colonel, I've never seen the men like this," answered Asa. "I couldn't even get Sergeant Rivers to assist, colonel."

Trowbridge looked at both men and then began walking again toward the duty tent.

As the three officers approached the tent, the colonel saw the surgeon in the adjacent tent still attending to Private Mills. He noticed the large number of soldiers milling around at a distance. There was a group near the remaining two wagons of the 56th New York. The private under arrest was no longer in the back of the wagon.

"Where's Lieutenant Wood?" the colonel asked, as he approached the duty tent.

The guard saluted. "He in da tent, cunnel, back near da prisoner," As the colonel walked toward his lieutenant, he saw four guards on the man, but the men were still trying to get at him.

"You men back away there!" shouted Trowbridge, to the several men confronting Lieutenant Wood. He watched as the men looked in his direction and then moved off briskly into the darkness.

"Wood, how long has it been like this?" asked the colonel, in a frustrated tone.

"Since about the time you left, Colonel Trowbridge," answered the lieutenant. "Mills has got the boys stirred up, hollering for revenge for him being stabbed. I tried to get the men back to their tents, but you see they won't listen, colonel. Surgeon Crandall can't seem to get the private to shut up either, colonel. And those teamsters ain't helping matters," he added, pointing in the direction of the wagons.

The colonel turned and walked to the medical tent. Sergeant Rivers was standing just outside the duty tent when the colonel emerged.

"Colonel, I's tried, sah, but da boys won't listen." the sergeant began. "Dey's upset about da prisoner, colonel. Somebody done told them ain't noth'in go'in be done to him, and da boys is mad, colonel. Dey's won't even listens to ols Prince, sur. Dey say dey go'in to burn da town, les somp'in done to dat boy. Dey's want'in him shot, colonel."

"Thanks, sergeant. Glad that you tried," responded the officer. He moved into the medical tent followed by Hyde and Child.

"Doc, is he going to live?" asked Trowbridge, seemingly unfeeling to what the doctor might say in the private's presence.

Crandall looked up and handed the instruments to the assistant surgeon and walked back toward the entrance of the tent.

"Colonel, he has lost too much blood. I don't think he'll make it 'til morning," diagnosed the doctor.

"Well, gentlemen, we need to make a decision," began the colonel. "If the boy's guilty and Mills dies, he's going to be shot."

"The boy said he stabbed him, didn't he?" asked the doctor.

"He confessed, but I still don't know the whole of what happened. He claims Mills attacked him," answered the colonel.

"I think I might say that, too, if I were that boy," added the doctor.

The men ain't going to be satisfied, now, 'til that man is shot. And I've already said that the wounded soldier won't last 'til morning."

"Colonel, maybe you better talk to him, again," suggested Lieutenant Hyde. "What was Mills doing at the station when he was supposed to be in camp?"

"Mills says he was just sleeping when this man cut him," added the doctor.

"You saying Mills only went to the station to find a place to sleep?" asked Asa, with a smile.

"I'll talk to him again. You men wait here," ordered Colonel Trowbridge.

As the colonel reentered the tent, he saw two men at the prisoner, taunting him. Lieutenant Wood was seated at a desk, looking exhausted. The prisoner was still seated, seeming to ignore the men around him.

"I'll ask you again, boy; did you cut my soldier?" asked the colonel.

Calvin looked up to see the colonel once more standing over him. "He attacked me and I had to fight him," came the reply.

"Where was he at when he attacked you?" came another quick question.

"He was aboard the train, colonel," Calvin answered.

"What was he doing aboard the train, sleeping?" asked the officer.

"He was scaring two ladies," he again answered.

"And you had to cut him, is that right?" asked Colonel Trowbridge, now accusingly.

""Your soldier is a big man, sir, and I couldn't fight him with my hands," Calvin answered.

"You know you killed that soldier?" stated the colonel.

"I didn't mean to hurt him that bad, colonel. It was a fight," Calvin again responded, this time with remorse in his tone.

Colonel Trowbridge stared at the man in silence for a long moment, then turned and went back outside the tent.

Calvin sat, his hands still bound behind him, now with none of the soldiers near him except for the guards. He stared at the ground once more. It seemed to him that his fate was sealed. He had held hope that the soldier would live, but that was now gone. He thought long and hard about the last several days. He regretted what was happening, but he would have no self–pity. If this thing cost him his life, so be it. He would do it all over again the same, wouldn't he? He thought of his mother. He thought of his sister, Mary.

Department of War Medical Records
Washington, D.C.

January 5, 1866
Lewis PO, Galveston, Texas

Dear Sir,

I am seeking the whereabouts of my brother, Calvin Crozier. I have been in touch with the War Department for several months and still do not have satisfactory answers. I was last told that your department might have records of his whereabouts. He was a prisoner at Camp Douglas until March 1865 and then moved to Point Lookout Maryland. I was told that you may have medical or hospital records that may help me find my brother. I cannot express to you how much he is missed and how anxious his family is. I was told that the prison records should have told me if he died as a prisoner of war. There has been no record found indicating that this is the case, and I am yet to accept that just because he has not returned home, that he is not alive. I need your help in finding my brother.

Sincerely,

Mary Crozier

# Chapter 12

"Let me pass. I'm here on Colonel Trowbridge's orders," demanded the captain to the guard, who had his weapon pointing in the direction of the mounted officer.

"Sah, the colonel say nobody can come into camp," responded the private.

"I have an order from your colonel, private," stated Captain Loomus, reaching into his pocket to produce the message from Colonel Trowbridge.

"I's can't read, captain," answered the guard,

"Then call the sergeant of the guard, boy," ordered the officer. "And be in a hurry about it!"

The guard turned and hollered the call across the field. Another guard picked it up and the word had soon reached Sergeant Jones.

"Lieutenant, a rider's trying to enter camp, sah," said the sergeant to Lieutenant Wood.

"That would be Colonel Tyler, sergeant," responded Colonel Trowbridge, now standing behind the sergeant. "Let him through, and make it quick," snapped the colonel.

"Yas, sur" answered the sergeant, as he ran back into the darkness. Shouts echoed across the field.

Captain Loomus was surprised to see all the men up and about as he rode into the camp of the 33rd US Colored Troops. Their excitement seemed excessive just having one of their men attacked. He walked his horse slowly toward the lighted tent just ahead. Corporal Green closely followed the captain.

He saw the colonel and three of his officers standing outside the tent, seemingly waiting on him. He reigned his horse to a halt and dismounted.

"I asked for Colonel Tyler's presence, captain. May I ask why he isn't here?" asked the colonel, his aggravation showing in his tone.

"Colonel Tyler sends his regrets that he is ill and can't leave his quarters, Colonel Trowbridge," responded the captain, offering his salute. "He sent me instead, colonel, to offer our assistance."

"Captain, I need decisions right now, ones that you can't make for the colonel," began Trowbridge.

"Then, I'll provide Colonel Tyler with the information he'll need to make the decisions you desire for himself," responded the captain with a smile.

"Captain, one of my men has been severely wounded; it appears that he'll die within the hour, according to my surgeon," began the colonel. "The guilty party has been brought into my camp and is now under arrest for the soldier's murder. As I told you and Colonel Tyler at the station, my men are in a high state of excitement, and this thing has got them to a fever pitch. We've already had men murdered while in the upstate of South Carolina, others shot, and all of us have been shot at. Shots were fired at us when we came into camp yesterday."

"Colonel Tyler had a report of that, sir," added Captain Loomus.

"We've finally caught one of the assassins, and the men are demanding his execution," continued the officer. "They're threatening to burn the town of Newberry, captain. Do you see why I wanted the colonel here?"

His words caught the adjutant off guard. He wasn't sure what to make of the colonel's men demanding this prisoner be shot.

"What are you going to do, colonel? We can't let your men start burning the town," asked the perplexed captain.

"I've had a meeting with my officers and we're all in agreement that the prisoner should be executed," stated the officer. "I want to know what Colonel Tyler's orders are on this matter, Captain."

"Colonel Trowbridge, you're not under our command, sir," argued the captain.

"I feel that I am, while we're here in Colonel Tyler's post, and I desire to know his orders, sir," the colonel again stated firmly.

"I can talk to Colonel Tyler about what you've said, but I tell you, his response will only be an opinion, Colonel Trowbridge," responded the captain, just as firmly.

"Then talk to the colonel, Captain Loomus. I desire an answer urgently," demanded the colonel.

"It'll take less then half an hour, sir," affirmed the captain. He saluted the colonel and mounted his horse. "Would you inform your sentinels to give me pass, sir, when I return?"

"There'll be no problem, captain," responded Colonel Trowbridge.

"I'm going back to my tent, gentlemen," said the colonel. "Send for me when the captain is back."

138

Samuel Bowers was one of the magistrates for Newberry District, and at this time of morning, Jake couldn't think of anyone else that might be able to help him more than his uncle. He hurried his buggy toward the Bowers home. He had no idea how long he had before they might harm that Crozier boy.

It had been only during the war that he had seen men do things as brave as that boy did, coming out to surrender himself to save a man he didn't know. That other sergeant might have prevented those boys from shooting him, if he had gotten there in time, but even then, he felt he would be dead now if Crozier hadn't spoken up when he did. He pulled the buggy to a stop in front of his uncle's house.

"Who's that at this time of night?" asked Samuel to his wife, who was also now awake from the noise at their front door.

"Sam!" came the shout from the front porch. "It's Jake! Wake up!"

Samuel slipped his trousers on and rapidly headed downstairs to the front door. Jake continued to knock and shout. Sam wondered what disaster had struck to cause Jake to be at his front door in the middle of the night.

"Jake, what's wrong, son?" asked the older man, excited with fear of what might have happened.

"I need your help, Sam. It's a matter of life or death!" Jake said.

"Well, I hope so, waking me up in the wee hours of the morning. Who's dying?" he asked.

"The soldiers have arrested a man and may be fixing to shoot him. I need your help, Sam," explained Jake.

"Hold on, boy, right there. If it concerns Federal soldiers, there ain't nothing I can do for you," responded the older Mr. Bowers. "I'm just a county judge, and I ain't got no influence with any Federal people."

"Just get dressed, Uncle Sam. I just need you to go with me to talk to some people about a boy they arrested tonight," responded Jake, with urgency. "I'll explain on the way. You need me to help you get dressed?" he asked, trying to hurry his uncle.

"No thanks, boy. I'm capable of still dressing myself," responded Sam, heading back up the stairs.

Jake paced the floor for what seemed like hours waiting for his uncle to return. He was anxious for Crozier's life; he knew the boy's friends were also worried, and he had taken it on himself to help. He owed it to help.

Sam Bowers came down the stairs, cane in hand, now fully dressed, looking the part of a dignified judge, be it just county magistrate. Jake helped his uncle down the steps from the porch and into his buggy. The two were soon off.

"You want to tell me what this is about and where we're going at 4 o'clock in the morning?" demanded Sam.

"A boy got in a fight with a soldier at the station tonight and they have arrested him, uncle," began Jake.

"I told you, ain't nothing I can to for nobody that takes on a soldier around here now and tries to get away with it," snapped Sam.

"Just listen a minute, Sam," Jake scolded. "This boy is just passing through, and he was protecting two young girls on the train from a black soldier. The soldier attacked him, and the boy cut him in self–defense. They sent a squad down to the depot to arrest him, and they grabbed me by mistake. Sam I swear, they were 'bout to shoot me when this Crozier boy came out of the station and gave himself up. If he hadn't done it, I think I'd be dead right now, Sam. I need you to go with me to their camp and see if we can see the colonel. I got to do something 'fore they shoot him, if they haven't already."

"All right, Jake. We'll do what we can," Sam offered. His tone didn't offer much hope.

Jake moved the buggy at a steady but dangerous pace in the darkness of the early morning.

Captain Loomus knocked quickly on the door and then entered the room where the lamp was still burning. Colonel Tyler was lying on his bed but only dozing.

"Henry, what's going on with those boys of the 33rd?" asked the colonel, removing his arm from his face.

"They've had an enlisted man severely injured in an attack by a man they now have in custody, Colonel Tyler. Colonel Trowbridge told me they wish to execute the man," said Captain Loomus.

"They want to execute him now, captain, in the middle of the night?" asked the officer, sitting up.

"I was told that their men are demanding that they execute him soon, or they'll set fire to the town, colonel," responded the captain.

"What's going on down there, Henry?" asked the colonel angrily. "Doesn't Trowbridge have command of his troops?"

"I was told that they're in a 'high state of excitement' and are demanding that the officers punish the prisoner," he responded.

Colonel Tyler lowered his head, shaking it in disapproval. He sat silently on the side of the bed.

"Colonel Trowbridge wants you to issue orders for him to execute the prisoner," the captain began. "I..."

"Issue orders!" shouted the colonel, now glaring at the adjutant. "He's not under my command. Can't the man make a decision for himself?"

"Colonel, I told Colonel Trowbridge that he wasn't under our command, but I think that he wants someone else to take responsibility," said the captain.

"Sounds exactly right, Henry. Is the prisoner guilty?"

"The colonel seems to think, so, sir."

"Did the injured soldier die?"

"He was still alive when I was there. I saw a surgeon sewing up the wounded man while I was talking with Colonel Trowbridge. The colonel said the surgeon didn't expect the soldier to live."

"Did he consult his other officers about the boy's guilt and what they should do with him?"

"There were other officers present while we were talking, colonel, and I was under the impression that they all agreed."

Colonel Tyler sat in silence on the bed, staring at the floor. Captain Loomus could add no more. There was a long pause before the colonel decided what he must do.

"Captain, go back to the camp of the 33rd and tell Colonel Trowbridge that he cannot let his soldiers loose on this town," he ordered. "Tell him I will personally see that he receives a court–martial if the town is harmed or any fires are set. Instruct him that if the only way he can control his troops is by carrying out the execution of their prisoner, then that's what he should do."

"Yes, sir, colonel. Is that all, sir?"

"Henry, you make sure that the colonel understands that they are not under my command, and I'm issuing no orders," the colonel added. "You make sure that his officers concur in the guilt of this man and that they are in agreement that the punishment is correct. If you see anything that suggests anything different, you have my authority to intervene on my behalf and do what you can to delay it 'til you can report back to me. Do you understand?"

"Yes, sir."

"Take an escort with you, Henry, and be careful," he added, as he lay back on the bed.

"Colonel Trowbridge?" called Lieutenant Wood, as he stood at the entrance of the colonel's tent.

"Come in, Henry. Why aren't you with the prisoner?" asked the colonel.

"Lieutenant Hyde is with him. That's why I'm here, colonel. Am I to keep him at the duty tent, sir?" he asked. "I'm having a difficult time keeping the men away from him."

"I've been in contact with Colonel Tyler of the 56th and I'm waiting further orders that will allow me to execute the man, lieutenant," he answered. "Asa, Ernie and Doc are all in agreement that he should be shot."

Henry Wood remained silent for a moment. "But Mills is still alive, colonel, and…"

"I'm afraid Private Mills won't see the break of day, lieutenant," interjected Trowbridge. "Doc Crandall has asked to send him to a hospital, and I've ordered the surgeon to make arrangements for transportation. I expect an answer from Tyler very soon about that prisoner, and when I get that word, he will be executed, and we'll be moving the regiment on to Charleston. Any other questions, Henry?"

"No, sir, colonel," answered the lieutenant. He turned and left the tent. He wasn't sure the colonel was right in his decision, but it wasn't his place to judge. He said the other officers agreed in the course of action, and that settled it. He suddenly felt bad for that Reb.

Lieutenant Wood was soon back at the duty tent.

"Those boys sure want blood, Henry," commented Ernie, as he walked over to where Henry had stopped. I've never seen them like this, even going into a fight."

"I know, Ernie. It's been this way since Mills was brought in," agreed Wood. "Before my guards were posted on the prisoner, I thought I was going to have to shoot some of our own boys to keep them away from him,"

"I'm glad you got the duty instead of me," the lieutenant added, with a slight smile. "I've got my hands full with my own company. Speaking of which, I'll see you later."

"Thanks, Ernie," Wood added, as he watched Ernie Hyde disappear into the darkness beyond the lights of the tent.

"Lieutenant?" came a voice from the rear of the tent.

Lieutenant Wood turned in the direction of Crozier. He was calling to him.

"What you want, Reb?" asked the lieutenant.

"It looks like things might be getting pretty bad for me, or am I mistaken?" he asked, looking up at the young officer in front of him.

"Can't truly say, boy," came the reply.

"I think you can," added Calvin, with a knowing expression.

"What you want me to say? That the colonel's going to turn you loose?" Henry asked.

"I need for you do something for me, sir. I want you to write to my folks for me," Calvin said.

This caught Henry off guard. "Write them about what?" he asked.

"Write my ma and pa and tell them that I'm being hung for stabbing a US soldier," Calvin asked.

"If I did that, how would I get it to them?" asked the lieutenant.

"There's a traveling companion on the train named Josh," Calvin said. "He's a soldier like me traveling home to Alabama. He can get the letter to Texas for me. I got a purse in my pocket that I wish for him to have, if you'll help me."

"Where are you traveling from, Reb?" Henry asked.

"I told you I've been sick. I was also in Camp Douglas for a while. We were sent to Maryland and we're trying to get home like the rest of General Lee's army," he responded.

Lieutenant Wood looked down at the young prisoner sitting in front of him. He stared at him for a long moment.

"I might do that for you, Johnny," answered the Federal officer. "Where's that purse?"

"In my right pocket. My sister gave it to me."

The lieutenant stooped beside the man and reached into the worn trouser pocket and removed a small leather purse. He opened it to see but two dollars Confederate, one green back, and a few coins. He smiled at the man as he started over to the small desk.

"The name is Calvin, lieutenant. Calvin Crozier," Calvin added. "And would you do one other thing, sir? Would you write my folks that I died doing my duty?"

The lieutenant looked at Calvin and frowned. One of the guards shifted his weight in agitation at what he thought he heard. Henry stared into the face of the young man bound on the ground before him. The eye contact was but brief. Henry's expression relaxed.

"I'll write your letter, Johnny," Henry said, walking away from the prisoner.

This time, as Captain Loomus reined his horse at the entrance to the camp just off Caldwell Street, the guard quickly stepped aside, offered a rifle salute, and allowed the officer and Corporal Green to pass. The captain trotted his horse again toward the lights of the large tent in the center of the camp.

As he halted and dismounted, a lieutenant came out of the tent to meet him.

"I'm the duty officer, sir. Colonel Trowbridge will be here shortly," said Lieutenant Wood, offering a hand salute. "A man has gone to get him. You can wait in the tent, sir,"

Captain Loomus walked past the officer into the tent. He immediately spotted the prisoner in Confederate gray sitting at the rear of the tent and guarded by four soldiers under arms. He walked back toward the entrance and looked to where the wounded man had been.

"The wounded soldier's been moved, lieutenant? Not bad news, I hope," asked the captain.

"The surgeon sent him to the hospital, sir," answered Wood. "You should have passed them on the street."

"I saw a wagon, one of our teamsters, I assumed, and another man in the seat." responded Loomus.

"That was Doc Stuart, our assistant surgeon," he added.

Two men approached from the captain's right, beyond the medical tent. Colonel Trowbridge was approaching with another officer.

"Captain Loomus, I hope you brought an answer from Colonel Tyler this time," stated Trowbridge. "This thing has drug out too long."

144

"May I speak to you in private, colonel?" asked the captain, looking toward Wood and Surgeon Crandall.

Colonel Trowbridge acted somewhat impatient but moved away from the tent.

"Colonel Tyler says that you must keep your men from burning any buildings in Newberry, sir," began the captain. "He said for me to tell you that if any damage is done to his post by your troops, he will personally prefer charges against you."

"What am I to do with the prisoner?" asked the colonel, angrily.

"The colonel says that if the only way you can control your troops is by executing your prisoner and if your officers are all in agreement with the sentence, then it's his opinion that should be your course of action," answered the captain.

"I asked for orders, captain, and all you bring me are opinions?" asked the colonel, still agitated.

"Colonel, I told you before, and Colonel Tyler wanted me to make it clear to you, that you're not under his command. It's your decision as to what to do with your prisoner and it's going to be your responsibility," added the captain.

Colonel Trowbridge turned away from the captain, staring into the darkness. He stood silent for a few moments.

"And what do you think I should do, Captain Loomus?" he asked.

"It's not for me to say, colonel. But if you're asking, I'll give my opinion, and understand it is just an opinion," answered the captain. "If in fact the boy's guilty of attacking your man and it's certain your soldier has received a fatal wound, then I'd have the man executed. If it's the only way you can keep your men under control, colonel, then execute him as soon as possible. Is he guilty of what you accuse him of?" asked Captain Loomus, directly.

Another pause by Trowbridge. "Oh, he's guilty, Captain Loomus. He followed us here from Anderson, waited for the right moment and mortally wounded Private Mills," he stated firmly. "He deserves to die for his deed."

"Then your dilemma is solved, Colonel Trowbridge," added the captain. "It appears my duty here is done, sir, and by your leave, I will report back to headquarters."

"Very, well, captain," responded the Colonel in a sedated tone.

Captain Loomus walked back to where the corporal was holding the horses. He mounted and the two men rode from the camp of the 33rd US Colored Troops.

Colonel Trowbridge walked back to the duty tent. Surgeon William Crandall and Lieutenant Henry Wood were standing by the entrance. The colonel looked at both men, but said nothing. He looked past the two officers at the man sitting on the ground. He stared briefly, then turned and walked back toward his quarters. A foreboding gray was becoming visible on the eastern horizon.

*July 18, 1866*

*Dear Diary,*

*It has now been so long since the war has ended and I still do not have the answers to what has happen to my dear brother Calvin. I have given up all hope now that he is alive. Ma has been strong and says I should not worry about Calvin, as she is certain God was with him and took care of him what ever his fate was. I do not understand why he has to be taken from us like this. God could have waited. I still miss him so much and I had hoped for maybe too long that he would walk in at anytime. I just wish now that someone could tell me what happened to him. I pray that someone was with him that knew him and cared about him and that he did not die alone. It seems that the best were taken by that cruel war. I pray my family never sees tragedy again nor do any of us live to see war again...*

*Mary*

# Chapter 13

Jake pulled the buggy to a halt at the corner of Platt and Caldwell Streets. Sheriff Houseal was calmly seated on the spring seat of his wagon, watching as the buggy came to a halt.

"Good morning, judge," Walt Houseal greeted, looking in the buggy at Sam Bowers. "Jake, you think you going to have any luck?" asked the sheriff.

"I don't know, Walt, but we're going to try," came the reply.

"Walter, I told Jacob, here, that I didn't think I could do much to help, but he's determined," commented the magistrate. "Neither of us looks forward to going into that field with those black soldiers in the middle of the night. Jake says those boys at the railroad station seemed determined to shoot somebody."

"You men want me to ride with you?" asked Walt. "I got the ladies settled in at the Gary's. I thought I might have to lock those other two boys up, especially the older one, but the two girls talked to them. That Crozier fellow seemed to be looking after them, too, as he made sure the ladies would tell them to stay away if he got arrested. That was the only thing that stopped them from getting into a mess they couldn't handle. They've bedded down in a shed in Doc Gary's backyard."

"Park your rig and you can ride with us," Sam answered.

Before he could respond, two horsemen trotted out of the semi–darkness and pass the three men. They were Federal soldiers, and they paid little attention to the three men as they passed. Jake, Sam and Walt stared as the two again disappeared into the night, leaving only the sounds of the horses' hooves behind.

Walt slipped into the rear seat of the buggy, as Jake snapped the reins. The horse trotted down Caldwell toward the distant lights flickering in the field beyond the railroad tracks.

"Halt! Yu can't come here," shouted the black guard, blocking the path into the camp.

"We've got to see your commanding officer," said Jake.

"Who yu?" asked the private, musket in hand.

"We're Judge Bowers and Sheriff Houseal of Newberry District. It's urgent that we see your commander," Jake again answered.

"Yu gotta wait here," said the guard. "Sergeant of da guard!"

shouted the soldier. "Strangers at post sev'n!"

Lieutenant Wood was on the way toward the colonel's tent when he heard the shouts coming across the camp. He turned to see Sergeant Jones leaving the rear of the duty tent, starting off in the direction of the shouts.

"Sergeant Jones!" shouted Wood. "I need you here."

Jones turned in the direction of the shout to see the lieutenant walking rapidly toward him. "Somebody trying to enter camp at post sev'n, boss," said the sergeant.

"Wait there, sergeant. No one is to enter camp," responded the officer.

"Dem local citizens, boss," Jones said as the lieutenant approached.

"You send a corporal and tell whoever is there they will have to wait until I see the colonel," ordered Wood. "And you remain at the tent, sergeant. I think the regiment will be breaking camp soon."

"Yas, sah, boss," answered Jones.

The lieutenant watched as the sergeant walked off in a new direction. He turned and retraced his steps toward Colonel Trowbridge's quarters.

When he arrived, Lieutenants Child and Hyde were already there, along with Surgeon Crandall.

"Took long enough for you to get here, Henry," commented the colonel, as the young officer entered the tent.

"There're local citizens trying to enter the camp, colonel. I've ordered the guard to hold them there until I saw you," explained the lieutenant.

"No one's to enter camp. As soon as you leave here, send word to the guard to send whoever it is away," said the colonel, agitated.

"Yes, sir," answered Wood.

"I want the regiment fed and in marching formation within the hour, gentlemen," began the commander. "Under Colonel Tyler's direction, I'm ordering the prisoner, Crozier, to be executed. Henry, detail a squad of men for the duty and make whatever other preparations necessary to get him shot and buried. I want everything prepared and ready by the time it's light enough to carry out the execution. Asa, you and Ernie make sure the men are formed and ready to leave just as soon as the execution is completed, even if they aren't able to finish their breakfast.

"Lieutenant Hyde, get Chamberlain to handle the tents and baggage. I want all supplies loaded back on the wagons and ready to move back to the station when the regiment is moved out," Trowbridge continued with his instructions. "We'll move the men further away from town, to where Captain Fowler and Captain Metcalf are camped. From there I want the men moved still further away from Newberry to a suitable location on the tracks where we'll wait for the train.

"Doc, I need for you to stay with Lieutenant Wood. I want you to confirm that the prisoner is dead," added the colonel, now looking at the surgeon. "After the execution, you accompany Wood to the station with the baggage and remain with the train.

"Lieutenant, take an adequate guard with you back to the station. Once the supplies are loaded, I want the train moving.

"Gentleman, I want that man dead and buried and the men out of Newberry before the sun comes up. Do you all understand?" asked Trowbridge.

The junior officers acknowledged the orders and quickly left the tent.

Lieutenant Wood found Sergeant Jones where he had told him to be. "Sergeant, send a corporal to the guard at post seven and order the visitors away. The colonel wants no one in camp. Also, select six men for a firing squad. The prisoner is to be executed at daylight. Assign a corporal to detail some of the pioneers to dig a grave. The execution will take place in the campgrounds, on the north end of the field near the tracks."

"Yas, sah, boss," answered the sergeant with a smile. "We's go'in shoots us a Reb."

"That's enough comments like that, sergeant!" scolded Wood. "We got a job to do, and the colonel ain't giving us much time to get it done, and you're not going to add to the excitement of the men by talk like that."

Yas, sah, lieutenant," he responded.

"You keep us waiting here twenty minutes, and now you tell us to leave!" shouted Jake, agitated at the black corporal standing in front of him. "I want to see your colonel!"

"Da cunnel say no body can come in camp. He says fo yu to leave," responded the soldier.

"Step aside, boy," demanded Jake.

"No, sa," responded the corporal, raising his weapon and pointing it at Jake. The other guard did the same.

"Better do as they say, Jake," commented the sheriff. "These boys mean business."

Jake stared at the two soldiers. He began to realize it was senseless to argue with them. He also knew they might be running out of time. It sounded like the entire camp was moving about, now dimly seen in the shadows of the breaking dawn. More fires were beginning to appear across the field.

Jake turned away and entered the buggy once again. He turned the horse back toward town and quickly moved away.

"What now, Jake?" asked Sam.

"We're going over to the college. I'm going to wake the colonel of the 56th up and see if he can't get that colonel of those black soldiers to listen to us," answered Jake with even more determination.

The sudden noise woke Mr. Kinard. He sat there in the rocker, listening, but heard nothing. Then he heard the noise of movement near one of his sheds. He picked up the pistol from the table and moved to the window. He could see two men moving in the dim morning light. He unbolted and opened the rear door. He could see other men moving under the open roof of the other shed.

"What you men doing there?" shouted Solomon. There was no response. "You better answer up, else somebody going to get shot!"

"Us's US soldiers," came an answer from somewhere near the outbuilding on his left. He pointed the gun in the direction of the response. A man emerged out of the semi-darkness, as he approached the backdoor.

"What you doing here?" asked Solomon. "This ain't no place you belong!"

"We's need borrow some tools, mis'a," answered the corporal.

"Not from me, you don't!" Mr. Kinard shouted.

"We's can borrow 'em ors we' can takes 'em, mis'a. Da cunnel done sent us to find tools to dig a grave," added the soldier.

Mr. Kinard stood silent for a moment. "Why should I believe you just want to borrow some tools?" he asked.

"We carrying 'nough baggage as is, boss. We's just wants to dig a hole, den yu's have 'em back," answered the corporal.

"I got a shovel and a pick in that building on the right, but its locked," replied Mr. Kinard. "You men come out where I can see all of you."

He watched as four other men moved out of the shadows into the gray light. Solomon's eyes had now adjusted and he could see the mix of their uniforms. The clothes weren't regulation.

"You don't look like soldiers to me. I think you just trying to steal something," snapped the merchant, now stepping back toward the door behind him.

"Na, sah, we's all soldiers. These boys here are just labors, mis'a," answered the corporal. "We's ain't steal'in noth'in. Just needs to borrow da shovel."

Solomon looked at the corporal for a long moment. He lowered the weapon and walked into the yard toward the shed.

The buggy turned from Adams Street into the lane leading up to the large, three story building of Newberry College. A soldier stood near the front entrance. It had been a long day for Jake Bowers, as the sky had now lightened, and the mist drifted above the many tents scattered in the field near the college building. The buggy came to a halt in front of the building, and Jake quickly emerged. He was followed by his uncle and Sheriff Houseal. The guard moved to block their way.

"We need to see the colonel; it's urgent," said Jake.

"You wait here, and I'll see about it," responded the soldier. The three men waited as the guard disappeared into the front entrance.

"Colonel Tyler?" came the voice through the door, followed by rapid knocks in secession.

"What is it, sergeant?" asked Captain Loomus. He had just dozed into a light sleep.

"Local citizens to see the colonel, sir. They say it's urgent," answered the sergeant.

"Captain, find out who it is and see if you can handle it," said Colonel Tyler, still lying on his bed.

The captain got up and once again reached for his trousers. "All

151

right, sergeant. I'll be there in a moment. Find out who it is," answered the officer.

The captain slipped on his boots and pulled his shirt over his arms as he rose from the bed. He was still buttoning the shirt as he walked down the hall toward the front entrance. The sergeant was coming back in the front door.

"It a Sheriff Houseal and a Judge Bowers, sir, and one other man. They want to talk to the colonel," said the sergeant.

The captain went out the front door to the porch.

"I'm Jake Bowers and I need to see the colonel," demanded the tall man in front.

"What's this about, that it demands the colonel's attention at such an early hour?" asked the captain.

"There's a man been arrested at the depot and the colonel of the colored soldiers won't let us see him, nor speak to the colonel about him," Jake said angrily.

"Sir, we believe the man acted in self–defense and we're afraid that he may be harmed before he can show his innocence," added Sam.

"And who are you, sir?" asked Captain Loomus.

"I'm Samuel Bowers, magistrate of Newberry District. But that's of little matter right now, young man. We need to see Colonel Tyler," he answered.

"Very well, gentlemen. Come in. I'll have to see if he's up," invited the captain.

Jake and the other two men followed the officer into the hall. They followed him to where an enlisted man stood outside a door on the right.

"Wake him up," demanded Jake. "We need to see him!"

Captain Loomus looked at Jake, somewhat irritated by his demanding tone. He entered the room and closed the door behind him, leaving the three men to wait again.

"Colonel, they're three men here, one is Sheriff Houseal and one a magistrate," said the captain, "asking about the man Colonel Trowbridge is about to execute. They say they need to see Colonel Trowbridge about the boy's innocence, but he refuses to see them."

"Damn, what now?" responded Colonel Tyler, as he sat up. "Give me a minute, Henry. I'll see them."

Captain Loomus went back into the hallway, where Jake and the others anxiously waited.

"Colonel Tyler will see you shortly. He's dressing. You can wait in that room, gentlemen," Loomus said, pointing to the room across the hall.

It was a long few minutes for Jake that they had to wait.

"Sheriff Houseal, what brings you out so early?" greeted the colonel, as he entered the room.

"Nothing pleasant, Colonel Tyler," responded the sheriff. "Jake here is convinced that the colonel of the colored troops is going to have a man he arrested tonight punished before he can prove his innocence."

"Jake, is it?" asked the colonel, now looking at Jake. "Tell me why this man that's been arrested is innocent. I understand he attacked one of the men of the 33rd at the station,"

"Self–defense, colonel," Jake quickly answered. "That man you arrested was protecting two ladies from insults from your soldier, when he attacked Mr. Crozier."

"How might you know this, sir?" asked Tyler.

"I was at the station. Those men were about to shoot me by mistake when Crozier surrendered" answered Jake. "I didn't see the fight, colonel, but I did see and talk to the girls that black soldier scared and who were there when the attack happened."

"Why did he have to kill the soldier?" asked the officer. "I understand the soldier wasn't armed."

Jake looked at his uncle and then back at the colonel. "Didn't know the soldier was dead, colonel," responded Jake. "But I do know it was a fight. One of the ladies said the boy commented that he didn't mean to hurt the soldier as bad as he was afraid he had."

"You got any idea why that soldier was aboard the cars where the ladies were, Colonel Tyler?" asked the older Bowers. The question put the colonel in sudden discomfort. He didn't answer the judge's question.

"I understand the man was an assassin and had followed the train from Anderson," said the colonel.

"There were two other traveling companions with the Crozier boy, colonel, and the three of them were on the train with the ladies who were attacked and that train just arrived in the night from

Winnsboro," argued the sheriff, looking at the colonel for a response.

Colonel Tyler looked at Sheriff Houseal, but said nothing. The three men waited.

Colonel Tyler walked to a desk across the room. He removed a paper and a pen.

"Sheriff Houseal, I understand that Colonel Trowbridge of the 33rd has already determined the prisoner to be guilty of trying to kill a US soldier and that he may have already ordered his execution," said the colonel, his head lowered, as he was now writing. "I'm sending an order with you that should get you in to see Colonel Trowbridge. I suggest, gentlemen, that if you believe this man to be innocent, you should hurry, as it may already be too late."

He handed the paper to Jake as he was heading for the door, and the other two men hurried to keep up with the younger man. In a few steps the three men were exiting through the front entrance of the building.

The roll of drums broke the early morning quiet. The men of the 33rd Regiment of US Colored Troops were rapidly moving into ranks, filling the width of Caldwell Street for nearly ninety yards. An air of excitement unnatural to the calm morning mist had settled over the landscape. The many campfires that had burned most of the night had formed a layer of smoke above the mist. Three Federal officers stood on the edge of the field waiting for the final act of the night's events to be played out. Near the north end of the field, a young lieutenant was giving final instruction to a sergeant, as a squad of soldiers under arms stood impatiently near by. A lone young man dressed in the remnants of a Confederate uniform stood in their midst, hands bound behind him.

Across the field was a civilian, standing next to an outbuilding behind his business on Drayton Street. Solomon Kinard had been standing there for some time. He had watched several men dig what he'd been told was to be a grave. Those men now stood a short distance from the hole, still holding the implements they had borrowed from him. He was curious about what was going to happen. He had watched a detail of soldiers move toward that end of the campground with a prisoner, a young man that Mr. Kinard did not recognize.

He continued to watch as a sergeant led the squad with their prisoner toward the newly dug grave. Mr. Kinard started to walk in their direction. He watched the sergeant take the prisoner, his hands still bound, to the spot where the hole had been dug. He saw the black soldier remove the slouch hat from the man's head and throw it on the ground. He saw the young man kneel, and the sergeant placed a cloth sack over the man's head. The task finished, the sergeant quickly returned to the detail of men carrying rifles. Solomon looked at the men standing in ranks in the road, stirring, all trying to get a better view of what was happening. On command, he saw the soldiers raise their weapons, and then the fire flashed from the ends of the muskets, quickly followed by the bellows of white smoke. The loud report of the guns echoed through the tree tops, sounding more like a small cannon rather then small arms fire. He saw the man tossed backwards from the impact of the bullets and then tumble into the opening in the ground. A leg and foot were still visible, but there was no movement. The smoke drifted upward as the men slowly lowered their weapons. Mr. Kinard continued to move closer, but was soon challenged by a guard rapidly approaching from his right.

"Yu halt, there!" shouted the sentinel. "Yu's wants ta get shot, too. Them boys just abouts ready ta shoots e'benbody now. Yu better stays back, mis'a."

Solomon stopped and watched as another man, one of the officers, moved from the edge of the road toward the grave. The surgeon bent over the hole, examining the body. Shortly he stood and walked to the other three officers. The men with the shovels moved to the open hole. Some of the men who did the shooting also walked to the site. The small group stood looking down upon their victim.

Mr. Kinard stared in bewilderment, then disgust, as one of the soldiers kicked at the man's leg and then jumped into the hole on top of the man's body and began to jump up and down. He was soon joined by another man. Kinard stood motionless as he saw the officers still watching the spectacle that was taking place in the field before them. The men suddenly began to take joy in trying to get the man's body into the small hole.

The men in the road began to react, some pointing, others laughing, and still others seemingly dancing in jubilation. They no longer looked like a military formation, but a mob. This commotion was allowed to last but a few minutes when two of the officers moved into the road, bringing the men to attention. They slowly stopped the celebration. The formation was dressed and the orders to move were echoed down the line. It was but a few more moments and they were in motion, marching away from town.

Mr. Kinard watched as the last few shovels of dirt were quickly thrown over the grave. The soldiers threw the implements onto the ground and ran to catch the regiment as it moved away.

Three wagons loaded with supplies rolled from the edge of the field into the street. They were heading back toward town. The young officer who had been in charge of the firing squad was sitting in the first wagon, along with the man who had examined the prisoner. The guard who had warned Solomon to stay back had now left, also aboard the wagon with several others. In a few more minutes the field and street were empty, leaving nothing but the early morning sounds. He looked toward the south end of the field and saw two dogs nosing among the debris that had been left behind. He looked back at the low mound of fresh dug dirt not too far distant from him. Its solitude was eerie and frightening.

A buggy slowly made its way along Caldwell toward the empty field. It stopped just after crossing the tracks and two men emerged. Solomon saw that it was Jake Bowers and Sheriff Walt Houseal. Walt stood by the buggy as Jake moved ahead into the field. Jake looked in the direction of Mr. Kinard, as he moved toward the freshly made grave. He stood above the spot for a few long minutes, then turned, reached down and picked up the faded hat, dusted it off on his trousers, and carried it with him back to the buggy.

Jake and the other two men had just turned onto Platt from Adams when they heard the volley of gunfire. Jake relaxed the reins momentarily, listening to the echoes over the rooftops of downtown Newberry. His reaction to the fatal sounding noise was as if a round had found its mark in him. The horse continued to move the buggy along the street.

"Jake, you, okay, son?" asked his uncle.

"They've killed that boy, Sam," came the response.

"You don't know that, Jake," added Walt. "Just keep driving; we may not be too late."

They turned onto Caldwell and saw the soldiers gathered in the middle of the street beyond the tracks. They appeared to be preparing to depart. Jake continued to drive right toward them. A guard was soon seen standing in the street looking in their direction.

"You better stop here, Jake," advised the sheriff.

"We've got orders from Colonel Tyler," he responded.

"You best stop here," he said it again with authority.

Jake reined the horse to a stop and the three men sat in silence, as they watched the commotion in the street. Other soldiers could be seen on the edge of the field, but on the right trees lining the tracks blocked their vision. Jake quickly searched the scene for the Crozier boy. The soldiers were already beginning to move ahead. It was just minutes before they had disappeared over a slight rise further down the street. Jake saw no sign of Calvin.

The men watched as wagons began to approach, driven by soldiers, with two officers aboard the lead wagon. Other men were in the back, sitting among the supplies and baggage. Again, Jake searched unsuccessfully for Crozier. The three men exchanged looks with the officers as they passed. Nothing was said, nor did they acknowledge each other.

Jake put the buggy into motion once again, this time moving at a reluctant pace across the tracks. The men spotted the mound of dirt not far from the tracks. Jake brought the buggy to a halt once again. He climbed from the buggy and started across the field. He saw Solomon Kinard standing behind his sheds. He looked at the makeshift grave. He saw the slouch hat on the ground.

"This couldn't have happened so quickly, and so unjustly," he thought. "Those people were looking for blood, and fairness and justice had nothing to do with it."

Jake stared at the spot of fresh turned dirt. He thought of the man who showed so much bravery and justice for him beside the train just a few hours earlier. He wondered if he would have been able to do the same for him.

He picked the boy's hat up and returned to the buggy. There was nothing he could do here.

Jim and Josh had been awake the entire night; neither could sleep. Josh's fever had finally subsided during the passing hours they had been in the shed. They were both anxious and restless and talking about it hadn't helped. Daylight had come and they were sitting silently wrapped in their own thoughts. They both raised their heads as the distant rumble of what sounded like a rifle volley drifted though the cracks in the walls of the small building. They both were on their feet and rushing toward the door in a split second. They went outside but now only heard a rooster crowing in the west. Josh began walking toward the street.

"Jim, you stay here with the girls," Josh said, as he began to walk faster.

"No! I'm not going to do that" argued Jim. "You come with me to the house to tell those people where we're going. They can look after the girls while we're gone."

Josh stopped and looked at his friend. He saw that any arguing with Jim would be futile.

"All right, but hurry," Josh answered.

They were soon on their way. Both girls were sound asleep, according to Mrs. Gary, and she said she would leave them that way as long as she could. She had cautioned them to be careful and to do as the sheriff had said.

The boys hurried off. They knew the sound of the firing had come some distance from where they were, and they were anxious to get there. Josh and Jim were aware that they were heading back in the direction of the train, but with daylight, nothing gave hints as to where they were. They just moved in the direction from which the sound had come.

Josh stopped to get his breath after a few minutes of hard walking.

"Josh, you better take it a little easier," advised Jim. "I don't need you any sicker right now."

Jim looked toward what appeared to be the center of town, but he could see nothing that could help him get his bearings. The sound of gunfire had come from the area beyond the large buildings on his left. The street they were on didn't lead that way, but there seemed to be a cross street not far ahead. He saw a freight car beyond some trees in the distance as the street turned to the left.

Josh started to walk again and Jim moved with him, this time at a somewhat slower pace. They saw a man standing on a porch watching as they passed. They soon turned onto Caldwell Street. Just ahead were a buggy and a wagon on the street. It was the sheriff and the foreman from the railroad.

"What's happened, mister?" asked Josh, again out of breath.

"Where you boys headed?" asked Walt Houseal, standing beside his wagon. "You supposed to be with those ladies."

"What was the noise we heard?" Jim asked anxiously.

"Boys, your friend's dead. He's been shot," said the sheriff.

"What do you mean 'dead'?" asked Jim. "There ain't been no cause to shoot Cal. He ain't dead!"

The two men in the buggy were silent, looking at the two young men standing restlessly facing the sheriff. Jake waited until the reality of the news had set in.

"I don't know why the soldiers shot him, but we were too late to stop it. We were told earlier that that colonel had sentenced him to die for killing one of their soldiers," added Jake.

"But he was defending himself," argued Jim.

"Did you talk to that colonel that done the shooting?" asked Josh, now with a growing anger.

"No, boys, he wouldn't allow us in his camp," answered Jake. "The colonel of the soldiers stationed here had written us orders to get us in, but we were too late." He pulled the paper from his pocket and handed it to Josh.

"I need for you men to go back to those ladies and stay with them," stated Walt. "There's nothing you can do here. They're in your care now, and I think that's what your friend would have wanted."

"Where's Cal?" asked Josh.

"There's a grave not far ahead in the field on the right," answered Sheriff Houseal.

Josh looked at Jake and his uncle sitting in the buggy. There were tears now in his eyes.

"Thanks, mister," Josh said, as he started past the men.

"You boys want a ride?" asked the sheriff, as he watched them walk away. There was no response.

Josh and Jim moved on down Caldwell toward the tracks crossing the road. The sun had now broken above the horizon on their left as they headed toward the field ahead.

# Chapter 14

Tom Grenaker struggled to stay centered on the mule's back as he crossed the tracks on Platt Street, looking toward the depot on his left. He could see the cars out of line not far beyond the station house. He saw the crew of men there, working. He stared briefly but could not spot Jake Bowers. That was unusual. He expected to see the foreman in the middle of the activity. He got the mule moving again and turned on to Tarrant Street. There were three wagons parked there, and black soldiers were busy loading freight from the wagons onto the cars of the special train. He continued to ride ahead. There would be time to get back to the accident sight, but now his interest was on the camp of the black soldiers. He had been wakened by the sound of gunfire, and he was anxious to find out what was going on.

He rode past Boundary, turning briefly to the west to get to Drayton and then on past Solomon Kinard's feed store. He noticed the front door was open and movement inside. "What was Mr. Kinard doing here at such an early hour?" he wondered. He decided to find out.

He tied the mule to the post in front and walked to the open door. "Mr. Kinard? That you in here so early?" he called.

"Who else it might be, Tom?" answered the older man. "I suppose it's that newspaper of yours that brings you out so early. Heard the shooting, I guess?"

"What happened, Mr. Kinard?" he asked.

"Those soldiers shot and killed a man a while ago. That's all I know," answered Solomon, still depressed at the scene he had witnessed.

"Who'd they shoot? You know why?" Tom quickly asked.

"Easy, Tom," he answered. "I told you I don't know nothing except they shot a man. Nobody I know. They buried him out back in the field where they were camped."

Tom moved to the back window of the store. He looked beyond the sheds and caught a glimpse of two men walking into the field. They disappeared out of sight behind one of the sheds.

"I'll be back, Mr. Kinard," said Tom, as he turned back toward the front door.

Solomon was surprised at the sudden departure of the man

160

always so interested in everybody else's business. He walked to the front just in time to see Tom and the mule disappear around the corner of the store. He went back inside, opened the back door and watched as Tom rode through his back lot into the field beyond. He was soon out of sight.

Tom managed with effort to get Boss round the pile of discarded equipment on the edge of Mr. Kinard's lot and over the shallow ditch beyond and then into the large vacant field. Evidence was scattered over the open ground of the recent presence of the soldiers. In front of Tom and his mule stood two young men, both ex–soldiers, from their appearance, standing by a mound of freshly dug earth. Tom moved his mule closer to where the boys stood.

"Is that a grave?" asked the reporter, nervously. There was no reply.

He slid from the animal's back and walked closer. "You know who those soldiers shot?" he asked.

"Yea, they shot our friend, Cal," came the sad response from the younger of the two boys.

"You know why?" he again asked.

"You mighty nosey, mister," responded Josh, anger still in his voice. "Any reason other than morbid curiosity of what you asking?"

"I own the newspaper and there's going to be a lot of people asking what I've been asking," Tom answered. "Don't you want them to know about your friend?"

"He didn't do nothing wrong, mister," answered Jim. "They had no cause to do this thing. Cal was a good man, and they shouldn't have killed him." His voice was about to break.

The reporter remained quiet for a few minutes as the boys stared at the pile of dirt in front of them.

"We can't leave Cal in this empty field, Josh," commented Jim. "This ain't no place for him."

"You know what happened?" again Tom asked.

After a long pause, Josh answered, "He got in a fight with a black soldier last night at the station. The soldier attacked him, and Cal had to cut him. It was self–defense."

Tom pulled a small paper and a pencil from his pocket. "Were you there?" he asked.

"Should have been...we should have been there," answered Josh.

"There's a man across yonder at that store that I think saw what happened. You want to go talk to him?" asked Tom, now looking for a better place to talk to the boys.

Josh quickly looked toward the back of the feed and hardware store. "Sure, mister. We'll go talk to him," answered Josh.

Tom led Boss by the rope as he walked along with the boys. "You men were soldiers. Was your friend?" he asked.

"Yea," responded Jim. "He was just trying to get home."

The three men moved into the back lot of the store between the sheds. Solomon was standing in the back door, watching as they approached.

"You see what happened, mister," asked Josh, as he moved ahead of Jim and the reporter.

Mr. Kinard looked at the two men in Confederate clothes. He quickly realized they must have known the boy he saw executed.

"Come on in and sit down. I saw what happened," answered Solomon. "I'm S. P. Kinard. I own this place. You boys know that man they shot?" he asked.

"His name is Cal Crozier," answered Josh. "We were traveling home together."

Tom quickly tied Boss to a rail and followed the men inside.

"Kind of late to be passing through," commented the older man. "Most of the boys have long since passed through. You been in prison?" asked Solomon.

"Yea, all three of us were, Camp Douglas in Chicago," answered Jim.

"You said you saw what happened?" asked Josh.

"Not much to tell, boys. Some soldiers woke me up before daybreak, wanting to borrow some tools to dig a grave, they said," began Solomon. "I went back out later and saw them preparing to leave. They bought your friend, hands tied, with a squad of soldiers to where the soldiers had dug the grave. Officers were there, so I guess it was ordered for him to be shot. They put him in front of the hole, and they fired on him. An officer examined him to make sure he was dead, I guess, and then they buried him.

"They didn't use no coffin?" interrupted Jim.

"They just covered him up in the hole. Borrowed my tools to do that deed and then left them for me to go get," answered Solomon. "It weren't a pretty thing to watch, boys, and I didn't know your friend. But it made me wish I had a howitzer with those boys lined up in the street like they were. They all marched away from town when it was done."

"I saw Jake Bowers out in the field earlier, Tom. You might want to ask him some questions, too," Mr. Kinard added.

"Can you tell me about your friend?" asked Tom.

"His name was Calvin Crozier," Josh began.

Mr. Kinard moved another chair to the small table next to the rocking chair and invited the men to sit down. He stood back near the door looking out toward the empty field as he listened to Josh and Jim tell the reporter about their friend. He heard them tell of the cavalry and then Camp Douglas. Then he heard about the ladies who were aboard the train. Solomon turned in anger as he listened to the story of the man fighting with the soldier when he found him in the car with the girls.

"I don't know your names," added Tom, as he filled his paper with notes.

"That ain't important, mister," Calvin Crozier is the name you need to remember. He was a special friend and special person," answered Josh. "We just happened to be traveling with him."

"I better go, boys," said Mr. Grenaker. "There were some of those soldiers still at the station when I come by and I might try to find out more from them. It looked like it might still be a while before they get your train fixed," he added. "Maybe I'll see you at the station before you leave."

The three men watched Tom as he quickly walked through the rear door to Boss. They watched through the window as he repeatedly kicked at the mule before he finally moved off out of sight.

"That boy's going to put himself in a early grave trying to keep up with everything that happens here," chuckled Solomon, as he turned away from the window.

"You reckon there's anyway we can get Cal moved from that place, mister? We ain't got any money," asked Josh, looking up at the man standing by the window.

"Don't worry 'bout that," answered Solomon, firmly. "He'll be given a decent burial and moved to the cemetery. I'll see to that."

**T**om rode down Drayton Street as rapidly as he could get Boss to move. He was anxious to get back to the depot. He could see the steam being released from the engine as it sat ready to depart. He turned off of Tarrant Street down to the train. There was no one at the controls as he passed the engine. He stopped Boss at the entrance to the passenger car. He slid off Boss's back, leaving his mule with the rope hanging to the ground and quickly tried to enter the train. A guard suddenly appeared on the platform and stopped him.

"Any officers aboard," he asked the soldier holding the musket.

"Yas, sah, buts yu can't come aboard," answered the private.

"Would you ask one of them to come out, then? Tell him I need to see him on urgent business," stated the reporter.

The guard stood still, not sure what to do. "Yu's wait there," he told the man standing by his mule.

It was but a few seconds before a young lieutenant came out the front of the car.

"What business you got here, mister?" asked Lieutenant Wood.

"Just want to ask some questions about the execution, lieutenant. I'm with the local newspaper," answered Tom.

"I can't talk to any reporter!" answered Henry. "You best leave before you get in trouble." He turned to go back into the train.

"Did the soldier that attacked Mr. Crozier die?" Tom asked.

Lieutenant Wood stopped and looked back at the reporter. The man on the ground continued to look at the officer waiting for a response.

Henry stepped back once again facing the reporter. He stood there a moment longer, and then moved to the bottom step.

BH

"He's in the hospital," he answered.

"He's not dead?" asked Tom.

"He's mortally wounded. He's not expected to live but a few hours."

"Did you talk to the man whom was executed?" Tom asked, removing his paper from his pocket.

"I told you I can't talk with any newspaperman," Henry said. "If you want information, you put that paper up."

Tom quickly put his notes back in his pocket. "Did you talk to Mr. Crozier?"

"He was my prisoner."

"Did he tell you he had defended two ladies from your soldier and that the soldier attacked him? Did he tell you it was self–defense?"

Henry Wood looked at the man, hesitating to trust him any farther.

"He told me that," responded the officer. "Said he would do it again if he had to."

"Then why was he executed?"

"I was following orders."

"Whose orders?"

"Colonel Charles Trowbridge is our commanding officer. He interviewed the man. He confessed to him and the colonel determined he should be shot. That's what he ordered," answered Henry.

"Any problem, lieutenant?" asked William Crandall, as he came out of the front of the car. The guard stood behind him, rifle in hand.

"No, Will, this man's leaving," answered Henry. "I told him he has no business here, and he's leaving. Just asking some questions about the train wreck."

The officer turned and walked past the surgeon and guard back into the car. Will stared at the young man. Tom took hold of Boss's rope and led him away from the train.

The engineer was now at the controls, preparing to get under way.

Tom walked his mule around the rear of the train to the other side of the tracks. He looked back toward the depot and saw the work crew still busy at work. He spotted Jake Bowers giving orders. He hurriedly led Boss to the depot and tied him there. He went to where Jake stood.

"The only thing exciting that's happened around here in weeks, since that house fire, and it's mid morning 'fore you come around to ask questions about the train wreck," snapped Jake, kidding young Tom Grenaker.

"I've been checking on that shooting near Halcyon Grove this morning, Mr. Bowers. You weren't here when I came by earlier, and Mr. Kinard tells me he saw you out at that man's grave," said Tom.

"Well, boy, it sounds like maybe I was wrong. You've been busy already this morning, I see." answered Jake with surprise.

"What do you know about what happened here last night?"

"Let's go inside and we'll talk," responded Jake, turning now toward the station house. "I'll be glad to tell people about what happened here last night, but not what they did this morning to that boy. He didn't deserve that, Tom."

"You men are going to need another jack there and some more crossties," Jake shouted to the small group of men working on the front wheels of the passenger car. "There's another jack in the shed. You might as well get two more of them out," he added, as he and Tom moved to the depot.

Jake entered the station house and walked over to where Benny had a fresh pot of coffee brewing. He poured himself a cup and moved to one of the benches. Tom already had his paper and pencil in hand.

"Tom, those soldiers were going to shoot me last night."

"What do you mean 'shoot you'?" How did you get involved?"

"I was here with my crew because of the train wreck," Jake answered. "I didn't know anything was going on at the time, when this gang of black soldiers came out of the dark and accused me of cutting one of their men. There was a sergeant in charge, but I'm not sure they were even supposed to be here. I tried talking reason with them but that was foolish. 'Fore I knew it, they had grabbed me and were threatening to shoot me."

"You mean they were threatening to arrest you and shoot you?" asked Tom, trying to clarify what Jake was saying.

"I mean those boys had their weapons cocked and pointed at men. You write down what I'm telling you."

Tom smiled, and looked back at his notes and began to write again.

"It was the first time I felt fear for my life since Farmville, Virginia, Tom. It was then that that boy Crozier came up and surrendered. He told them I hadn't done anything. He said he had fought with their soldier and that he was the one they were looking for. He made them turn me loose 'fore he would even admit he had done it."

"They grabbed him and I thought I was going to be a witness to a murder when this other group of soldiers came up and took control," continued Mr. Bowers, now more excited. "There was a sergeant with them that was pretty tough. He stopped them from hurting that boy then and there, even had one of his own arrested 'cause he wouldn't listen to him. I heard Crozier tell him he had fought with their soldier in self–defense. The sergeant told him to be careful what he was saying, as those boys were looking for blood."

"What happened then?"

"Crozier told me I had better get and to tell his two traveling companions to stay away. He told me there were ladies in the station who needed looking after. They left with Crozier, going back to their camp. Tom, I'd be dead if that boy hadn't surrendered himself when he did. There's no doubt about it. I saw the look in those boys' eyes; they were about to commit murder!"

Tom was busy writing, listening to Jake's every word, and trying to think of the next question all at the same time.

"Did you see the execution this morning, Mr. Bowers?"

"I went back to the station house and stayed with the two young ladies until Crozier's friends came in," added Jake. "That older boy wanted to go straight to their camp, but with the help of the ladies, we managed to keep him at the depot. Crozier had told the girls to make the two men stay away from the soldiers."

"What did you do then?"

"I made them promise to stay with the girls, and I went to find Sheriff Houseal. I got him out of bed and told him what had happened. When I told him about the soldier attacking the girls, he wanted to get Doc Gary and Rebecca to come with him to the station. By then I wanted to do something to help that man."

"What'd you do?"

"I got Sam Bowers to go with me to the camp of those black soldiers, but it didn't do any good. We finally saw that Colonel Tyler at the college about it and he gave us orders so we could see that other colonel, but it was too late, Tom. They shot him 'fore we got there."

"Your uncle Sam went with you?"

"He and the sheriff both went with me, but we were too late. Did you see those two friends of his?"

"I left them at Mr. Kinard's store," answered Tom. "I suppose they're still there. Where are the two ladies?"

"They're at Doc Gary's."

Tom rose from the bench, put his notes back into his pocket, thanked Jake, and then walked back out the front of the depot toward his mule. He was mounted and had Boss moving as fast as ever heading in the direction of Dr. Gary's home. As he passed the funeral house, he noticed Mr. Kinard coming out the front door with Mr. Wiggins. Tom soon turned into the front drive of Dr. Gary's. He saw Josh and Jim sitting near a wood pile in the rear of the house. He tied Boss to a hitching post and climbed the steps to the porch. The doctor soon answered the knock at he door.

"Tom Grenaker, what are you doing at my door this Friday morning?" asked the distinguished doctor.

"Doc Gary, I'm here to see if I might talk to those young ladies from the train."

"I guess you know about all that happened by now, Tom?"

"Most everything, Dr. Gary. I would like to speak with the young ladies, though."

The doctor moved out the door, pulling it shut behind him.

"I think it might need to wait, Tom. The girls haven't been up long and they were just told what happened to that young man who was traveling with them. My wife's with them now. You best come back later."

For once, Tom took "no" for an answer graciously and went back down the steps. He went around the house to where Josh and Jim were sitting.

"I saw Mr. Kinard at the funeral home just now. Do you know what he's doing?" asked the inquisitive reporter.

"He said he was going to get Cal moved to the cemetery," answered Jim.

"You boys all right?" asked Tom, showing true concern for the first time.

There was no reply.

"I spoke with Mr. Bowers, and he told me how Calvin kept him from being shot by surrendering himself last night," commented the reporter. "It looks like that friend of yours will soon be quite a hero around here."

"He was already a hero. He survived that war, the prison, and we owed our lives to him, mister," answered Jim. "You can't add anything to what we already knew."

Mr. Kinard had driven Mr. Wiggins by the cotton shed to get Sam and Willy to help them remove Calvin's body and prepare a new grave in the cemetery. Sam and Willy had been working for Mr. Wiggins for some time now as gravediggers. They had told Mr. Wiggins that they would dig a new grave but refused to dig up a body. Solomon had finally told Mr. Wiggins he would do the digging. They had a coffin in the rear of the wagon and had now reached the field. Mr. Kinard was surprised to see several men there, standing over the grave. One of them was Earl Morris.

"We heard what happened this morning and came out to see the dirty work of them black soldiers, Solomon," commented Earl, as the two men brought the wagon to a halt behind the grave. "You going to dig that boy up, Mr. Wiggins?"

"Looks like Solomon here is," answered the undertaker. "He wants me to get the body ready for another burial this afternoon."

"You can help me Earl, if you would. This boy don't deserve to be in this ground," Mr. Kinard said.

"I ain't never dug nobody up, Solomon, but there's always a first," answered Earl, helping remove the shovels from the wagon. The other men were moving away.

It wasn't long before the three men had the body removed from the shallow grave and loaded into the coffin. Earl rode back to the funeral parlor with the two men to help.

Tom sat patiently outside the office of Colonel Rockwell Tyler. He had requested an interview with him and had been waiting nearly half an hour. Captain Henry Loomus came into the hallway where the man sat.

"The colonel sends his regrets, but he does not wish to discuss anything concerning the 33rd Regiment," said the adjutant. "He said he doesn't have any knowledge of the details of the incident and cannot assist you in any way."

"Would you please tell Colonel Tyler that I know he met with Sheriff Houseal and Judge Bowers earlier this morning and that he does have knowledge of the incident," answered Tom. "Tell him it's justice to the citizens of Newberry to relate information about what occurred this morning."

The captain did not respond, but returned to the inner office. Tom waited again for a response, feeling certain that he might now get his interview.

"The colonel says he will not be able to see you now, and to tell you the army will issue an official statement later on the matter," stated Captain Loomus, as he reentered the hallway.

Tom was disappointed, but knew he had hit a dead end road with the colonel of the 56th New York for now. Without any further words, the man left the building heading back toward the railroad station. He also had a train accident to investigate.

Sarah Dekalb sat numb from all that had happened during the last hours. She had tried to eat the late morning breakfast that was sitting in front of her, but she only dabbled at it. Rebecca Gary had been kind and understanding to her and to Jenny, but she wasn't in any mood to eat.

She looked at her sister and saw the tears still on her cheeks as she ate the eggs, grits and the ham biscuit on her plate. She was glad to see her eating.

She had left the bedroom with Jenny still asleep and slipped downstairs to find Mrs. Gary to see if they had any news about when Calvin would be released. She had spotted Josh and Jim through the window, sitting outside the shed near the woodpile. There was no hint from them what was going on.

She found her host in the kitchen. When she asked about Mr. Crozier, the expression she saw on the older woman's face said it wasn't good. She was not prepared for what she heard the woman say. Jenny came into the room before Sarah had recovered herself and immediately knew there had been tragedy. Jenny had just now been able to stop her crying.

Sarah felt sad for the young man she had gotten to know just briefly. It was hard knowing how much he wanted to get home. And to have it end in such injustice terrified her as to what the future held for them when they would reach home. She would not think about that. She was glad to know that Calvin's friends would be traveling the rest of the way with them.

"It looks like your train may be leaving this afternoon, ladies," said Doctor Gary, as he entered the room.

"I hoped you wouldn't go back to the depot until this thing is settled," said Rebecca Gary, slightly scolding her husband.

"The black troops are gone now, and this thing will clear up soon," he told her. "Girls, Mr. Crozier's body has been moved to the funeral home, and there'll be a burial this afternoon. One of our citizens is seeing to that," the doctor added.

"Can we see him?" asked Jenny.

Mr. and Mrs. Gary were surprised by the question.

"No, girl, it's best you don't do that," answered the woman. "You talked about how pleasant a smile he had. It's better that you just remember him that way."

Jenny looked at her sister. Sarah again had tears in her eyes.

There was a knock at the back door, and Doctor Gary went to tend to it. He soon returned.

"That was Mr. Crozier's two friends," he said. "They're going back to the station. I told them we'd look after you and would bring you to the station later."

"**M**r. Bowers, what caused the cars to come off?" asked Tom, who had just walked up behind Jake.

"Look down the track a ways, and you'll see what the train hit," answered Jake. "Somebody put those ties on the tracks last night."

"Who'd do that?"

"Don't know, Tom, but I'd say those black troops had something to do with it."

"Anybody get hurt?"

"Just a few people shook up, but nobody seriously. The Crozier boy hurt his leg, and I think even the ladies he was with were bruised. Doc Gary came down to the station after it happened. Come to speak of it, I guess I was surprised you weren't here, Tom."

"Mr. Kinard is seeing that Crozier is being reburied in the cemetery this afternoon."

Jake stopped and looked at the young man. He was glad to hear Tom's news.

"He's already had him moved from Halcyon Grove to Mr. Wiggins' place," added the reporter.

Jake turned back to his work and said no more. The newspaperman moved toward the wood scattered along the track further down the rails.

The sun was shining brightly on this cool September afternoon. A crowd of men and women were gathered outside the funeral home on Platt Street. Word spread rapidly over the small community about the death of this soldier on his way home and the circumstances of what had happened. They were there now to pay their respects to this unknown man and to escort him to the cemetery. When Jake Bowers approached the funeral home, he was surprised at the crowd that was gathering.

Jake had been without sleep now for more than a day and a half. The physical strain from the work at the station was exhausting, but the emotional turmoil had drained him. The Anderson train would finally be departing, and he knew he needed to be there. But when he heard about what was being done for the Crozier boy, Jake was determined to help escort him to his final resting place.

As he parked his buggy on the curb, he looked up to see Colonel William Lester heading toward him.

"Jake, I heard you were injured. Are you all right?" asked his long time friend.

"I'm not injured, Will. No harm was done. Just tired and exhausted. This thing with this Crozier boy has been unsettling."

"I heard he kept you from being hurt worst at the depot last night. What happened, Jake?"

"He saved my life, colonel. No doubts on that. Those soldiers were about to shoot me when this man surrendered. He was still in Confederate clothes, Will, trying to get home from Maryland, I was told."

"I heard he was a soldier passing through. Looks like this war will never end for some of our boys."

The two men joined the crowd that stood on the street waiting. It wasn't long before Mr. Wiggins appeared on the porch with the Rev. H. H. Murphy and Silas Johnstone. They waited but a few more minutes before the hearse moved into the drive from behind the building. The preacher, mayor, and Mr. Wiggins walked ahead of the procession as the crowd slowly followed.

As the group moved down Platt, others came from their houses to witness what was taking place. Some knew, but others had not heard about the shooting and watched out of curiosity. The procession moved to Caldwell and on toward the Village Cemetery. As Jake walked along with the others, his attention was drawn to the distant field ahead on his right. He could see the now empty hole in the ground. He stared in that direction until the procession turned off Caldwell toward the graveyard. His thoughts were of his visit there earlier in the morning.

The hearse turned into the cemetery and the crowd was soon gathered around a newly dug grave. Dr. Murphy said the prayer and the people watched, as this stranger was laid to rest.

Dr. John K. Gary and his wife, Rebecca, stood on the platform of the Greenville-Columbia train depot waiting the departure of the delayed train from Winnsboro. Aboard the cars were two young ladies that they had become affectionately attached to during their brief and unexpected stop in Newberry. Standing beside the Garys was the railroad foreman, Jake Bowers, watching, as the final call was made for the train's departure. His crew had worked hard for the past fourteen hours getting the repairs made, even without him there to help much of the time.

Jake could see the two girls as they looked back at them through the window. The young one gestured a wave. In the seat behind them sat two young men in Confederate clothes. They were escorting the ladies to their home in Georgia. Jake had arranged for them to have coach fare the rest of the way to Macon so they would be close to the girls.

He stared at the two friends of the man who had saved his life. He was saddened that he didn't know him as these two men had. He would have liked to.

He continued to watch as the steam belched from the engine just ahead of the passenger car, and the train slowly went into motion. Jake Bowers stood silently watching, listening to the lonesome sound of the train's whistle. He felt he was now the only man in Newberry who had any idea of the character and bravery of the young man named Calvin Crozier -- the young man whose name was to be written in stone in the history of this small, southern town.

*March 23, 1901*

*Dear Mrs. Rogers,*

*I just recently read of your story about your brother, Calvin Crozier. It is sad to know that for so many years and through no fault of your own you did not learn until just recently of the story of your brother. I regret to inform you that I might have prevented that had I but put forth just half the effort you did in your effort to locate him. I was with your brother the day he was killed in Newberry, South Carolina. I was attached to the 33rd US Colored Troops under command of Colonel Charles Trowbridge who ordered your brother's execution. I spoke with your brother while he was in our custody. I was the Officer of the Day the night he was arrested. Early in the morning of the 8th of September when he realized what the outcome of his arrest was to be, he asked me to write to his family for him. He asked me to write that he was to be shot for killing a US soldier. He asked me to write that he died doing his duty. He asked me to have the letter given to a traveling companion that was on the train. I did write the letter but I was unable to find an opportunity to locate his traveling companion. I spent some time after this* incident was over trying to locate his family in Texas unsuccessfully. Maybe I did not look hard enough because I did not want to face up to my part of the affair. I was ordered to carry out the execution of your brother, which I did even though I felt he might be innocent of any crime.

The letter I wrote to your family lay in a chest for many years before I finally destroyed it.

The man your brother cut in Newberry did not die of his wound. Colonel Trowbridge was charged and tried for the murder of your brother. His commanding general in October of 1865 charged him with the crime of murder. I do know he was acquitted of the crime by a court-marshal and that General Charles Devens disapproved of the results of the court's action.

I am including a purse that he asked me to send by his companion. The contents are those as I received it. The purse has been in the chest where my letter was originally stored.

I personally regret the killing of your brother and I regret my part in it. I must say that I was following orders of my commander, but youth and fear did more to prevent me from stopping the outcome of the events of that day in 1865.

I hope that my letter may help you put a closure to your efforts to find your brother,

Sincerely,

Henry Wood
Johnstown, Pennsylvania

# Epilog

Quoted from the Weekly Herald, September 13th, 1865...

"Killing; -- The most of our readers are, -- ere this, in possession of the reports telling of the diabolical occurrences of last Friday morning, which resulted in the killing, or murder, of Mr. Calvin Crozier, late a member of the 3rd Kentucky Cavalry, under Morgan's command, by the 33rd colored troops, in command of Col. Trowbridge. The facts, as we hear them are these: Mr. Crozier, long a prisoner, was returning to his home in Texas, and arrived at this place sometime in the night of Thursday and had two young ladies under his care. A portion of the colored 33rd had been here several days, waiting for the remainder, which got here Thursday evening. An obstruction on the track near the depot, supposed to be done by some of these colored troops, threw a portion of the train off. Leaving the car a short time, and returning, Mr. Crozier found a Negro soldier in there in such close proximity to the ladies, that he ordered him out, which the other in the most violent manner refused to do. An altercation ensued, in which the Negro was cut on the back of the neck. He then left. Sometime after and while the cars were being righted, a squad of Negro soldiers came up under a sergeant, in search of Crozier, and seizing by mistake Mr. Jake Bowers, in charge of the hands, threatened to shoot him; the right man however, promptly appeared and declaring that Bowers innocent, gave himself up. A part of the squad were for instantly shooting him, while others objected, and insisted on taking him to Headquarters, which was then done. The report then is that he was taken before the Colonel and acknowledged what he had done, and that he would do the same again; and that he was then told that he must die for it. He was then taken under strong guard a few yards from camp, and a hole being dug, was ordered to kneel. At this point Mr. S. P. Kinard, who lives near, and who loaned the implements to dig the hole approached near the spot and saw the flash of the guns as the Negroes fired upon Crozier, who immediately fell. Mr. Kinard tried to get nearer, but was warned by a sentinel not to do so, as the regiment was much excited and that he might get killed. He then went round and saw them jumping upon the body which was too large for the hole. All this time the regiment was in line, drums beat, and it was evident that it was in readiness to move, which it did, a short time after, a few miles down the road to wait for the cars, thus getting out of the way. Further than this, we know nothing, but that an inquest was held and much evidence elicited, which evidence, however, is withheld from us, as not being fully complete in showing that the colonel of these Negro troops was full cognizant of the deceased, that it could possibly be otherwise admits a considerable doubt, and in as such, calls loudly for examination and satisfaction. We understand that the facts will be submitted to the Secretary of War. The deceased is said to have been a most estimable young man, brave, and generous, as was clearly shown in giving himself up when he might have escaped.

During the morning, Friday, our citizens had the body taken from the hole where it was partially covered and placed in a neat coffin, preparatory to final interment, which was done in the afternoon, a very large respectable and sympathizing procession of ladies and gentlemen following it to its final resting place in the grave yard."

The "Weekly Herald" was the Newberry publication owned and operated by Mr. T. W. Grenaker and Mr. R. H. Grenaker in 1865.

The Fifty–Sixth New York Regiment of Infantry was relieved of duty in Newberry in mid October of 1865 and returned to Charleston, S.C. Shortly after their return to Charleston, Major General Charles Devens, Commander of the Military District of South Carolina, filed charges against Colonel Trowbridge for the murder of Calvin Crozier.

The court convened on November 6, 1865 and stayed in session four days. The court acquitted Colonel Trowbridge for the crime, but General Devens submitted the finding back to the court for further consideration, with a letter attached that is quoted as follows:

> "Respectfully returned to the Court–Martial of which Brevetted Brig. General W. T. Bennett is President, for reconsideration. The execution of Calvin Crozier seems to me, an act without form of law or justifiable cause. That Crozier had committed an act worthy of death is not now even pretended in the defense, how then can this officer who caused him to be executed be held guiltless?
>
> It is earnestly urged on the Court–Martial that this act is one which ought not to go unpunished.
>
> `Signed Charles Devens, Major General, Commanding."*

The court upheld their acquittal. Major General Devens forwarded the results to the War Department in Washington with a cover letter attached. The letter is quoted as follows:

> "The findings in the above case are, disapproved. Calvin Crozier was executed summarily by Lt Col Trowbridge for the murder of Private Mills 33rd U.S.C.T. who was not only not murdered, but is today alive and well. It was in my opinion, a most unjustifiable act, and indicates, a weakness in yielding to momentary clamor and excitement unworthy of a brave and judicious officer. This case has been returned once to the Court who tried it for reconsideration and the Court having adhered to its previous decision, the General Commanding feels compelled to order Lt Col C. T. Trowbridge 33 U.S.C.T. to be released from arrest and returned to duty."
>
> *Signed Charles Devens, Major General, Commanding."*

The Thirty–Third US Colored Troops were released from active duty on January 31, 1866. Lieutenant Colonel Charles Trowbridge was held on active duty until March of that year.

The people of Newberry did not know this information concerning the court–martial of Colonel Charles Trowbridge until 1994.

Colonel Charles Trowbridge removed himself to Minnesota and died there in December, 1903. Although notice of his death was published in the "Newberry Observer" at that time, his death was not mourned in Newberry, South Carolina.

As seen in Major General Charles Devens' letter, Private Gloster Mills did not die from the wound he received on the night of September 7th, 1865. Nor is it documented in his record that he was wounded.

The man named Calvin Crozier was not buried and forgotten in the town of Newberry. In fact, the grave in the Old Village Cemetery was not to be his final resting–place.

In 1891 the citizens of Newberry had Calvin Crozier's body exhumed and reburied at Rosemont Cemetery on College Street (previously Adams Street). Donations were sought and collected to erect a suitable monument over his grave at that time.

The inscription that the citizens then elected to write on the monument is as follows:

On the front face:

CALVIN CROZIER

BORN

At Brandon, Miss.

August, 1840

Murdered at

Newberry, S.C.

Sept 8, 1865

On another face:

After the surrender of the
Confederate armies, while on
the way to his home in Texas,
was called upon at the rail–
road station at Newberry,
S.C. on the night of Sept. 7,
1865, to protect a young white
woman temporarily under

his charge from gross insults
offered by a Negro Federal
soldier of the garrison
stationed here

On another face:

A difficulty ensued in which
the Negro was slightly cut.
The infuriated soldiers
seized a citizen of Newberry
upon whom
they were about to execute
savage revenge
when Crozier came promptly
forward and avowed his own
responsibility for the deed
thus refusing to accept safety
by allowing a stranger
to receive the violence
intended for himself.

On another face:

He was hurried in the
night time to the
bivouac of the regiment
to which the soldiers
belonged, was kept
under guard all night,
and not allowed com–
munication with any
citizen, was condemned
to die, without even the
form of a trial, and
was shot to death
about day light the
following morning
and his body mutilated.

The history of Calvin Crozier was again not laid to rest, when in 1900 a letter written by Bill Arp was published in the "Atlanta Constitution," referencing the deed that occurred in Newberry, South

Carolina, on September 8, 1865. It aroused more questions than it answered. In response to this, an article was written in the "Confederate Veteran" in January of the following year, telling the story of the events in Newberry.

It was from this article that the remaining survivor of the Crozier family, Mrs. Mary S. Rogers, in Blum, Texas, found out what had become of her brother. Twelve members of the Crozier family perished in the Galveston hurricane and flood in September 1900. Apparently, Lieutenant Henry Wood never got the message to Calvin Crozier's traveling companion; else it was never delivered to his family.

In Newberry a chapter of the United Daughter's of the Confederacy was named in his honor, and in 1913, the Calvin Crozier Chapter erected an additional marker at the original burial site in the field near Halcyon Grove.

The Sons of Confederate Veterans have honored the memory of Calvin Crozier over the years by naming units in his honor. Two such groups were named the Calvin Crozier Camp, Tyler, Texas, and the Cal Crozier Camp, Will's Pond, Texas.

In 1992 the owner of the land that was the site of the Crozier murder approached the Calvin Crozier Chapter of the UDC and asked if the marker that was placed there in 1913 could be moved. The UDC contacted the local camp of the Sons of Confederate Veterans in Newberry for assistance with the relocation of this marker. The John M. Kinard Camp #35 of the SCV gained approval for the marker to be placed beside the Confederate Monument in downtown Newberry. The marker was removed to this location before the end of that year.

It was during this time that an application was made to the South Carolina Department of Achieves and History for approval for a roadside marker to be located near the original murder site to honor Calvin Crozier and telling of the events that occurred near there in 1865. During the two year process of providing the Department with required documentation of the event, it was discovered that Colonel Charles Trowbridge of the Thirty-Third US Colored Troops was court–marshaled for the murder of Calvin Crozier.

The roadside marker approved by the SC Department of Archives and History was erected and dedicated on September 10, 1994. Mrs. Sherry Davis and Mrs. Mary Lund of the Texas Division of the United Daughters of the Confederacy represented Texas at this dedication. Members of the Texas Division, SCV, and the Texas Division, UDC, assisted the John M. Kinard Camp #35 in providing funds to pay for this marker. It is now located in Newberry on Nance Street approximately a hundred yards east of the original murder site.

Newberry College has thrived, back in its original location, since 1877, as a nationally renowned and accreted Lutheran College.

Calvin Crozier's final resting place is in Rosemont Cemetery on College Street near Newberry College. It is located under the shade of a magnolia tree near the street.

It is rare that one man's presence for such a short period of time can have such a positive impact on a community as that of Calvin Crozier. His act involving violence in the protection and defense of others produced a sad but generous reaction by the citizens of this small community. His story is one that deserves retelling. It is one where character and courage of one individual can not only have an immediate positive effect on events as they transpire, but also can carry over upon future generations.

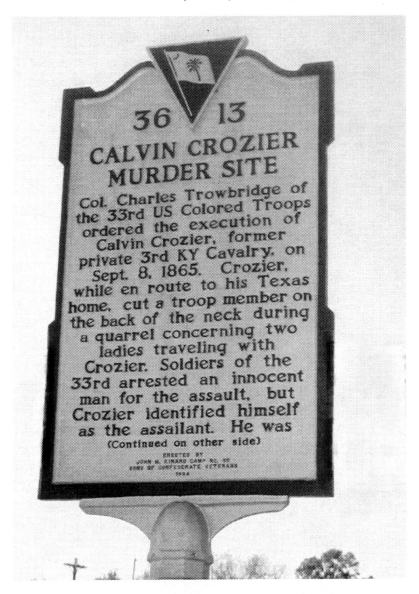

The Calvin Crozier Marker on Nance Street (front)

The Calvin Crozier Marker on Nance Street
(reverse)

Site of original train station in Newberry, S.C.

*CH*

Sketch of Lt Colonel Charles S Trowbridge

Letter of Major General Charles Devens

Calvin Crozier grave, Rosemont Cemetery

# Bibliography

Davis, George B., Major U.S.A., Leslie J Perry, and Joseph W. Kirklein, 1895,
*War of the Rebellion a compilation of the Official Records of the Union and
Confederate Armies*, Washington, Government Printing Office.


"Calvin Crozier", *The Confederate Veteran*, January, 1901


Higginson, Thomas Wentworth, originally published in 1870, republished in
1984, *Army Life in a Black Regiment*, Corner House Publishers,
Williamstown, Mass., 01267


Military Records, National Archives, Washington, DC


O'Neall, John Belton and John A Chapman, 1892, *The Annals Of Newberry, in
Two Parts*, Aull & Houseal, Newberry, S.C., reproduced in 1949,
Edwards Brothers, Inc, Lithoprinters, Ann Arbor, Michigan


Pope, Thomas H, 1973, *The History of Newberry County, South Carolina*,
University of South Carolina Press, Columbia, S.C..


Taylor, Susie King, 1988, originally published by the author, 1902, Boston

*Murder in Newberry, South Carolina*

Mass. *Reminiscences of My Life in Camp with the 33rd US Colored Troops, Late the 1st South Carolina Volunteers*, new edited publication, edited by Patricia W. Romero and Willie Lee Rose, in 1988, *A Black Woman's Civil War Memoirs*, Markus Weiner Publishing, New York

*The Weekly Herald*, September 13, 1865

All picture credits belong to the author

ISBN 1-41205755-8

9 781412 057554